Praise for *We Are Pirates*

"Exuberant . . . Fresh and funny . . . Although the novel is a raucously funny adventure, it's also a tragic exploration of the restlessness in all of us, of the ways we want to claim our happiness like buried treasure that might change everything. *We Are Pirates* is about how we try to forge our own destinies, and if we're lucky, become heroes of our own stories." **—Caroline Leavitt,** *San Francisco Chronicle*

"Arresting . . . What drives *We Are Pirates* is a current of love and Handler's strangely beautiful ability to show how even in a chaotic world, our lives have a way of converging if only we stop to notice." *—Elle*

"Daniel Handler keelhauls the ordinary outlaw-family-at-sea tale." *—Vanity Fair*

"Compelling . . . Engaging . . . *Pirates* develops a darkly comic rhythm as it moves along . . . An incredibly brisk read . . . Near impossible to put down." *—USA Today*

"The author of four previous novels and, under the name Lemony Snicket, 'far too many' books for children, Handler is superb at excavating truffles. But what would a novel be if it didn't also try to choke you with a few indigestible clods of earth? Part of the fun of *We Are Pirates* is watching its characters refuse to take responsibility for their unhappiness, preferring to think of themselves as victims, from whom something (happiness, money, prestige, etc.) has been stolen . . . Written with an unflinching eye for comedy and horror . . . *We Are Pirates* is an American story." *—The New York Times Book Review*

"*We Are Pirates* will dazzle, disturb, and delight you. It might even do things to you that don't start with the letter D, like remind you what it's like to be young, or convince you that Daniel Handler can do anything." —**Jess Walter, author of** *Beautiful Ruins*

"Daniel Handler—aka Lemony Snicket—is one of the funniest people on the planet and his new novel is further evidence of his gift for offbeat, razor-sharp wit . . . *We Are Pirates* is high-flying fun and Gwen may be one of Handler's most endearing protagonists." —*San Jose Mercury News*

"Sails against readerly expectation to brilliant effect. Gloriously cut loose from much in the current book market, *We Are Pirates* is a pirate adventure for grown-ups set in modern-day San Francisco . . . It is a swashbuckling, wonderfully eccentric message in a bottle for those seeking a social order beyond the realm of traditional authority . . . Handler's yarn, replete with as many twists and turns as the classic pirate stories, captivates from start to finish, but it is his stylistic exploration of the piratical yen for elsewhere which most cleverly shanghais the imagination." —*The Independent on Sunday*

"A macabre, darkly human portrayal of family dynamics and growing up in a world running low on adventure . . . peppered with black humor." —*Booklist* **(starred review)**

"There is no writer quite like Daniel Handler. Somehow he manages to work at the intersection of irony and wonderment, whimsy and menace—a space I'm not sure I knew existed until I read his work." —**Jennifer Egan, author of** *A Visit from the Goon Squad*

"Handler's wry prose keeps even the darkest passages from tipping off balance. The author treats language the way some treat fashion, tooling intentionally jarring or ugly phrases to striking effect." —*The Kansas City Star*

"Full of whimsy, adventure and intrigue. There are dastardly grown-ups and children in peril, moments of high camp and utter despair ... Beneath all the trappings of make-believe and fancy dress, there is a poignant, serious story about a girl's need to find her true self, shackled to her desire to escape from the world—and the irreconcilable, sometimes bloody conflict between those two yearnings ... The exhilarating sections dealing with this caper are the book's highlights, the prose full of high-blown pirate speak that does little to hide the sincerity of all those on deck." —*The Telegraph*

"Honest and funny, dark and painful, *We Are Pirates* reads like the result of a nightmarish mating experiment between Joseph Heller and Captain Jack Sparrow. It's the strangest, most brilliant offering yet from the mind behind Lemony Snicket." —**Neil Gaiman**

"Daniel Handler turns whimsy into wisdom and the fantastic into the great. He is, of course, a genius." —**Lorrie Moore, author of** *A Gate at the Stairs* **and** *Bark*

"Handler is a master at depicting the existential chaos all his major characters are living through, and with warmth, sympathy and considerable humor at that. The reader will delight in Gwen and old Errol's escapades ... Affecting, lively and expertly told. Just the sort of thing to make grown-ups and teenagers alike want to unfurl the black flag." —*Kirkus Reviews*

"Can a couple of teenagers, a befuddled old man, and a nursing home orderly really steal a boat and wreak havoc in San Francisco harbor? Sure, says Handler, crossing and mixing genres—dark and light, YA yarn and midlife doldrum—while making readers root for his 20th-century privateers ... Jaunty and occasionally jolting, [an] honest take on the discomforts of youth, midlife, and old age, and how ineffective we are at dealing with them." —*Publishers Weekly*

WE ARE PIRATES

WE ARE PIRATES

A NOVEL

Daniel Handler

B L O O M S B U R Y

NEW YORK · LONDON · OXFORD · NEW DELHI · SYDNEY

The author would like to thank the following people: Lisa Brown, Otto Handler, Charlotte Sheedy, Ron Bernstein, Nancy Miller, Suzi Young, Andrew Sean Greer, Dave Eggers, Amanda Ducat, Nina Seligson, Laura King, Lauren Cerand, Jeffrey Fisher and Susan Rich. Parts of this novel were hashed out at the MacDowell Colony, to which the author also tips his hat.

Bloomsbury USA
An imprint of Bloomsbury Publishing Plc

1385 Broadway	50 Bedford Square
New York	London
NY 10018	WC1B 3DP
USA	UK

www.bloomsbury.com

BLOOMSBURY and the Diana logo are trademarks of Bloomsbury Publishing Plc

First published 2015
This paperback edition published 2015

ISBN: HB: 978-1-60819-688-3
PB: 978-1-60819-776-7
ePub: 978-1-60819-775-0

Library of Congress Cataloging-in-Publication Data

Handler, Daniel.
We are pirates : a novel / Daniel Handler. —First edition.
pages ; cm
ISBN 978-1-60819-688-3 (hardcover : acid-free paper)
1. Teenage girls—Fiction. 2. Treasure troves—Fiction. 3. San Francisco Bay Area (Calif.)—Fiction. I. Title.
PS3558.A4636W4 2015
813'.54—dc23
2014021908

2 4 6 8 10 9 7 5 3 1

Designed by Katya Mezhibovskaya
Typeset by Hewer Text UK Ltd, Edinburgh
Printed and bound in the U.S.A. by Thomson-Shore Inc., Dexter, Michigan

To find out more about our authors and books visit www.bloomsbury.com.
Here you will find extracts, author interviews, details of forthcoming events, and the option to sign up for our newsletters.

Bloomsbury books may be purchased for business or promotional use.
For information on bulk purchases please contact Macmillan Corporate and Premium Sales Department at specialmarkets@macmillan.com.

FOR MY SISTER

Is it better to be here or there?
—Robinson Crusoe

WE ARE PIRATES

Part One

CHAPTER 1

Imet Phil Needle on Independence Day, two hundred something-something years since America had freed itself from British rule and just a few days after the pirates had returned from the high seas, at a barbecue commemorating that troubled time. I wasn't invited. The party was out under the cold sky, with a view of the bridge. At the time this story takes place, the bridge was called the Bay Bridge, and it connected San Francisco to points east, where the country was originally founded, except during rush hour, when it just clutched cars in a long, metal standstill. The air was thick and no fun to stand around in. I stood around Phil Needle, who met my eyes only for a moment as he said the thing nobody could believe.

"We are pirates," he said, and his glance scuttled away. "It's an American story, really, with an outlaw spirit. Leonard Steed, starting out in his private railway car, riding through someplace, when out the window there's a cotton gin rusting in a field just outside a tiny black town. He has the train stop. He walks into town and negotiates it, because of 'Cotton Gin Blues.' You know that song?" Phil Needle didn't pause long enough for anyone to answer but himself. "Legend has it the Devil came for Belly's soul and Belly looked at the cotton gin and wrote 'Cotton Gin Blues' right on the spot and won it back. That song changed Leonard Steed's life when he heard it at Harvard. He rode all the way back to Los Angeles, and you can still see it there in the lobby of his building. Leonard Steed just took that little piece of treasure just like Belly Jefferson took his soul back from the Devil."

Phil Needle stopped, surrounded by quiet astonishment, and took a sip of beer from the bottle. Nobody had been listening after "We are pirates." I had to get away, too embarrassed to look at him. The pirates' voyage had just ended, and caterers require two weeks' notice to cancel, so they didn't cancel. Not a big time frame, this story. It had begun, the history said, around Memorial Day. It was over now, and I walked across the courtyard. Phil Needle's condo was in a shiny building everyone knew now as the home of the pirate. It was on the sixth or eighth floor, with an outdoor court-yard he shared with neighbors, hovering high over the streets to avoid the noise and dirt. It was landscaped with trees and benches and a small waterfalled pond and a brick barbecue with sausages from kindly treated animals. They were Jews, the Needles, but there still wasn't enough food. Not a single person had declined the printed invitations, and the Needles hadn't thought to expect all the people like me, who had tagged along just to lay eyes on them, after hearing the extravagant and ridiculous accounts of the pirate exploits.

I went inside. The living room had a huge window showing me the bridge and the water and the wide boulevard of the Embarcadero, a land of roller skates and tourists holding hands. Under a staircase was a grand piano with an orchid on it, sharing a pot with a little flag. It was surprising he could afford a place like this, but at the time this story takes place, most people bought places they couldn't afford. Just eighteen months earlier, when the building was built, an advertisement was hung out for all the traffic to see: IF YOU LIVED HERE, YOU'D BE HOME NOW. They lived here. They were home now.

In the kitchen one last caterer hurried out, sliding shut the door behind her. Behind glass the party was like the sound of the sea. I opened the dishwasher and shut it. A shopping list said they needed three things, and inside the refrigerator everything had been pushed up against the walls, like furniture in a ballroom. On the bottom shelf was a plastic holder of four cupcakes from a bakery. Two were missing, and the other two looked old. I knew there wasn't going to be a cotton gin, but I kept looking.

I stepped past a bowl of water for the dog and found the room where people had put their coats. A home office with a couch from a long-ago apartment and a desk chair for people with bad backs. On the wall was the silhouette of a window with tree branches shivering in the breeze, but the wrong wall. The answer was on top of an almost empty bookshelf: a tiny projector, squat as a telescope, shining a false window onto the wall of a windowless room. We lived in an era in which we could do anything. Further down the hallway was an unmarked door to the room where Marina did her paintings. I didn't open it. At the dead end, I entered a bathroom I wasn't supposed to be in. It was clean, but the towels weren't nice and hung unfolded and damp from the rack as if someone had cried into them. I pulled back the shower curtain and saw crumbs from where Marina had shaken out a tablecloth, tumbled out in a trail winding to the drain. I ran the tap and sent them to the sea, and then sat on the toilet, pants up, lid down, and saw in the wastebasket a handful of junk mail torn in half. The image of Phil Needle, sitting on the toilet and going through his mail, was so clear and so obvious that I no longer felt in the diaspora of this story. I was invited. I could be in this bathroom. He was no longer a man I didn't know. I could see him tall in the mirror, a glimpse at his fine sharp gray hair, his body not bad from jogging. Contact lenses, he thought, made him look younger. He worked in radio, and if someone were to ask Phil Needle about the radio business he would have three things to say, but nobody asked him. People sometimes thought badly of him for the things he said—*We are pirates*—but nobody ever took into account all of the things he withheld out of tact or kindness, all the times he pulled over to the side of the road to let the ambulance go roaring by to its emergency. One time, Phil Needle tripped over a small rug as he entered a café, and he *straightened the rug* so no one else would do the same thing. He sometimes walked across the street against a red light, but never when small children could see him and follow his example.

Phil Needle blinked in the bad light of the bathroom, his least favorite one, looking at the towels. Little blue boats on the ripply embroidery of the sea's surface—Marina must have found them. Phil Needle was a man whose story was always getting away from him. It was Memorial Day, a time to think of soldiers and sacrifice, and in the living room his wife and child were waiting. He had planned to use this time to decide what to say, but instead he had thought about the barbecue some weeks ahead, and skimmed the mail he'd taken off the kitchen counter. It was all junk. He threw it out into the wastebasket, which was empty except for the wrapper from a brand of candy bar he didn't like. He washed and looked in the mirror. Gwen, his daughter Gwen, was stealing things. And now he had to say something.

×

It's so easy to steal things. Octavia was fourteen, just like Gwen, but she was taller and prettier than Gwen. She walked forcefully, in this long, flared coat, almost a cape, with deep, cavernous pockets, and a pair of boots that meant business. Gwen had seen a guy outside the Fillmore, an ancient rock club her dad took her to once with free tickets from work. The jagged gleam of the streetlights shone on a piece of actual metal on the toes of this guy's boots as he looked at her and sneered a little like she was a kid, licked his lips. The boots Octavia wore could kick that guy in the balls.

Just like Gwen, Octavia was okay for a long time, and not just when she was a kid. Twelve and thirteen she was pretty happy. Or *naive* was the word Octavia thought for it. Then one day boredom just set upon her with a fierceness. There was nothing to do in the condo. She had to get away, but the neighborhood was lame and she wasn't allowed to take the bus alone. Up and down the Embarcadero, the tourists took joke pictures in front of the ugly statues, flying all the way from Japan or Germany to make the same stupid poses everybody made. The cars moved across the bridge to somewhere fun. Even the ocean seemed to be having a better time, waving and crashing and making cappuccino foam on the pilings. She was mad at the ocean, how stupid was that, jealous of its schedule and its freedom when she couldn't even get a bus pass. Eventually she was always at the drugstore.

When Octavia was *naive*, the name "drugstore" was wrong, because drugs were just one of the things, way in the back where the people coughed and waited in cheap chairs. But one day she was old enough to get it. The store *was* a drug, with the rush, the dizziness, the spending money to do it again, how it messed up your body and made your mind feel cool and false, all the stuff they warned you about with drugs that she was going to find out for herself the second she was allowed to take the bus alone. Her grandfather once said, running an errand with her, "Only in America are there places like this," and now she felt patriotic. She loved to go to the drugstore here in America land of the free.

But it wasn't free the day she had no money. Not a cent. It was Memorial Day, and in this part of America there was a rack of candy bars discounted. It was the land of opportunity, so she took one. It slipped into the deep pocket of her cape and she spun around on the heels of her cool boots and walked right back out. Tourists were laughing. Maybe it was funny in France. She raced home and hid in the ugliest bathroom to eat it like a wolf with a baby animal, smeared all over her teeth before she thought to look at the calories. Gwen would have thrown it up again, but Octavia just threw the wrapper away and flipped her hair a little. Gwen could not stand it when her father tucked her own hair back behind her own ears without asking.

She was careful and got better at it quick. The enemy wore red vests so they were easily spotted, and they were busy stacking cans and ringing people up and some of them were retarded. The chocolate still flickered in her blood when she went back into the drugstore for another adventure. It was still Memorial Day and the aisles were quiet. She was methodical, and her method was taking everything and putting it into her pockets. Lipstick in Savage, Scarlet Fever, and Jealous Rage. Barbecue potato chips and red licorice coiled inside a plastic pouch like rope on a ship. A handful of nail polishes—she had to be quick, couldn't choose the colors— and then back around the corner for a bottle of remover. Glitter for her face and neck, batteries she hoped were the right kind, thick pleasing markers, soap with flowers, actual flowers, forced into it. She remembered suddenly what it was called—shoplifting—and pictured lifting the whole place, the aisles tilting and tumbling their baubles and trinkety treasures into her pockets. Pink razors for her burnt leg and then a key chain she thought Naomi would like, and when she realized she could steal for other people it was an avalanche, a chew bone for Toby II, more stuff for Naomi, a stuffed bear and a tiny license plate that said NAOMI. Three flasks of perfume, curvy and shapy like internal organs in her pockets, and she was done with Mother's Day for ages. Her father liked the electronic things, which were behind locked cabinets, but she grabbed a slick stereo magazine and managed to slip it into one of her boots. It would be a way to warm him up for taking the bus by herself. By now she was thirsty and rounded a corner to open a fridge and grab an iced tea in a bottle that felt so good in her hands. It was One Universe Green Tea, which the label said was good for the immune system and for Octavia's skin. No one had stopped her. No one had spoken to her. It was smooth sailing. All for one and one for all.

Where does trouble come from? How do you get into it? It was no trouble to steal any of these things, and the thief was untroubled during the entire easy adventure, her immune system and her skin flushed and glowing. But of course it was a lie. One Universe Green Tea was a soda company in disguise, moving aggressively among young people to get a large share. There was no one in the whole One Universe who was concerned about young girls' immune systems at this time in American history, and the bottle Octavia held was cool and wet from refrigeration, slipping against the sweat on her hands so when the guard said "Miss?" it shattered on the floor. Instinctively she knelt down to pick up the pieces and a razor fell out of her pocket, and one of the nail polishes, and the guard reached down. For a moment Octavia thought he was going to embrace her. She should have kicked him in the balls. But he unbuttoned her cape and held it up as if he wanted to try it on, several more items clattering to the floor, and then spotted the magazine sticking out of the top of her boot. He took that too, and it unrolled open and her heart cut its elevator cables and plummeted to where the chocolate was seething. She had grabbed the wrong magazine. This wasn't the stereo thing. This was *Schoolgirls*, with girls too old for school dressed up in plaid skirts and terrible pigtails, with their legs open and lollipops in their mouths. You could see their cunts even on the cover. The slow tide of tea reached Octavia's knees as the man stood over her in disgust.

She had to say something. "I—"

The guard grabbed her arm by the elbow and wrenched her down the aisle to a door she wasn't supposed to go in. He forced her through a room where two guys in red vests were eating noodles they had heated up in little cups. They stared as she dragged by, and the guard dropped her coat on the table and *Schoolgirls* too, and then the guys grinned at each other and at the magazine and at her, and the guard shoved open another door and pushed her into a seat that was still warm. There was an empty bag of chips identical to the one she had taken, and a peach iced tea and a bunch of the same markers in a mug with the name of the drugstore on it. It was his chair, the guard's. She looked up at the TV screens. Of course they had cameras. Of course they had been watching her. She couldn't even think of how she thought that wouldn't be so. She had never thought the idea of getting caught was even possible, back when she pushed the door into the store. Ten minutes ago. Now there was nothing else but getting caught. He slammed the door shut and said something to the guys and his footsteps walked away. Octavia shuddered and her throat felt hot. She grabbed one of the markers and wrote SHIT on the back of her hand and then, when she was done staring at it, did not cry. Over her head the big square light told her what it thought of this: *flutter flutter.* She wiped her knee and the door opened again.

"What's your name?" the guard barked. A man with greasy hair and a white shirt was standing next to him.

"Octavia," Octavia said.

"Octavia what?"

"Octavia," Octavia said, "Needle." She was tired of thinking up things.

"You live around here?"

She didn't answer. What did it matter? On the television screens, one of the guys was mopping up her mess.

"Sure," the guy in the shirt said. "She comes in with her mother, her father, and by herself."

She didn't answer that either.

"Pretty girl," the guy in the shirt said. The guard reached down and adjusted his belt. Octavia stopped clasping her hands together and put them down and the two men looked at what she had written on her hand.

"Gwen," Gwen said. She couldn't do it. She couldn't even

explain why she thought of herself as Octavia during the adventure, but she certainly couldn't do it any longer. Her boots didn't mean business. She wasn't taller or sexier than she was. She was Gwen, and she was in trouble.

"Octavia, I could call the police or I could call your parents," the guard said.

"Memorial Day," said someone else, one of the guys in vests maybe, Gwen couldn't see.

"Stay out of this," said the guy in the shirt.

"I'm just saying the cops aren't going to come," said the person who was supposed to stay out of it.

The guard adjusted his belt again, which was gross. "Octavia, what is your parents' phone number?"

"My dad's at work," said Gwen, but the men just looked at her. Even the guy staying out of it leaned his head in. It was the guy she thought it was. Her father at work was not the answer to what these people wanted from her. She was going to cry, as surely as she was going to get caught. They called her dad, Phil Needle, and her dad called her mom and her mom came and got her out of the drugstore. It had all happened so fast that the tourists were still laughing outside—not the same ones, but Gwen swore she recognized them anyway. They were all, everyone out there, the same.

×

Phil Needle needed a new girl. He had to finish the Belly Jefferson story. *Riding the Rails* was working. Ratings on *Heavy Petting* were solid. Lots of one-time-only repeat business. His engineers were all right, young guys who might come in late or arm-wrestle over the free tickets the promoters sent, but okay. The stringers only talked to him when he didn't pay them. Dr. Croc was all right. Phil Needle felt confident about America, or whatever he was going to call it, but he had to finish the Belly Jefferson story, and he couldn't do that without a girl.

His first girl had a sarcastic smile. When Phil Needle would walk out of his office and stop at her desk, whatever he asked her to do, staple things, give her opinion about an idea he just had, wrap up the other half of his sandwich, she always did it. She did everything. But she smiled like she had a better idea, and fled one Friday after only two years, with a note he still kept crumpled in a ball in the bottom of a drawer:

> This job is not meeting my needs. As of 5 PM today
> I resign.

Instead of a signature, she'd left the key to the office at the bottom of the note, and when Phil Needle picked it up, he saw there was an image of a key underneath it. She'd made copies of the whole note, probably to prove she left the key if it ever came up, though of course Phil Needle, on the advice of Leonard Steed, had the locks changed anyway, in case she'd copied the key before she'd copied the key. He never uncrumpled the ball, but he still wrote her letters in his head: *Dear Renée, What are your goddamn needs?*

His second girl had cancer, diagnosed just weeks after she was hired. She worked hard enough except when she had tests, or treatment, or was recovering from tests or treatment. The guys all rooted for her, and Phil Needle even sketched out an audio diary, "Jenna's Story," which he thank goodness never got around to pitching to the Keep Healthy people, because one day her boyfriend came to pick her up and Phil Needle finally got to shake his hand and say how happy everyone at Phil Needle Productions was to hear that Jenna was in remission, and he wondered what Phil Needle was talking about, and everything you can extrapolate from that story is true. The third girl was the one who walked into Studio B, where Allan was on break from his all-night mixing session for the Sinatra anniversary piece and masturbating. Phil Needle Productions now had a knock-first policy, and Phil Needle had placed an ad in all the necessary places, written with some coaching from Leonard Steed:

> Dynamic, re-inventive company looking for smart, energetic, quality-minded person for an adminis-trative support position with limitless possibilities. Meet our needs and we will meet yours.

Phil Needle felt good about the entire final draft except maybe *re-inventive*, a term Leonard Steed used that hadn't taken off yet. His consulting company was called Re-Edison. Nineteen people had responded to the ad, but only two of them were girls. Phil Needle wanted a girl at the desk, a pleasant, young girl who would greet people who walked into the offices, like Phil Needle, with a smile and on good days a wink.

The first applicant was a drunk. Or at least she was drunk at the interview, and drunk at the second interview Phil Needle sched-uled for her as another chance, because anybody might get drunk at the first interview. In order to project himself as part of a dynamic, re-inventive company, he told the second one, Alma Levine, that he needed her to come in for an interview bright and early Monday morning. She suggested eleven o'clock. He was too embarrassed to get back to her and say he forgot that Monday was going to be Memorial Day, and so now he sat in his office listening to "(Water on a) Drowning Man," a song by Belly Jefferson, for inspiration and because he wanted to. Belly Jefferson had died in 1970, just when he had been rediscovered. He left behind a number of illegitimate chil-dren who became perfectly legitimate businessmen with rights to Belly Jefferson's image and likeness and any portrayal of him in any media, because at this point in American history they could do such things. They were interfering with the outlaw spirit Phil Needle was trying to embody.

Phil Needle had an idea. It was a huge idea, like a craggy island rising out of the water while the ocean fizzled obsequiously around it. It was a radio show. It would be about America and it would be broadcast everywhere, in people's cars and homes and computers. The show—he didn't know what it was called yet—would embody the American outlaw spirit. So far Leonard Steed liked this idea very, very much.

It was his destiny, he knew it was, but if the boat was to reach the destiny, he needed an American story that would launch the boat of the show across the ocean of radio. A practical, smaller version of this was that Phil Needle had to produce a sample episode in order to officially pitch the show to Leonard Steed. Steed had advised this as his consultant and told him this officially as his producing partner. Phil Needle Productions was contractually obligated to split its profits with Leonard Steed, and additionally Phil Needle had hired Leonard Steed as a consultant through Re-Edison. That added up to a substantial investment, but Phil Needle felt with this show he could live up to it. But to live up to it he needed a story, and his story was "Belly Jefferson, an American something."

Phil Needle hadn't told Leonard Steed that the episode was about Belly Jefferson. Phil Needle scarcely ever stopped thinking about the day he would fly down to Los Angeles, walk through the lobby of the Steed Building, past the cotton gin, go up the elevator to Leonard Steed's office and then sit down in front of Leonard Steed and have him listen to an episode he, Phil Needle, had produced about the man who sang "Cotton Gin Blues." Usually Leonard Steed was the outlaw in that room. That day, it would be him, Phil Needle, and within months of that day his new condo, with the view of the bridge and the water that was supposed to inspire him, would perhaps not seem so unaffordable as to make his stomach sink. Surely that day could come. But to reach this day he had to clear his desk of these papers lily-padding all over one another, and to clear his desk he needed a new girl, and so it was not beyond reason to say that it was his destiny who walked into his office at eleven o'clock. He watched her walk past the desk she'd sit at if the job was hers and knock on his open door.

"Knock, knock," she said. She seemed like she looked cute, with trendy shoes and a slightly lovely top. "Are you Phil Needle?"

"Yes," said Phil Needle, and turned the music down.

"I'm here for the interview? I'm Alma Levine."

"Right," Phil Needle said, and scurried the papers around his desk for her résumé as she sat down. It was two pages long, but the second page contained just a short list of hobbies. This was possibly the fault of the printer, which Phil Needle hoped never to use, once he had a new girl. She would print it for him. He had assumed her name rhymed with *mine*, but she'd said *mean*. "Alma," he said.

"Spanish for *soul*, Hebrew for *virgin*," Alma Levine said, for clearly the millionth time.

Phil Needle blinked. "Virgin?"

"None of your business," said Alma Levine, the millionth punch line. "I don't like it either. Everyone calls me Levine."

"Levine."

"Right." Sticking out of her bag was the tube of a rolled-up magazine, and Phil Needle wondered what magazine she read on the streetcar. But he had a first question planned out already. "It's quiet here today," she said.

"It's the holiday," Phil Needle said.

"Did you forget it was Memorial Day when you scheduled me?" she asked. "I wondered about that."

Phil Needle flipped over Alma Levine's hobbies so he could cover Belly Jefferson's face. It was best not to think of his destiny at this moment. "Yes," he said, more sharply than he'd planned.

She frowned at him, but it was a sympathetic frown, as if he'd spilled something but she was going to wash the shirt. "You're the boss," she said. "You shouldn't be doing the calendar."

"That's right," Phil Needle said in slow amazement, looking at his desk. He had a list prepared but could not find it in front of him, only another list, from a brainstorming session with Leonard Steed. Perhaps this proved his point. "Managing the calendar is not the half of it," he said. "Much, much less than half. There's administrative duties, the phones and the mail and scheduling our engineers—we have three engineers, Allan, Ezra, who we call EZ, and Barry. But all those things aren't the half of it."

"The mail, things like that?"

"Yes, but that's not the half of it," Phil Needle said again. His first question was supposed to be about the applicant's most unforgettable experience, but they had veered off topic and were talking about the job. The conversation they were supposed to be having was like some landmark that had just bobbed out of sight, and for a second Phil Needle felt a little dizzied. "If the position is offered you, you can think of yourself as a bouncing board, or a kind of shadow. I'd need you by my side." He paused for a moment and felt like he'd said something creepy, but Alma Levine was nodding and he could detect no trace of sarcasm. *Dear Renée, look at this girl's face. This is how you nod at a boss.*

Phil Needle clapped his hands together and fingered his fingers, his wedding ring a tiny ripple in the room. "Tell me something about yourself."

There was a pause, and during the pause Phil Needle thought, *Now she'll say "What do you want to know?"*

"I graduated from college two years ago," she said. "I majored in philosophy. I took ethics for so long that I got tired of it, so I'm done with that. Right out of college I met a guy at a show, Ray Droke."

"Ray Droke?"

"Why, do you know him?"

"No."

"He ran this marketing agency, Ray Droke Marketing. He

moved offices and I started answering phones, but then a few months ago I quit."

"Why did you quit?"

Levine paused and then sighed and then paused again. "I had a problem with the boss."

This was probably the worst thing you could say in an interview. Phil Needle looked down at her résumé and saw that Ray Droke was listed as a reference. But below the résumé, there was another item that should not have been in front of him: the printed invitations for the barbecue he and Marina were throwing on July 4. They did it every year, but this year, because there was no girl, Phil Needle was supposed to look at the invitations before Marina had them printed, but he hadn't had time to look at them, and so nobody had noticed that the invitations left off Gwen's name. Usually the invitations were signed "The Needles," and then below it "Phil—Marina—Gwen," but now it was just "Phil—Marina—nothing," no daughter, because there was no girl. The phone rang.

"Hello?"

"I'm looking for Phil Needle," said a man in a loud room.

"This is Phil Needle," Phil Needle said, and looked at Alma Levine. She pointed to the door and cocked her head. Phil Needle gave her a silent *No, don't leave.*

"Your daughter Octavia, sir," said the voice, "has been caught shoplifting. We have not decided whether or not to press criminal charges."

"There must be some mistake," Phil Needle said sternly, and nodded at Levine.

"It's no mistake, Mr. Needle," the manager said. "I am the manager. We caught her red-handed. Listen, sir, I have a daughter myself. That's why I'm calling."

"But I don't have a daughter named Octavia," Phil Needle said. There was no way to make this sound like an impressive and professional call.

"Do you have a daughter, maybe eleven-twelve years old?"

"Fourteen," Phil Needle said, getting annoyed on Gwen's behalf. But he heard the manager ask the question *Is your real name Octavia?* in the noisy room, and it was at this moment in American history that Phil Needle knew his daughter had been stealing. His contact lenses suddenly felt dry and present. He thanked the manager. He apologized. He said she would be fetched. He appreciated the kindness. He agreed that daughters were a handful. Yes. Maybe twenty minutes. He had to call Gwen's mother. Her real name was Gwen. Tell her, don't tell her anything, thank you. Goodbye.

"I have to cut the interview," Phil Needle said, "short. My daughter—"

"I heard," Levine said. "I'm so sorry."

It sounded like Gwen was dead. Surely Alma Levine did not think that. "She was stealing," he said, and thought of a way to make it part of the interview. "What do you think about stealing?"

"I think it's wrong," Levine said flatly. He could not disagree. Stealing was wrong. If you were caught they filed charges, or called your father. Phil Needle looked at her and tried to reinvent the day. He needed a girl, and here was one. Maybe she hadn't had a problem with her boss. She'd said so, yes, but his daughter had said Octavia. People had to say something.

"It *is* wrong," Phil Needle said, and decided to hire Alma Levine. "Start tomorrow," Phil Needle said. "Let's start tomorrow." The boat of his mind sailed quickly forward to the conversation he had to have with his wife, his daughter, on the sofa in the living room of the condo he could soon afford. He would buy something to eat, so they could eat something while they talked this over, the fact that she was stealing things, cupcakes. He wrote CUPCAKES quickly on the back of the invitation to the barbecue, in such large letters that Levine looked down and read them, and he turned the invitation back over, and could see on the horizon the barbecue on the Fourth of July, when if all went well he'd be celebrating his success and his outlaw spirit. Stealing things. It was wrong. He picked up the phone.

"Yes," said his new girl.

×

When Gwen was born Phil Needle planted a tree. This was in their old place out in the Sunset, and the girl at the nursery told him the tree was a native one that would thrive in his yard, but it died when Gwen was five. He and Marina decided to replace it in secret, so she wouldn't cry. Digging up a stump at night, with a healthy native tree perched next to him with its roots in a bag, was how Phil Needle thought about being a father. It was like taking care of something, or digging something up, fixing it without the other person knowing it, with something identical to what it was that had gone wrong in the first place, or something. Phil Needle didn't know what it was. Fuck that tree.

He entered the living room with his shirt untucked, holding two cupcakes. Marina and Gwen were quiet on separate couches, Gwen's legs long on the coffee table and Marina holding a small pillow over her lap. Toby II lay with his body curled up on the floor. Everyone looked at the cupcakes. Phil Needle sighed, knowing from the moment he inhaled that he was already doing it wrong.

"Why did you do this?" he asked her. "Why are you stealing? Is it true?"

"It's true all right," Marina said. "They caught her red-handed. You wouldn't believe all she had in her pockets."

"So it's true," Phil Needle said, losing ground.

Gwen shrugged. "Yes," she said. "I don't know, Dad. I was just—I didn't know what to do."

"I told her, call a friend and I'll take you there," said Marina. "I said go out to the Embarcadero."

Gwen looked as though she was going to snarl at her mother, and Phil Needle didn't know how to take this. They had moved out of the Sunset to this beautiful place, with a view of the water and the Embarcadero right outside, full of safe tourists and smilers on roller skates, so Gwen could have someplace to go. Down the way was a farmers' market and she could take an interest in cooking, for instance, and surprise him when he came home from work with something she made herself from a recipe on a cooking show, while Marina set the table for a change. There was a gym in the building, whenever she was ready, and of course every day they drove her to school. She would never have to take the bus, had been the plan. Not like the Sunset, where every day it was waiting in the fog, squeezing in next to strollers and people with big bags of bok choy. Why wasn't Gwen into this plan? He could see her moving, if you looked closely at her shoulders, a shivery motion like an extra cup of coffee. He tried to remember the first time Gwen looked so mad she was going to cry, this furious fierceness that had pounced on her while he wasn't looking.

"I understand that you can be bored," he tried at Gwen, "but stealing is wrong."

"I *know* it's wrong," Gwen said, like this had happened ages ago. "I never did it before."

Marina barked this laugh she did sometimes. Toby II looked around without moving. "I looked in your room," she said. "*Everywhere.*"

"*Mom*," Gwen said. She stood up.

"You know her cupboard?" Marina asked him. "It was just *stuffed* with stuff."

"I buy things there all the time!" Gwen shouted. "That's unfair!"

"I threw it all away," Marina explained to him.

"That doesn't seem right," Phil Needle said. "If it's hers, then, well, or if she stole it, well, then it's property of the store."

"*I didn't steal it!*" Gwen stepped over the dog and looked at them. Even Phil Needle could see that she was trying not to cry. "I just did it, I don't know. And it's not even stealing. It *isn't*. It's not stealing unless you leave the store, and they caught me before that."

"*Gwen,*" Phil Needle said.

"It's *not.*"

Phil Needle tried to picture what in the world his daughter wanted from the drugstore, its hideous lights, its buzzing fridges and all the retarded people wandering around in vests making him uncomfortable. He leaned forward and tucked her hair behind her ears, which she had always loved, even though it fell loose again when she shook her head. "I said I was sorry," she said.

"You didn't say you were sorry until I asked you to," Marina said.

"Yes, I *did*," Gwen said. "In the drugstore I did."

"When I asked you to."

"I didn't say it because you asked me to."

"Heaven forbid you'd do something because I asked you to," Marina said.

"*I said I was sorry,*" Gwen said. "How many times do I have to say it?"

"Once," Marina said, "and mean it."

Phil Needle tried to turn his cupcake into a Scotch on the rocks with the power of his mind. He did not know anything about a girl who would steal things from a drugstore. Gwen didn't seem like she could be this girl. He pictured a shoplifter, and it was somebody more glamorous, more methodical, than this shaking thing with one foot on the coffee table and the other on tiptoe on the carpet, quivering and annoying the dog. He patted Gwen's knee and then Toby II's head. He knew of course that she had not been sorry while she was throwing makeup into her pockets. She was sorry later, at the moment she got caught. If people were sorry beforehand, they wouldn't do things.

Gwen had been talking this whole time, through clenched teeth, in a rough whisper that sounded like she was firing someone. "And I *did it*," she spat, "and it was the *only time*, and I said *sorry*. You never *believe* me. You won't let me take the *bus* by myself. I never get to go *anywhere*. You didn't even ask me about the *barbecue*."

Phil Needle thought about this list of things from his daughter, but he had no idea what any of them were. It was as if Gwen had emptied her pockets of everything but the reason she had stuffed things into her pockets, although to be fair, Phil Needle had not been listening for a minute that could have been crucial.

"If something's bothering you, honey," Marina said, "then—"

"Maybe it's none of your business, *Mom*," Gwen said.

"All right, all right," Phil Needle said. It was the tone of voice on *Mom*, as if Gwen's mother was not really her mother but somebody else. Everyone was nonsense. Still, he had to say something. "You will be," he said, but *you will be punished* sounded dramatic, or maybe filthy. "There will be punishment, which we will decide on, and in the meantime, for starters, you're grounded." He'd never grounded anyone in his life. "You can't go out"—how did it work?— "or talk on the phone, except for school."

"And swimming," Marina said.

"Except for school and swimming," Phil Needle said, but Gwen was already standing up again, her mouth shaking open and her hand with SHIT written on it rubbing at her crying eyes.

"*I knew it!*" Gwen said, storming off. "*I knew you'd take her side!*" It was a real storming off, his daughter thundering and leaving and roaring with tears through the kitchen to the bathroom nobody liked but everyone used. Marina tossed the pillow off her lap, leaned forward and put almost all of a cupcake into her mouth. He hadn't thought one was hers. He thought one for Gwen and one for himself because Marina was trying to be skinny for the barbecue.

"What," Phil Needle said, listening to his wife's lips smack, "was that?"

Marina shook her head with her mouth full.

"She gave the drugstore a fake name? *Octavia*. I guess she was trying not to get caught."

"She was already caught," Marina said. "And the magazine." She reached behind a pillow on the sofa, not the pillow she had been holding, and threw the magazine on the coffee table, rattling the cupcake. *Schoolgirls*.

"Well, she's trying to shock us," Phil Needle said. He could not take his eyes off the girl on the cover of the magazine. He was under the impression that they couldn't be like that, spread so wide, at least not on the cover. She had one hand between her legs, not to cover herself but to stretch herself open even further. She looked like she was explaining exactly where it hurt. He was guessing. "I mean, Gwen's not into schoolgirls. She *is* a schoolgirl. If she wanted to see naked schoolgirls, she'd take a bath, or ask Naomi."

"Naomi?" Gwen had a friend, this girl Naomi who hung around the condo with her eyes everywhere like she was itemizing the place. "You think Naomi's involved." Marina was thinking about it. "I don't like the way she looks at us."

"No, I just mean, I mean, Gwen didn't steal that to look at."

"She didn't do it to shock us," Marina said. "She didn't know she'd get caught. She *stole* it. It's *shocking* is what it is."

"Maybe she was trying to steal another magazine," he said weakly, and Marina just looked at him until he thought of something else. "Why do you have it? How did you get it?"

"*Gwen* stole it," Marina said.

"But what's it doing here?"

"I paid for it," Marina said.

"Why did you want it?"

Marina licked the last of the icing off the wrapper of the cupcake and then looked wildly at Phil Needle's. "I can't believe I ate that," she said. "I can't believe you brought those damn things home." Marina slid down the couch and grasped her belly with both hands through her shirt. "I wanted to show it to you."

"You didn't have to show it to me," Phil Needle said irritably. "I know what naked schoolgirls look like." He heard himself and grinned over at Marina in her ugly pose on the couch. She agreed to laugh, and they both shrugged to indicate that something was over, but Phil Needle could not for the life of him think of what it was.

"Do you really think this is an isolated case?" his wife asked him.

Phil Needle looked out to sea but was distracted by his own face in a photograph sitting on top of the piano, among the ones of his ravenous wife and the little thief they'd conceived. He could not hear if Gwen was still crying down the hall. "She seems isolated," he said finally, and got up without his cupcake or wife. He walked through the kitchen and passed the office and the room where Marina did her painting and paused for a moment at the door to the bathroom. He walked very quietly on the carpet, but he could not hear anything when he got there. He could open the door, or knock on it, and in the small room try to hug her and make her feel better. She would be crying into those dumb towels. He could tuck her hair, again, behind her ears. But he had to decide on a punishment. She would be punished, and, or, also, maybe, she hated him. So Phil Needle walked away and stood for a minute in the office doorway looking at the projection of the fake tree rattling against the fake window and the desk with the last of the invitations. On the other side of the wall, Gwen was furious, with furious words on her hands, although of course Phil Needle did not know, and could not have known, the terrors on the horizon, the bloodshed and the ravaged citizens. And yet at that moment he might not have been surprised. He felt unready. He had raced home to face the alarums of trouble, stopping only for cupcakes, and then had not been able to make himself useful. He'd said nothing. He'd ruined his wife's diet. He was in a room by himself, sinking into his old couch to stare at a window that wasn't even there. He was a landlubber, with no sea legs even in his own house, and his daughter, his baby, was storming in the next room, unhinged, unanchored and grounded.

CHAPTER 2

Don't start with Gwen. She lay grounded and alone in bed looking up. In her old room in the better house, there were stars on the ceiling. They weren't real stars, of course, and they didn't even look like real stars, but they were stand-ins, a reminder that over the roof was the sky, full of airplanes and other planets. Her new ceiling was white and reminded her of nothing. In a few minutes everyone would start with her, but right now it was 5:51 A.M. She was supposed to get up at 5:45, but the clock radio her father had bought for her, at this point in her life, ran the numbers too quickly when you were setting it. Her father had said it was her responsibility to get herself up on time, though Gwen could not see how that could be true. It wasn't her responsibility. It was everyone else who wanted her to go to every single place she went.

They were playing Tortuga. "You Ain't Hittin'." This was one of the few things she liked. She held an imaginary cigarette to her lips and blew white smoke at the ceiling. Her room was still ransacked, with drawers gaping open and empty because her mom had thrown all her stuff out, thinking it was stolen. Well, it was stolen now. Everything had been stolen from her. Tortuga, who grew up on the streets, she was pretty sure, would understand. Over the sound of his smooth, angry voice and the throb of the song she could hear her father faintly peeing, something she never heard in the old house. It was embarrassing, but then her father was always embarrassing. Also her mom, her school, the Embarcadero, her clothes, her own voice on the phone, the color orange, television, old music, the coaches, fancy food, being Jewish, blue jeans, clips in old women's hair, sweat, kids, long sweaters, and everything else except six tracks on the Tortuga album. She stood up and looked at the view of the water and the bridge. Already people were driving. Gwen was going to have to grow up and get up in the morning and drive to a job. In a minute everyone was going to start with her and it was never going to stop.

In her new bathroom she washed the last of the ink off her hands. It went down the drain to stain the ocean. On the other side of her bathroom mirror was her dad's bathroom mirror, so it felt like he was staring right through the mirror at her messy hair and bad breath. She was always a mess, because she had to get ready for school in the locker room at swimming. She didn't want to be a Marionette anymore.

Her dad was making her toast as usual. Gwen felt the weariness of waiting forever for someone to finish a simple, menial task, just so you can say thank you and move on. "Am I still grounded?"

"You were grounded yesterday," said her mother, of course. "For stealing. There's punishment for you, and yes, you're still grounded also."

"Except swimming," said her father, to cheer her up. The top of his swimming trunks was peering over his wide, pale blue jeans. Gwen had heard him tell people that the two of them swam together because it produced better results. "You think that little Glasserman kid will be fast today? What's his name?"

Cody Glasserman was fast most days. He was skinny as a stem, but he'd beaten all the boys in Competitive. Her dad talked about him for some reason. He wore a tight, smooth swimsuit, so Gwen could not look at Cody Glasserman at this point in her life. "I don't know," Gwen said, and her father finally finished the toast and slid the plate over to her. They stood side by side at the kitchen counter while her mother stared out at the courtyard. Toby II was making embarrassing noises at his bowl.

"I don't hear you saying thank you," said her mother.

"I just *got* it," Gwen said sourly. "Thank you for the toast." Her father had put too much butter and swirled honey on top of it.

"What was that?" her father asked.

"Thank you for the toast," Gwen said, worse.

He held up his hands like he was getting arrested and it was fun. "No, no," he said. "I mean what were you listening to this morning? I heard the thump, thump. It sounded pretty cool."

Thump, thump, she almost pitied him. "Tortuga."

"Tor-whata?"

"I'm really into him," she said. "If you get Tortuga tickets, I'll totally go. Don't give them to Allan."

"Okay."

"Can you really?" Gwen asked him. Or, she thought, are you another one torturing me. "Can you really get tickets to that show?"

"Let me get back to you," her father said, and Gwen knew what this meant. She slapped the toast in half and forced it into her mouth, picking up her backpack and sliding the sliding door open. The air was boring, neither cool nor hot.

"You forgot your juice," her mother said.

Why didn't they say what everyone knew, that Gwen was a mistake? She strode across the courtyard feeling the burn on her leg. Gwen rode the elevator down to the garage level to sit in her father's car, the second-best part of the day. She spat half the toast in a garbage can full for some reason of batteries, but couldn't get herself to stop chewing the rest. It was delicious. She wanted it. She deserved it, for having to get up and for her parents' thinking she stole a dirty magazine. She clicked her father's car unlocked and got in. It wasn't her responsibility to remember the keys. It was a favor she did for him, because he never remembered them. She did people favors. Where were hers? Her mother had said last night, dishing out the punishment, that Gwen was ungrateful. It was not ungratitude. She sat and waited for her ride to something else she did not want to do, bobbing her finger over and over on the thing that opened the door to the condo parking garage, three floors up, like she was poking a bruise to see if it still hurt. Down here the signal was too far away to work. It was a useless device, with a useless button. What did this longing matter, or the sky far, far above this dark place underground? What did it matter where she *wanted* to go? Nothing would change, and in twenty minutes she would be changing and getting stared at in the locker room, for her burn.

The burn had been there forever, like an island on Gwen's leg, with the odd torn boundaries of sea-smacked land. It sat there for years, familiar on the horizon to anyone who surveyed the region. But then like America it was discovered, under the flag of Naomi Wise.

"What is that?" she said, pointing her finger as close to Gwen as she could without touching her. Gwen was taking her bra off under her shirt.

"What's what?"

"On your leg."

"I told you about it."

"I never noticed it before."

This was unlikely. Naomi Wise noticed everything. She and Gwen had become friends, if they were still friends, when Naomi had leaned forward one day and murmured about Stacey Gleason: "That's the same outfit she wore to the party Friday." Gwen had not been invited to the party Friday, but she grinned anyway as Stacey stood oblivious with her face in the wind. Only the most popular had been invited. Naomi had risen to fame by inventing the fad of tying your hair up with a bikini top. At this point in her life Gwen knew that was idiotic and important. She could not afford to lose

Naomi and had tagged along at a studied, careful pace since then. Gwen was not the most popular. She was somewhere between twenty-ninth and thirty-fifth, in her estimation, and in Naomi's. Naomi was ninth.

"I was four," Gwen said patiently, "and I reached up for a doughnut and spilled a carafe of coffee. It was boiling hot. It was a second- and third-degree burn. I ruined my grandmother's birthday, because we all had to leave the hotel and wait in the emergency room."

"Now I remember," Naomi said, with a nod Gwen didn't like. Naomi was her best friend. She was very excited a lot. She watched everything. She scouted, and Gwen's role was to be there, in the right place at school or on the other end of the phone, when Naomi returned with the little secret animals she had caught, and to tie them up in the shed, or split them open so Naomi could mess around with their insides. It was often mean, but it was always fun, and there was so little fun when you couldn't take the bus by yourself. Lately Naomi's breathless excitement had become a little wary, and their phone calls were curdled ever so slightly around the edges of the sentences. Gwen could see the way this would go but had no maneuvering skills to make it go any other way. She had no other friends at school, really. It was complicated. Gwen watched Naomi now, staring at the burn again, and knew she would go down in this ship.

"Can't doctors fix something like that?"

"Maybe when I'm older," Gwen said, and then thought of something to say. "I'm in trouble. Grounded."

Naomi nodded like this, too, was something she remembered. "Why?"

Gwen felt she could not close her eyes without seeing *Schoolgirls*. "My mom's mad at me. And my dad, he took my mom's side. As usual."

"But what did you do?"

Gwen stood up in her suit. She could remember a time when she did not worry about her hair. Her face was clear, but she felt all the pimples that were yet to come, standing on their marks waiting for their cues, a crumb in her teeth, her body stuck everywhere with pins like a well-worn map. The burn stood out worse now that Naomi had claimed it. "I took some stuff," Gwen said finally. "From the drugstore."

"What, like shoplifting?"

"I don't know. I was bored."

"What did they do?"

"I'm grounded. I'll have punishment."

"They could have filed charges," Naomi said, like a pro. "What's the punishment?"

A hair dryer went on, and two toddlers from the toddlers class screeched with delight as the hot air hit them, and an old lady, part of a slow, smiley troupe called the Aquadettes that was the most embarrassing thing in the world, tucked her ancient, scary breasts away. "Can I tell you something too?" Naomi murmured in Gwen's ear. Gwen nodded in the noise. "I have a crush on someone. Someone who's here."

Gwen wasn't interested. This happened all the time, someone who was here, no matter where here was. "Who?"

Naomi grabbed Gwen's arm and they dragged together toward the pool. Naomi hadn't taken any of her clothes off. "I'll show you."

"You haven't changed."

"I'll tell Coach I have my period. I want to sit and watch him. I saw him yesterday at practice."

"We had practice yesterday? I thought it was a holiday."

"Optional. He's so hot."

"Coach is not going to believe you. You just had it."

"Ew, are you keeping track?"

Gwen had the sense to laugh, and Naomi gave her a little shove as they rounded the corner to the pool. It was a hard shove, on purpose maybe, and Gwen had to shuffle her legs a little to keep from falling to the concrete, and slap her hand against the tile to balance as Naomi rolled her eyes and went to the bleachers. Gwen didn't mind. Gwen had fallen in love with Nathan Glasserman.

Cody Glasserman had a brother. Gwen watched him muss Cody's hair as he strode toward the pool, a tiny loop of black cord around his ankle. His hair was long and shivery blond, and his little smile was crooked. Gwen kept her hand on the tiles. What was he doing here? A new Shark midseason? Cody slapped him back on the leg. It would be damp, with tiny, tiny hairs that fluttered their way up under the leg of his wrinkled suit. His arms gripped the curve of the ladder that rose out of the deep end of the pool and he casually lifted himself off the ground, his legs out straight like a pier, as he laughed at something Cody said. A shiver ran down Gwen like a drop on a windowpane, stopping between her legs with a sudden, breathy *snap!* She got for the first time why the girls in *Schoolgirls* opened themselves like that. If he walked right toward her now, took her hands to vanish around the corner to some private place, she would say yes before he even asked.

"I want you in the water!" Coach said. "Marionettes, lane four! Sharks, one through three! Freestyle, twenty laps, twenty-five for Division Three!"

The girls and boys moved. Gwen found herself in a herd of Marionettes of different ages, all skinny, not one with a burn on her leg. The boys and a handful of girls who would never be popular took lanes one through three, along with a few desperado dads like her own father, who looked for her in the hurry. She ducked his gaze, and Cody's, and tossed her towel on the bleachers nobody sat in, because of a WET PAINT sign that had been up all year but still made people nervous. On the opposite bleachers Naomi was watching her, until Coach strolled between them.

"What's with you, Wise?" he asked her. Naomi looked down at her jeans and then back up at Coach in an imitation of shyness.

"My period."

"You just had your period."

"*Coach.*"

"Don't *Coach* me, Wise. You think I was born yesterday?"

Gwen looked down and put her swim cap on. Coach's sweat-pants were bunched up here and there like haystacks in a field. She would guess that, no, he had been born a long time ago. She stepped closer to the water and waited for her turn. Nathan was gone into the froth and the lapping. She could not hear what Naomi was saying, but Gwen knew that she would stay at the bleachers just like she wanted. She saw Coach flick his hands at her, *I give up,* and blow his whistle at the rest of them to show he wasn't being a good sport, a little shriek in the splashy echo, and then she was up.

Desire propelled her through the warm-up. She was fast. She couldn't stop thinking about him. She was in love for the first time. The world tilted through this boy, as if through a prism, blue and foamy and full of possible dates. She was grounded but would see him every morning at the pool, and by the time she could go out again maybe he'd ask her out. She'd have to plan how to talk to him, get dressed quickly maybe and hang out outside until her dad was done with his stupid comb. She could picture him smiling at some-thing she said, his hair still wet from the shower, where he had been naked. She thought for the first time in a year about Allan, this guy who worked for her father. The reception girl had walked in on him touching himself. Her dad had told her this, for some reason, and even used a hand gesture that she'd never seen before and tried for weeks to get out of her mind after she saw it, this tubular movement up and down on an invisible penis. She knew all about it now. Boys did it every day. The trick, Naomi said once on the phone, was to make them do it about you.

She breathed and kicked and thought about a dating guide she and Naomi had read in a magazine. She imagined him pondering the questions boys were supposed to ask before asking a girl out: Will she feel safe? Will she feel comfortable? Will she be interested in the date activity?

Coach blew the whistle. Backstroke. Gwen got a glimpse of him two lanes over when she flipped over and then had to stare high at the ceiling. One of the lights was burnt out, the sunlight smoggy through the skylights dirty with leaves. She counted tiles like always, he loves me, he loves me not, arching her back so her chest looked okay if he happened to glance over. She turned around and pretended not to see her dad giving her a goggled thumbs-up under a sign with a shark on it.

The Sharks raced, split into age groups at statewide meets. Marionettes were different. Coach warmed them up, but when laps were over the Marionettes moved to the smaller pool with Tammy King, the choreographer, because the Marionettes were part of the National Alliance of Synchronized Swimming Youth Division. They performed their routines competitively, but they never won the competitions. They were low in Technical Merit. Gwen didn't care. She had joined the Marionettes because it was a place to hide. She was a good swimmer, she knew she was, but once you were old enough, you couldn't be a girl and race. It meant you were a lesbian. Any girl who swam joined Marionettes when she was old enough, Gwen learned several years after she was old enough. Naomi had told her. She went too fast into the turn-around, and so did the boy in lane three, and they ran into each other, hard, their bones knocking a gong in her ears. She grabbed the side and sputtered, blinking wildly to see if Nathan Glasserman had seen her.

"You okay?"

It was Nathan Glasserman.

Gwen made her gasp sound, like a choking breath. The boy two lanes down, some other boy, turned around and Gwen saw that he had ugly legs. "I'm okay," she said. "Just, uh, surprised."

"Me too," he said. He shook a droplet halo from his hair and gave her the grin she'd seen before. "I'm Nathan."

His name was Nathan. "Gwen," Gwen said, after biting her lip on *Octavia.* "You're new, right?"

"Not new, just here with my brother to stay in shape. I'm on the school team, but the season's out. What do you do?"

"For a living?"

Nathan laughed with his head back, all bright teeth and a neck she could encircle while slow dancing. "No, I mean what do you compete in?"

"Oh, I'm Marionettes."

"That water ballet thing?"

"Yeah, sort of."

"Some of those girls are hot," Nathan said, and then tugged a piece of blond over his eye. Gwen saw he hadn't meant to say that. "Are you on a school team too?"

He could not think for a second, *for a second,* that she was a lesbian. "No."

"How old are you?"

"Fourteen," she said.

He smiled again. "Maybe you're too young for me to talk to." His teasing her was so many things at once: Gwen's desire for him, her shame at her desire, her embarrassment at her shame. They were jamming up traffic in the lanes, so Gwen had to move to the line of buoys that separated them. She was very close to him. She glanced over at Naomi, just a few feet away on the bleachers, and saw with some triumph that *now* she was watching.

"So what do you do?" she asked.

"Little of this, little of that," he said. "Coach says I'm better at length. I might quit, though. Feel that?"

He held up his palm and she put her palm against it. She had no idea what he was talking about. Warm and wet. Out of the corner of her eye, Naomi's hands moved.

"Not sure."

"On my fingers. They get too wrinkly, it messes up my calluses. I play bass in a band."

"What're you called?"

He laughed again. "Satan's Ass Cheeks," he said. "Not my choice. We're kind of, I don't know, funky boom, the drummer says. You like Tortuga?"

"My dad's in radio," she said. "He's getting me tickets."

"Tickets, like more than one?" Nathan said. "Take me."

"Maybe," Gwen said, instead of yes yes yes yes yes yes yes.

Nathan reached out and found a little slip of hair that had escaped from her swim cap. He moved it around on her cheek. He hadn't said how old he was, but he must have been a junior, not off to college in the fall but old enough to flirt like this. "Then I'd owe you a favor," he said.

Now Tammy King blew the whistle. "Marionettes into the small pool," she said. "Moonlight Dance."

"My brother has your info on the roster," Nathan said. "I'll call you or something, okay?"

Gwen could not speak. She nodded like a diving board. He was the flower of the Jewish Community Center, slipping his smile under her suit, arousing selfish lusts and vanities in her breast. Bless the dirty sunshine, the four lanes, bless even her father and even on the days he blew water out of his nose. She pushed herself up with her elbows and dripped down joy and gratitude on the concrete while Nathan kept looking at her.

"Wait, you have something on your leg."

Happiness is not whatever they tell you it is, a weightless bright light that lives private inside you. Everyone can see it. It is laid out for the world, stacked on shelves underneath the glare of everyone's gaze. It belongs to somebody, each parcel of happiness, just one person at a time. Gwen had just realized what this meant. It meant, of course, that people could steal it.

"You just noticed that?" Naomi Wise had perfected a tone of casual disbelief that made stutterers out of heroes.

"Uh," Nathan said.

"It's freaky, isn't it?" Naomi stretched her legs and rose off the bleachers so she was standing over Nathan, smiling in expectation. "We all call her *Spot*."

"Spot." Nathan couldn't help it. "Good one. Good one."

He let loose another laugh, and Gwen's hope let loose too, landing somewhere in the water, ruffled and raging from stupid swimmers. Her bare hands clenched at her side, the hair he'd touched dripping down her face thicker than tears. She was a mistake, a burned and ugly mistake. Her head swiveled quickly, unattractively, to see who else was watching. A few Marionettes hurried by, pretending not to have heard, and Cody Glasserman, tiny skinny in his silly suit, stood just steps away with his hands on his hips, watching her with eyes wide and canine. The roar in her head, the thundering unfairness, the appalling malevolence of the whole wide world, her fury rising like some fish long thought extinct. *Good one.* So everyone knew, everyone a thief. She was a burnt bridge and she could never set foot in this place again.

×

Phil Needle, culprit and rascal, looked up from his list. There were several items crossed off, indicating deeds he had done, although to be fair, these were items he had just thought of, that he had already done, and then written down and then crossed off. Nevertheless his spirits were hoisted high. He was embodying the outlaw American spirit, clearly hopefully visible with Levine standing in the doorway. She didn't knock. She wasn't very good at that part of her job, or any other part. The reason Phil Needle had hired her was that there was no reason, really. Now she was here.

"You said staff meeting at nine thirty. It's nine forty."

Phil Needle looked at his computer in silent agreement. "Is everyone here?"

"Everyone except you. And you-know-who, I guess he's late."

"Dr. Croc."

Levine cringed. He knew she hated to say his name. "Dr. Croc," she said.

"Okay," he said, and stood up to talk to his crew. Levine led the way. Her first morning he had asked her to proofread a letter he wrote to the Belly Jefferson people. Leonard Steed had suggested, if you notice yourself using one word over and over, the strategy of substituting the word "fruitcake" for the word you can't stop using, and then going through the letter and reinventing the word differently each time. Phil Needle was having trouble with "inspiration," and he thought he'd had it licked. Levine had found no typos, but as it turned out the letter contained six unchanged *fruitcakes*. After questioning, Levine had revealed that she thought the letter was somehow about fruitcake. She still worked here. Phil Needle was young once himself, and the Belly Jefferson people were so confused by the letter that they had called him, and after explaining what had happened, as well as two or three other stories about Levine that he invented on the spot, they had all laughed together on the phone, and now, just as he had planned, the first episode of his new show was almost complete. *Dear Renée, I bet your needs still aren't being met, and Phil Needle Productions is veering closer to its destiny.*

His loyal men, Allan and EZ, were laughing when he walked in. "Hey boss," EZ said. Levine did not like to call him EZ, and called him "Ezra," with a tiny flick of scorn. "Listen to what went down at the dry cleaners."

This was for a radio ad he'd agreed to produce, Incredible Cleaners. "We're incredible!" in the booming, joyful tone of the voice-over actor they'd hired had been ricocheting through Studio A for the past two days. They'd used a stringer to interview the owner of the place, and Allan was pasting together a kind of mission statement that would provide a sober balance to the actor's hysteria. Allan pressed PLAY and Phil Needle heard the shy, reedy voice of this stringer they kept using.

"So, sir, why did you choose the name Incredible Cleaners?"

"*Why the hell do you think?*"

The crew laughed and cued it up again. Levine smiled widely and guiltily. "How did that happen?" Phil Needle asked.

"There's nothing usable," Allan said. "I've been trying to cherry-pick for a day now. The whole thing's like that."

"Did he realize it was an advertisement for his own business?"

"I don't know what he realized," Allan said.

"We shouldn't use that stringer anymore," Phil Needle decided.

"Maybe now's the time for your cross-flowering?"

"What?"

"I'm not using the right word. You know, bees and flowers."

"Pollination," Phil Needle said. Leonard Steed had helped him develop an idea that sometime he should surprise a client with a new kind of ad. The ad would be honest. It would have no bells and whistles, no catchy jingles, no statements of purpose. The only sound in the ad would be the testimonial of Phil Needle of Phil Needle Productions, saying that the client needed no bells and whistles, no catchy jingles, no statements of purpose, because the client was so good that Phil Needle of Phil Needle Productions was a customer. Cleverly, Leonard Steed pointed out, the ad had something flying under the radar, an ad buried in the ad for Phil Needle Productions. He hadn't used this idea yet, but it appealed to him. "*Cross-pollination* is the word. Yes, let's do that."

"The thing where you are just going to say you're a customer?" EZ scratched his nose. "Do you like Incredible Cleaners?"

"Yes, I like them," Phil Needle said. "They clean clothes."

"Do they clean *your* clothes?"

"They pay me to produce an ad," Phil Needle said, "and I use some of my money to clean my clothes, yes." Incredible Cleaners was across town.

"I guess that's the American way," EZ acknowledged.

"*America.*" Allan snapped his fingers. "I had an idea for the America show, another episode we could do. The Olympics. That's an American story."

"But it's boring," EZ said. "The stories are all the same. All those kids, practicing every day, in honor of some family member who hadn't lived to see the day."

Phil Needle knew now why his daughter had quit swimming. She was bored. All she had to do was say so, but maybe she had. He looked at his hands, jealous of the Olympians, the smile they had when they'd just predictably done something real hard real well. "Do we know what we're calling this America show?" Allan asked him.

"No," Phil Needle said. "That's the first issue for the staff meeting."

"I vote *America, America,*" Dr. Croc said, limping into the studio. As always he was carrying too many bags. He was a fat man, almost as old as Phil Needle, and just looking at his hat Phil Needle wanted to weep. "After the song."

"You're late," Phil Needle said.

"I ran into this guy on the streetcar," Dr. Croc said, and handed Phil Needle a printed card. "He's a plumber. He said he'll always give us a deal, if we ever need a plumber. He won't rip us off. He wants to be our go-to guy. Today's consumers like that kind of deal."

Dr. Croc walked into the office with a go-to guy's card almost every week. A long time ago, for a short stretch, Dr. Croc had been the host of a briefly somewhat popular morning radio show in New York City. The show was called *The Dr. Croc and Whiskers Show,* and Whiskers was a woman who sounded young and sultry on the air but was actually middle-aged and always eating pineapple slices from plastic cartons. Phil Needle had the occasional fill-in shift in the afternoons, lunchtime dedications that would arrive via fax in the office, and he'd wait his turn, watching Dr. Croc laughing through the soundproof glass, and one night at the opening of some club—"Come buy Dr. Croc a drink!" said the promo—Dr. Croc gave Phil Needle some cocaine.

For a time, drugs made New York City a wondrous sea for Phil Needle, and Dr. Croc was his first mate of appetite and fortune. But in a few months the microphone kept staring at Phil Needle in the booth, and he felt his unreliability creeping out of his skin; there was a look white people shared on the subway, when other people were misbehaving, and the more drugs he took the less often they shared it with him. The elevator was more crowded every day, because of some new business on the floor below, Orthodox Jew after Orthodox Jew pushing Phil Needle against the grimy mirror before finally leaving him all alone in the box for one more floor. It was a sign. He cut down on the drugs over a week's vacation back in San Francisco visiting his parents, and returned to New York steady enough to convince Dr. Croc, now sober and fired and scared, to work for him at the new company Leonard Steed had convinced him to start, and to meet his wife, almost immediately after finally ending things with Eleanor.

Eleanor.

"We have guys," Phil Needle said gently to Dr. Croc now, gently and wearily. "We rent this office, Croc. We don't have to take care of the plumbing."

"Today's consumers didn't know that," Dr. Croc said, taking the card back. Referring to himself as "Today's consumers" was a joke he used to do on the air, and he couldn't stop doing it.

"So, sir, why did you choose the name Incredible Cleaners?"

"*Why the hell do you think?*"

"I'll cross-pollinate after the meeting," Phil Needle said. "You can cue it up for me and I'll do it in Studio A."

"This is Studio A," Allan said blankly.

Phil Needle nodded in agreement. "And right now," he said, "I want a status report on Belly Jefferson."

"The interview's done," EZ said. "We just need background."

"I'll do background," Dr. Croc said. "I want to learn how. I could do it tonight. You know, they call me Mr. Batteries, because I can run all night, so let me do it."

"They already call you Dr. Croc," Levine said patiently. "They can't call you Dr. Croc *and* Mr. Batteries."

This was a way Levine kept talking. Phil Needle felt that Dr. Croc wanted to learn more about the craft of radio, and Phil Needle was willing to be a resource. Also, Dr. Croc hardly did anything around the office. "Could he do that?" he asked EZ. "Could he do background?"

"If you tell me more what you need," EZ said reluctantly, scratching his head. "I put your questions in yesterday afternoon, and Barry finished with the actor last night, so—"

"I told you," Phil Needle said. "He's not an actor. We're not making something up here. It's an interview with Belly Jefferson. Belly Jefferson was a real person. These interviews actually happened."

"In the thirties," Levine said. Phil Needle turned around and looked at her, remembering what Leonard Steed had suggested he say when an employee of his said something he didn't like.

"Ouch," said Phil Needle.

Levine stopped smiling. "What?" she said.

"Look, it's hard to say this, because I'm afraid you'll take it as criticism."

She leaned against the wall. The boys exchanged a look. "*Is* it criticism?"

"See what I mean?" Phil Needle said. "This is an important project, Levine. It's riches for us if we pull it through. I need my whole crew standing with me."

"You told me you wanted my take on things."

"I do."

"Well, it seems strange to me. If you want to tell a genuine

American story, why do we have an actor pretending to be this dead blues guy?"

"Belly Jefferson was an American outlaw," Phil Needle said. "It wasn't like today, when musicians are always giving interviews." He waved his hands at a shelf of old episodes of *Riding the Rails*. "This was a rare conversation that Belly Jefferson had with someone from the Smithsonian, but the original audio is not of a quality we want to associate with Phil Needle Productions, and so we're re-creating the original interview."

"And you're saying it takes place at a blues club that's not even real," Levine said.

"Fiona's is real," Phil Needle said. "I've been negotiating with the owners for five days."

"But you can't *go* there," Levine said. "It's not like Incredible Cleaners."

All Phil Needle could think of was that he didn't go to Incredible Cleaners either, but the phone rang before he had to say anything. Thank you, powerful angels in the sky who occasionally do something to help. Levine leaned across Phil Needle to answer it, but their bodies did not touch.

"Phil Needle Productions. Yes, may I ask who—yes. Hey, I thought it was you. How are you? Yes. Yes. Me too. Okay. Yes, he's right here." She stopped giggling and put the phone to her chest. "It's Leonard Steed."

Leonard Steed! Phil Needle talked to him every day and still it was like electric pants just hearing the name. "I'll take it, of course," said frantic Phil Needle. "In my office. Put him on hold." Phil Needle ran a hand through his kempt hair and twitched his way back down the hall, past the plant they never moved. Why didn't they? Why didn't they? Why didn't they move the plant to the window like he had once said? "Leonard," he said, shutting his door with his foot, but he'd pressed the wrong button and tried again. "Steed, how are you?"

Leonard Steed was the somethingth-richest man in the

country or the world. He was rotten rich. He lived in a house as big as a house, to which Phil Needle would never be invited, despite several promises of future invitations. He had long hair on the back of his head and no hair in front, just a huge round space over his calm, pretty eyes, where he did his thinking, and long shirts half-unbuttoned that always seemed to be blowing in the wind. He was an outlaw and a rapscallion, a fortune finder and a problem solver, and Phil Needle was very lucky to know him, although Leonard Steed had told him once that all luck was skill.

"Who am I talking to?"

"Phil Needle."

"Good, good, good. How are you, Needle?"

"I'm good."

"I'm hoping so. Needle, Roger Cuff let me down."

Roger Cuff was another man in radio, with a long, shiny yacht he sailed into remote corners of the San Francisco Bay because, he once told Phil Needle in a whiskey whisper at an industry party, his twenty-three-year-old girlfriend liked to scream when he put it in her ass. He was another client of Leonard Steed's and had an idea for a show Leonard Steed said he liked first best.

"He let you down?"

"Down like the blues," Leonard Steed said with a staticky sigh. "You know his show idea, *What's on Your Mind*? I took a listen to the episode he finished and it's a no-go."

"What's wrong with it?"

"What's wrong with it is that people are apparently thinking about nothing anyone wants to hear. I mean, he found some guy outside a hospital and had him talk for a full forty-five seconds about his wife who was probably going to die. Who wants that? I don't want that. I want his wife to live, Needle."

"Of course."

"I thought a show that asked ordinary people to speak their minds would feel outlaw, you know?"

"Absolutely."

"And I placed so much confidence in Roger Cuff that I only listened to the show on the way out here, and now I'm out here, Needle, and I can't give them this. And so I called you because I know you have ideas."

"*Yes,* I have ideas." In Phil Needle's jumpy mind's eye he saw Cuff's yacht splitting in half as his ship sailed forward through the foam, Cuff, panicked and desperate, gripping one half of the boat, the girlfriend wet and frantic on the other half. Only time to rescue one of you.

"That's what I figured, Needle. That's why I co-produce your shows and why I took you on as a consulting client. Not a lot of people understand this business. It's not like how it was when I graduated Harvard. Everything's a dying art now."

"Don't get that way, Leonard." This was a scene they played about once a week, Leonard Steed the despairing king, Phil Needle the inspiring young ruffian. "I just finished my episode today."

"This thing you won't tell me about?"

"It's a surprise."

"Sure, but it's a show I want?"

"I think so."

"Don't *think so.* Answer me. Is it a show I want?"

"Yes."

"A good yarn?"

"Yes."

"A rich spoil?"

"Absolutely?"

"It has that energy?"

"Yes."

"That outlaw spirit?"

"Yes."

"That American thing?"

"Yes."

"Bring it to me, Needle."

This was his day, his chosen time. He felt sick with luck.
"Yes, okay."

"Get on a plane down here tomorrow."

"You want me to bring it in person?"

"Needle, I got no basket for my eggs. I need a desperado to come down and get me out of trouble. It's RADIO, remember?"

RADIO was Radio Artists and Development International Organization, a word problem Phil Needle could never remember because the *R* in RADIO stood for "radio," as if the whole thing was nothing more than a mass of cells splitting and resplitting instead of what it was, which was a professional organization that met once a year in a beachfront hotel in Los Angeles. Leonard Steed was on the board and was the one who got the networks involved, so what had begun as a few days of socializing had become a monstrous band of cutthroats and swaggering, misbegotten bullies plotting ventures well into the night. Phil Needle always came back with a sunburn.

"You told me it wasn't a good idea to go this year."

"I told you that as a consultant, Needle, but as a producing partner I'm telling you to fly down here tomorrow and bring me that show. I have one shot with the network at Saturday breakfast and I'm not giving them a man worrying about his wife."

"Okay."

"What does that mean, *okay*?"

"Yes, I will go."

"This is a downhill battle, Needle. They want something from me. You have a show you've been telling me I will like because it has everything we were just talking about. We walk in that room together, Needle, and no treasure will be denied us."

Phil Needle held his head in his hands and opened his legs wide in his chair. He had not made money for the first two years after New York, and the first time he finally did, with a six-ad campaign for Frankie's, he cried. The second time he bought some things. Third time cried. Fourth time bought some things. Fifth time bought some things. Sixth time bought some things. Seventh, eighth, ninth, tenth time bought some things, and then alternated buying and crying until this very moment. He thought about what to say, the line he could utter into the phone that would bring this treasure closer. "Yes," he said.

"Good," Leonard Steed said. "That's the other line. See you tomorrow."

The phone clicked off. Levine came in without knocking. "Just who I wanted to see," he said. "That was Leonard Steed."

"I know."

"How do you—"

"I answered the phone."

"Right. I need to go to Los Angeles tomorrow, for RADIO."

"Radio?"

"Radio Artists and Development International Organization. Book me on a flight first thing tomorrow morning."

Levine handed him an envelope. "I got the tickets like you asked me," she said.

"Already? But I just—"

"Tortuga, tomorrow night. Two tickets."

"You're pretty good with the promoters," Phil Needle said.

"So you'll keep me around?" She asked it like it wasn't a question, and then stood on tiptoes to take her bag off the hook on the back of Phil Needle's door. Her skirt rose very, very slightly, and Phil Needle wanted to touch on that briefly—the reason, if there was a reason, why Alma Levine kept working here.

It was the end of her first week, and everyone had gone home except for Phil Needle, who had been talking to the Fiona's people. Their club, Fiona's, had hosted some of the greatest American musicians on its stage, thanks to their estates, who agreed to license the likenesses and music of various artists on posters, shirts and recordings from the Fiona's archive. Only one photo existed of

Fiona herself, laughing at a speakeasy with a long strand of pearls dangling into her drink. Six weeks of research had failed to turn up the woman's actual identity. Actual clubs, in the tradition of the original Fiona's, were due to open over the next five years. Phil Needle had lost the bid to reinvent several jazz recordings into "Live at Fiona's" by adding crowd noise and a master of ceremonies, but after much negotiation he had the right to reinvent interviews as taking place at Fiona's in order to bolster what the Fiona's people called "mutual authenticity." The first interview would form the centerpiece of the Belly Jefferson story. Phil Needle hung up the phone and almost skipped out of his office, past Levine's glowing computer. He moved to put it to sleep when he noticed a folder on the screen marked "Personal."

> We never speak a word but I can feel your eyes searing into me whenever I walk into the room. Your hands look passionate and your mouth always seems hungry in a way that touches me deep inside. One night we're alone, late, taking a break from a deadline and we talk about how the world feels so wild at this time of night, reckless and free of all rules and inhibitions. You say we could do anything on a night like this, anything we wanted. I ask what you want to do. You unzip your pants. You ask me what I want to do. I close my eyes before I answer.

The story ended there, on the second page, and of course Phil Needle was not so foolhardy as to think it was about him. But, he thought afterwards, neither should he automatically assume it was about somebody else. The document had disappeared from the folder, and Phil Needle had not had the opportunity to see if Levine had hidden it elsewhere so he could read the answer she gave, if any.

It was like an interrupted broadcast, still crackling in the air some-place. "I want you to go with me," he said now. "I could use an assistant at a conference like this."

"You want me to go to Los Angeles?" she asked.

"I know it's last-minute," Phil Needle said, "but we're going to be pitching the America show. It's big and I need someone there. Can you go?"

"Okay," Levine said.

"Okay?"

"So, sir, why did you choose the name Incredible Cleaners?"

The crew laughed again and again. Levine was looking at him the way she looked at everyone in the office. In his hand were the tickets he had been given, and Levine was looking right through his contact lenses into his eyes. *You ask me what I want to do.* "Yes," she said.

"*Why the hell do you think?*"

Phil Needle tried to imagine the answer.

CHAPTER 3

Dear San Francisco Chronicle,

I am writing to you as a former sailor of the United States Navy. I have seen war and been a prisoner many times both in Malta and Devil's Island but never have I been treated so badly as in J.Bonnet which according to my research is a government-run facility both national and international. Help.

Not a word of this letter was true. Gwen listened to it, her eyes blinking and shivering, and wanted, ravenously, to steal something again. This was her punishment, not just having to be here but to be here and not want to be. It was not fair is what it was. She wanted to write it on her hand, NOT FAIR, but the only pen she could see was in someone else's hand.

"That's worth a comment," said the woman named Peggy. The office was very wide, and the wastebasket was full of the discarded tissues of someone who had been crying very hard. It was in the center of the building, like an internal organ, reached from hallways full of women pushing their own empty wheelchairs, and women in wheelchairs pushing themselves.

"It sounds like he doesn't like it here," said Gwen, who didn't blame him.

"That's what I mean," Peggy said, with a click of her pen. By the way, she was as big as a house. "We don't have the resources for full-time companionship. This is where we rely heavily on our volunteers."

She beamed at Gwen, just *beamed* at her, and Gwen could tell for sure that she was supposed to say something. "What?"

"You'll be his companion."

Gwen looked at her for a second.

"Of course, you must know something about Alzheimer's disease."

At this point in American history, Alzheimer's was a brain disease, degenerative, with no cure and no hope, just a slow gray fade. Gwen nodded quickly and tried to look solemn. When she was a child she thought it was "old-timers disease," which made a horrid sense.

"His condition isn't full-blown. His attention wanders, and you'll hear a lot of stories that aren't true." She held up the letter. "He writes to the newspaper every day. It's an accident waiting to happen. He fought against coming here, but after the Fall, of course, he didn't really have any choice."

Gwen didn't have to ask about the Fall. It happened to all old people, the Fall. They fell and then everything changed, seats in the shower, ramps at the front door. They fell and never quite got up again.

"He's not dangerous, of course," Peggy said, with a smile that sort of was. "Nor is he likely to harm himself. He's just getting into small trouble. A little hoarding, a little theft from the terrorists."

Gwen sat up straighter. "He steals things? From—?"

"Just candy. He has diabetes and can't eat everything, so you have to watch him when you go out there. We keep snacks."

Gwen decided that she must have said "terrace."

"He's really got the spirit of rebellion, but I guess we shouldn't be surprised. How long are you volunteering with us?"

Gwen didn't feel it was volunteering, not if she was being made to do it, but all her arguments about this had been chopped off long ago at the knees. "How about five weeks?" her mother had said, and her father just sat there. "That's a nice even number."

"Independence Day," Gwen said. "Until then." It was so far away, July. Weeks. Time just refused to pass. Gwen's life stubbornly refused to go on and take her to her own apartment with beanbag chairs in the living room where all her new friends could relax. Naomi was gone. Texts to her had blipped to nowhere, and Gwen had been reduced, in school's last days, to tailing Naomi trying to catch her eye. It was like grabbing an eel barehanded. If they could roll their eyes together it would mean they were reconciled, at least partway, that Nathan Glasserman was now water under the bridge at the pool. But Naomi even wore sunglasses at her. Every hallway was miles long until school stopped, Naomi far and out of reach. Her first swimming teacher, Miss Crudy, would hold out her hands as Gwen kicked and blew bubbles. "Almost there," Miss Crudy would say, and hold her hands out. "Almost there, almost there," but she'd be walking backwards the whole time, until Gwen had been lured the entire length of the pool with the promise that Miss Crudy was just inches away. Liars, Miss Crudy, all of them.

"Of course," Peggy said, "even after your, um, volunteering span, you're always welcome here."

The *um* meant Peggy knew it was punishment. So everyone knew. "I don't think so."

"Well, think of who you're helping."

Gwen clenched her hands so she wouldn't grab a pen.

"I want you to enjoy your time here. Enjoy it! I just need you to sign something."

If respect is shown toward the rules that were developed in response to the requirements of Federal, State, and Local Law and the requests of our clients, Jean Bonnet Living Center will be a much more pleasant and safer place for all. If rules are not respected, penalties will be assigned. Gwen, dizzied by the way they wrote this, was already penalized. Below the logo for the place, which was a silhouette of whoever the hell Jean Bonnet was, was "A Better Place," in flouncy letters all curled up like dental floss when you were done with it. She scrawled her name, Gwen Needle, and watched Peggy look at it before gesturing to someone Gwen had not known was in the room, a man with black shiny skin, enormous like a stack of pancakes in white pants and shirt, overflowing on a chair in the corner. "Manny here will show you the way."

"Okay," said Gwen, but Manny did not look like it was okay. Every wrinkle in his pants was scowling as he stood.

"Manny here is invaluable," Peggy said, her smile so bright and false that Gwen decided it didn't matter if *invaluable* meant valuable or worthless.

"My name's not Manny," the man said.

Peggy needed a better laugh. This one sounded worrying, a brittle falling down stairs or a wrong crackle when the Band-Aid was torn off. "We talked about this, Manny," she said. "The residents find it easier to remember than anything Jamaican." She swiveled to make Gwen a co-conspirator, but Gwen would stand with Manny through hell and blazes before nodding in agreement with this lousy wreck of a woman. "He makes wonderful tea," she was saying, "for all our guests sometimes. It's very traditional. Catnip."

"Cat*mint*," Manny said, but Peggy was cocking her head at her cardboard folder as it told her it was time for them to leave. "Manny here will show you the way and let you two get to it. If either of you need me, you know where to find me."

Manny gave the woman a look of disgust, and Gwen realized he hadn't yet looked at her. Peggy gave them both a little wave with the fingers she wasn't using to hold the folder, and Gwen followed him down the hallways. They passed two women who had walked their wheelchairs to a bench in order to sit on it, and a man in a chair who just sat there like a collectible. Manny said hello, gently, to one of the women, calling her Silver, although that might just have been her hair. Maybe he only hated fools, so Gwen tried not to be one.

"What part of Jamaica are you from?"

Manny shook his head. "Haiti."

"Isn't that—"

"It's a different country, white girl."

"I know that," Gwen said, though she hadn't been one hundred percent on that. From around a corner Gwen could hear a loud, scraped voice saying "Raisin! Raisin! Raisin! Raisin!," each time like it was starting all over, and she rounded that corner, and she was led through that door, and "Raisin! Raisin! Raisin!" was what he was saying when they found each other.

"Errol," Manny said.

He looked up from his chair, which he had moved closer to the sun. Gwen could see its wake across the bad rug. He had a plastic tray across his knees like an airline passenger, and on the tray was an overturned bowl and a small mountain of cereal he was picking through. The raisins were isolated in a line, as if they'd soon be marched off. Gwen was relieved. It was not crazy, to pick out the raisins, she hoped it wasn't.

"Cereal for lunch is ridiculous," he said to Manny, as if an argument were already in progress. "You're fired."

"You asked for cereal," Manny said, "and I don't work for you."

"For breakfast, I thought it was. Curse me."

"This is Gwen, Errol."

"I know who it is."

"She's volunteered to be your companion."

"I know who it is," Errol said again. "Leave me alone if you're not going to help."

This was, to Gwen, a very perfect sentence, just the thing she thought all the time. Manny backed out of the room and they sized each other up. The air between them felt awkward and managed, as if they were estranged, instead of being strangers. Gwen felt the familiar jitter, buzzy and smiley, of being next to old people. Her mother didn't like it either, she realized. That's why she'd chosen this for Gwen's punishment.

"How'd you get here?" Errol said finally.

"My mom drove me."

"No, I mean which way did you take?"

"We just took, um, Hill Street."

"Hill Street, no fucking kidding."

"Uh-huh." Was swearing against the rules? She had signed that thing.

"I mean I can't believe they called it Hill Street."

"Uh-huh."

"It is an insult," Errol said, with mild fury. "I guess I'll go my own way."

"I guess so," Gwen said. "I don't know what that means."

"It means, what do they teach you in school? Are you here for some kind of project?"

"No, punishment."

"Good, I'm glad. I don't like the school project kids. You know you're going to die when they come at you with a tape recorder. *Tell us about the Navy.* You want to know about the Navy?"

"No."

"Good. Are you here for some kind of project?"

"Punishment," Gwen said again, but felt bad about it and so added, "I'm your companion," which made it worse, but Errol didn't notice or forgot that he did notice.

"What'd you do?"

"Stole stuff."

Errol was putting a pinch of cereal in his mouth, and now he coughed long and hard at it. Gwen took a step toward him, but no more. He coughed and coughed, but Gwen did not do anything and could not think what to do. "As I live and breathe," he said.

"Are you okay?"

"What did you steal?"

"Candy, mostly."

"That's just what I'd steal. Did you steal it from here?"

"No, from a drugstore."

"What did you steal?"

"Candy, mostly."

Errol stared at her for a moment and then grinned. "From where?"

"The drugstore."

"Did I ask you that?"

"It's okay."

"I have a problem with my memory."

"That's okay."

"It's not a big problem. I worry about it, though. What's that river?"

"What river?"

"The big one."

"Mississippi?"

"Not the Amazon, the one in Egypt."

"The Nile."

"That's it. *Se-nile*. I made it up to remember. I worry about it, though. I have a problem with my memory. But I used to remember everything, even when I was a kid. What do you think about that?"

Gwen could not think about that. Errol surely had always been old. Gwen could not imagine him younger than he was. "I guess it's funny how life turns out?" she tried.

"Not last I checked," Errol said with a snort. "Raisin! Raisin! Want to help me?"

Gwen smiled. She felt as if something, a balloon, was untied from her and flitting toward the ceiling. She took another step forward and found a raisin.

"Raisin," she said.

"Raisin!"

"Raisin!"

"Raisin! Do you really want to know about the Navy?"

"No."

"Good. Raisin! I hate talking into the microphones they bring around here. When I have something on my mind I write the newspaper. I write them every day."

"Raisin! I know—Peggy told me."

"That Peggy's fat. I don't like her."

"Me neither."

"*Don't*," he said deliberately, "*don't like her.*" Gwen started to answer, but Errol lifted his fist and slammed it down into the tray. Cereal went everywhere, and the bowl bounced off a wall to spin on the floor, clattering, clattering, clattering, grumbling to a standstill. They looked at each other.

"Well," he said, as if he were telling her something that she of course knew already, "I'm not going to do it for you."

There was something about the quiet, perhaps because of the crash before it, that stung Gwen's eyes, but she knelt down to try and sweep up. "You don't have to do that!" Errol barked. "They have a staff! You're a companion, right?"

"Yes," Gwen said, still on the ground, and Errol's eyes slowly fell on her and smiled.

"I know you," he said.

"Yes—Gwen," Gwen said.

"That's it," he said. "I don't like this place."

"Yeah."

He opened his fist and one last raisin knocked its way down. *Raisin!* "Keep busy and keep your mind off your problems. *Make friends!* That's not going to keep my mind off my wife. She's dead."

"Of course not," Gwen said, getting mad at whoever, Peggy probably, had told him this. "Of course it wouldn't. Friends don't help."

"No, they do not," Errol said, with a fierce nod like he knew all about Naomi and her daggery ways. "Do you know? Do you know how she died?"

Gwen said she did not know.

"I didn't talk about her for two years after. Nobody likes to hear bad things. It was about a year. *Can't hoit*, she said. Do you know that joke? Those were her last words. We were joking when we met. We laughed like you wouldn't believe. *Can't hoit!* Those were her last words. They sent this lady at the hospital. Vera put her trust in her. Did I tell you this?"

"No."

"Dying in the hospital, so much pain. You wouldn't believe it. Like a dam breaking. They gave her everything. *Can't hoit!* she always said. And then this lady . . . "

This lady, as far as Gwen could tell, came to the hospital and sat at Vera's side. "Picture a trampoline," this lady said, holding the hand of Errol's wife, Vera. "Imagine that you're on a trampoline, up and down, up and down, up and down." The woman's voice was a traffic drone, lulling in its irritating pitch. Vera had been in pain for a long time. "You're jumping up and down on this trampoline, up and down, up and down. And now, Vera, now why don't you get off the trampoline? Why don't you get off for a while?" This lady worked for the hospital. They paid her to do this, to walk into people's rooms and talk them off the grit and jar of staying alive, the pain with each bounce. "Why don't you get off for a while?" She died just hours later. They killed her, those murderers, those terrible people with their smiling ladies.

"If any *man* dared that," Errol said, with a bit of froth, "I'd smite him by thunder, all right. By thunder I would. So they sent a woman to kill her, while the doctors went about their business as usual. *Can't hoit!* It is an insult."

"I know."

"We were joking when we met."

"You said. What was the joke?"

Errol wasn't listening. His eyes were very clear, very direct, completely focused on some lost punch line that nonetheless made him grin. Gwen waited in the nice space that had suddenly arrived.

"Thank you," Errol said quietly. "A nice memory is a nice thing."

"Sure," Gwen said.

"I don't like it here," he said, and then with both hands fished into one pocket. His fingers fought for a while and then handed Gwen something.

"Can you," he said, "please, mail this for me?"

The envelope had SAN FRANCISCO CHRONICLE written on it, nothing more. "Sure, of course," Gwen said. "That's easy." She could mail these every day. There was a mailbox right in front of the drugstore. They had a sign near the register about Lucky Seniors. Lucky Seniors receive our Lucky Senior discount. Let us know if you are a Lucky Senior. The awful words they throw at you. Gwen wanted to snarl at them; her hands itched to take whatever things they didn't want you to have.

"Did you really steal things?" Errol said. "Did I ask you that already, or somebody else?"

"No, I stole things," Gwen said.

Errol laughed. "Tell me all of it," he said. "I want a complete account of all the treasure."

"Really?"

"I'd be most happy."

"It was mostly candy."

"That's just what I'd steal. You want to read to me?"

"Sure, okay."

Errol pointed to a saggy shelf near where the bowl had fallen. Each step Gwen took toward it was a crunch of cereal. *Treasure*

Island. Marauders. The Dark Schooner. Mutiny! Piracy! The Aquarians. The Sea-Wolf. Captain Blood. Captain Black. Captain of the Black Flag. Seaward Sinister. Mardi. The Darkest Wind. Treasure Seekers. The Raid upon the Waves. White-Jacket. The Tempest. The Sea Witch. She had never heard of any of them. There were lots more. Gwen dubiously took out a book of poetry; old people probably liked poetry.

"I don't like it here," he said when she stood up again.

"I'm mailing your letter," Gwen said. "I'm going to mail that letter to the paper, Errol."

"It's not a big problem. I worry about it, though. What's that river?"

"Senile," Gwen said very quietly, but Errol drooped even at the whisper of it. The sun seethed down on the back of his bald head and the strange curl of a bulge on his neck, which was pillowed with white hairs. Gwen hadn't expected it would be like this, but of course it would be. Even with a happy childhood, or *naive* is the word Gwen thinks for it, you'd slowly start to be embarrassed by everything in the world, and eventually the weight of all these things, years and years of burdens and rebukes, would just collapse in your lap like a bag of heavy water, and your shoulders would sag from carrying all of it, and of course your shirt would be too small, plaid, buttoned too high and too tight, and of course your shoes would be ugly in some way that was demanded of you by the keepers of your prison hallways, and of course your face, Errol's face, would show all this, old in the land of the free, old and reined in with people punished to be your companion. These people, all of these people like Errol and herself, with their happiness stolen, every scrap of it, cast off with nothing they wanted. Surely there was a way to steal some back. She opened the book.

"Oh captain, my captain," she read uncertainly.

"No, no, no," Errol said, pointing at the pirates on the shelf. "Read me something else."

×

An easy way to broadcast a hero, Leonard Steed told him once, was to have the hero do something nice for a child right away, so the audience can see he's a good guy. The Belly Jefferson interview opens with Belly telling a story about teaching a kid the guitar—a story that was not part of the original interview, but one Phil Needle added to the show to make the heroism authentic. Phil Needle swirled honey on his daughter's toast before bumping it over to her. Gwen was staring out the window and biting into an apple. She was wearing a blue shirt with a green design, gray jeans, something with a hood tied around her waist, and some boots he had never seen before that Marina kept glaring at.

Gwen put the wounded apple down on the table. The bites were perfect.

"Are you going to eat that, Gwen?"

Gwen scowled at her mother and then shoved the whole toast into her mouth like she did. It looked like she was eating a sleeping bag. Her hair was tucked safely behind her ear, but what else was safe, squirreled away? Today, June whatever-it-was, Phil Needle was flying down to Los Angeles to seize what was his to be seized. But he worried about leaving Gwen. School was out and she had nothing to do but a punishment Phil Needle did not like to think about. Without swimming—why had she quit, could she just tell him that?—they didn't even spend time in the same body of water. With Marina it was worse. Last night they'd raged at each other until Gwen had stalked upstairs, where Phil Needle was hiding and trimming his nails. She had a pen in her hand, and before he could even look at her, she'd grabbed his wrist and written I HATE HER and was gone again with that music, Tortuga, turned up loud and muffled in her room. He'd scrubbed and scrubbed at it and there it was, still bruised on his skin. It looked like he'd had his hand stamped at a club.

"Are you?"

"What?"

"Are you going to eat that, Gwen?"

"I'm eating *toast now*," she snarled, and then turned to Phil Needle with very fake calm. "Thanks for the toast, Dad."

This fancy kitchen he could not afford, and it was a minefield.

Marina wouldn't quit. "Because if you're not going to eat it—"

"I'm *going to eat it*."

"—then you're wasting apples."

"I'm *going to eat it!*"

"They cost money. They don't grow on trees."

Phil Needle looked down at the front section of the newspaper, which at the time this story takes place showed a photograph of a senator who was resigning his position in order to spend more time with his family. Phil Needle also wanted to spend time with the senator's family. Look at them! Such beaming daughters! Not like Gwen, who was giving her mother a look of such violent nonchalance—*I don't give a fuck*—that she might as well have said it out loud.

"Talk to her," Marina said to him. "I'll finish your suitcase." Her robe ruffled with every step out of the kitchen. Gwen glared at everywhere. Phil Needle wished he could give her a tiny package with whatever it was inside, whatever her scowling little soul desired, but he couldn't. He couldn't, and since he couldn't, would she just goddamn stop?

"I know," he said, and sipped the last of his coffee, "that you're having a hard time right now."

Gwen replied that right now her time was fine.

"But I know, since the time at the drugstore—"

Gwen said that the drugstore thing was a long time ago.

"But you're having a hard time, am I right?"

Gwen said that he wasn't necessarily right all the time, okay?

Before Gwen he knew such people. To them he said: *Sleep it off.* Or: *Go get laid.* Or: *Sorry, it won't happen again, boss.* Gwen turned to him now and asked him to leave her alone. He wanted to. Instead, he took the envelope off the stack of papers he had ready for his voyage. They were in a neat stack, just the sort of stack he had hoped his assistant would put them in before he had to travel on business. He'd stacked them himself. He put the envelope down in front of his daughter and waited for her to ask what it was.

"It's tickets," he said finally, to his silent kid. "Tickets to Tortuga, like you asked me for. Tonight. But Gwen—" Gwen's wide, joyous eyes were already wary around the edges, eyeing the worm, knowing surely that there was a hook somewhere. "You know you can't go to the Fillmore alone. There are two tickets here, one for you and one for your mother." He put down his mug, reeling it in, the job of a parent, to steal his child's happiness after offering it as a possibility in the first place. "I haven't told her about it. I know you guys have been fighting, and so I want you to go together. You can either make peace with your mother or these tickets will go to waste."

Gwen didn't say anything. She did not say it was not fair, or that Phil Needle was the lowest viper that had ever crawled. She just stood, making up her own mind, her face as blank as a light switch. There she was. And there was his wife, with a *bonk-ruffle bonk-ruffle*, wheeling his suitcase down the stairs. And out in the courtyard, a young woman, hardly more than a girl, was standing near the benches, peering around as if she'd just woken up. Were homeless people in his building? With the fees he paid?

"I put in one more shirt," his wife said, "if you have to stay past Sunday."

"There's no way," Phil Needle said. "The conference is over with the weekend." The young woman was heading toward his door. Should he call the police? It was six-something in the morning.

"I hope it goes well," Marina said. She patted Phil Needle's hand, but she was also looking out the window. It wasn't until the girl started to knock that Phil Needle realized it was Levine.

"There you are," she said when Marina slid the door open. "I'm sorry, but I need forty dollars."

"What?"

"I'm really, really sorry," Levine said. Gwen had already retreated behind him, like she used to as a shy toddler. "I took a cab here and it's outside waiting. I forgot my purse at home. I can't believe it."

Phil Needle pointed to her purse. "That's not a purse?"

"That's my clothes," Levine said. "I packed light, just under-wear, et cetera. I figured we didn't want to check anything. I'm sorry."

"You'll need ID for the airplane," Marina said. "Phil, who is this?"

Phil Needle felt as if a jar of marbles had just been dropped on his floor. "This is Levine," he said, and reached for his wallet. "This is who works for me."

"The meter is running," Levine said, and stepped closer to the money. "It's nice to meet you, Mrs. Needle," she said to Marina, with a slight smirk at the robe.

"Oh, call me Marina," Marina said, the *Oh* in a tone she reserved for people who forgot their purses at home. Phil Needle curled up the bills.

"Here, go and pay your cab," he said.

"You're not taking a cab?" Marina asked.

"No, I'll park the car in the short-term lot."

"Do they let you do that for a whole weekend? Maybe you should just take that cab."

"*I'll do it,*" Gwen said, with sudden ferocity. In a flash the money was out of Phil Needle's hands and Gwen was sprinting across the courtyard. "*I'll do it!*" she called again, and then disap-peared toward the elevator. Marina frowned after Gwen and then looked down at Phil's inked hand.

"Were you holding a pen?" she asked him.

Phil Needle looked at his hands, and then at his wife, and finally found himself meeting Levine's amused eyes. All these wrenches, around which he had built his works. Holding a pen? A bag full of underwear, et cetera? Somewhere, a trophy was being made—forged—for him, and all he had to do was get out of the house to get it. It was like a million performances he had seen, where someone else got all the glory and ovations on stage. Some people clap, and stand, and then others decide to join them in the clapping and the standing and then other people have to stand up just to see what's going on, and the last stragglers agree to join the ovation, just because everyone else is clapping and standing and destiny has arrived. He was leaving the house. He was embarking. He did not notice, that Friday, on the counter, that the tickets he had given Gwen were already gone. He did not notice this because it was his destiny being forged for him this morning, not that of his daughter, who was already downstairs and opening the door of the taxi. Could not someone give this man a hand? It was his turn, if someone would just start clapping for him. If one person would just applaud his efforts, Phil Needle was sure his ovation would begin.

CHAPTER 4

Everything's ugly in an airport. Phil Needle rose on the escalator as if descending into rapids, the area lousy loud with bustle and cross-purpose. Hordes of church teens, bronzed European mothers with children but no bras. All these people and he'd never sleep with any of them. He looked with real regret at a young woman with tight, eager legs, hurry-hurry-hurrying her way out, her bracelets rolling down her arm to clatter against the handle of the bag rolling behind her. (That's one who died, on Roger Cuff's boat.)

"What are we on?" he asked Levine.

"What?"

"What did you book us on?"

"Winter Air."

"What?"

"Winter Air."

"What's that? What's Winter Air?"

"It's the cheapest thing on the computer. It was really cheap."

"I've never heard of Winter Air." He took a little bite of doubt while Levine headed toward a big neon *I*, for "Information," and stood in front of a sign with birds on it who were thanking Phil Needle for not smoking. He tried to think of a title—*American* something, *Visions of America*, which sounded nice until he thought of vision and radios. Levine, over at the I, pointed one way; the guy at Information pointed the other. The announcements were a scuffle of interrupts, someone's name called for, called for, called for, until Phil Needle began to be emotionally involved with Catherine Vogel and why she couldn't meet her party at the baggage claim area.

Alma Levine returned and led him. In one of the odd angles of the airport, where the architect's trapezoid met the budget, was a counter for another airline, with a banner reading WINTER AIR hung over the original's logo. The effect was startlingly Third World, and the woman behind the counter looked like his mother, who was dead. Phil Needle didn't want to think about it. She was on the phone.

"I'm just kidding," she said, and hung up. "I should tell you straight off that I'm American. There's some problem on the tarmac, so I'm just here as a stopgap."

"I'm going to Los Angeles," Phil Needle said hopefully.

"One or two?"

"Two," Phil Needle said, pointing at Levine.

"No, no, what flight number?"

"One," Levine said, and then, "I left my purse at home."

The woman clickety-clacked many, many letters into the computer, as if writing a paragraph about the plane. "Ooh," she said, with a toothy frown. "The plane's delayed. This is the problem I was talking about."

"How long?" Phil Needle asked.

"We're not supposed to know until nine."

"It's nine-oh-seven," said Phil Needle, and the clock on the wall.

"You know what I mean," the woman said, also like his mother. "Is there anything else I can help you with? The flight's canceled."

Catherine Vogel, Catherine Vogel. "What?"

"Just now," said the woman, typing again. "This happens a lot with Winter, I have to tell you. Let me see if I can put you somewhere."

Phil Needle found it was too early in the morning to summon the outlaw spirit. "Yes," he said, and wanted a banana muffin. "I really have to get somewhere."

"I'm American, like I said, so this will take a sec."

"I appreciate it."

"Just a sec. Okay, the two flights are collapsing."

"What is that?"

"Winter is collapsing them, One and Two. Unfortunately, Two is also delayed. All progress is incremental, huh?"

"I hear that," Levine said with a solemn nod. Phil Needle was not sure what language everyone was speaking.

"When are we leaving?"

"About an hour."

"An hour's not bad," Levine told him.

"Exactly," the woman said. "You can get a hot dog and go to the bathroom. Is your ID in your purse?"

"*Everything,*" Levine said, "is in my purse."

"And you?"

Phil Needle looked back at her. He, no, was not in Alma Levine's purse. "And me what?"

"We'll get you squared away," the woman said to Levine, and then to Phil Needle, "Identification."

Oh. Phil Needle handed himself over. At this time in history, this was done.

"There you go. Departs Gate D-Fifteen."

"D?"

"No, B."

"Wait, C? Cookie?"

"Yes, Cookie-Fifteen," the woman said, and Phil Needle

opened his eyes from a dream in which Eleanor was so sad and ghastly that he could not remember the rest of it. He was on the plane now, rattling down the state, the rigmarole with Levine at security over and blurred and leaving him in an aisle seat, having written, he saw slowly, "Possible Titles" on the top sheet in a new notebook, and "America," and given way to dozing. Levine was across the aisle with her head tilted forward so she could see out the window, half-blocked by the arm of the man next to her. The man's arm was in a cast, a stabilizing mass of plaster used by doctors at the time this story takes place, stabilized for some reason at an upward angle so it looked as if he was waving, or holding a hand puppet: *Hello! Hello!*

The flight attendant knelt down to sift through a drawer full of tiny bottles stored in a wheeled cart. She found the vodka and then she smiled at him with happy teeth. "Something to drink?"

"Ginger ale," Phil Needle said, Eleanor's ranting still in his ears and eyes.

"Do you want the can?"

"What?"

"The can?"

"Sure."

"I think I'll have ginger ale too," the woman next to him said brightly, and fanned herself with the information about what to do in an emergency. She had a bright red jacket on, pinned with a badge for a candidate who had already lost, but Phil Needle had found her warm when she rubbed past him on her way to her assigned seat, in the uneasy intimacy of their unfair close quarters. "My name's Jane."

"Phil Needle," Phil Needle said. In a minute he and Jane would learn they had the exact same birthday. The flight attendant handed him two cups of ice and two cans of ginger ale, like he and Jane were supposed to work things out for themselves.

"Are you traveling alone, Phil?" Jane asked.

"No," Phil Needle said. "She's with me." The cart went by and both of them could see he'd gestured to Alma Levine, who was carefully pouring the tiny bottle of vodka into her cup and saying something to the puppet guy.

"I'm alone," the woman said, startlingly not asking who Alma Levine was. "I won't be alone when I get there, though. I'm meeting somebody."

Leonard Steed said that whenever he sat next to someone on an airplane, he viewed them as an average American and tried to pitch ideas for programming to see what an average American would like. Leonard Steed had his own plane, of course, but still Phil Needle tried to steer the talk that way. "Do you listen to the radio?" he asked.

Jane shook her head, although it wasn't clear she was actually saying no. "Don't you want to know who I'm meeting?"

You don't care that I'm with a much younger woman who's drinking at ten in the morning, but "Sure."

"Guess."

"Boyfriend."

"That's right," she said, chuckling and sipping ginger ale. "Wow, first guess. Now guess what he looks like."

"Tall," Phil Needle said. Bubbles in his drink popped on the surface. "I bet he likes to listen to the radio."

"I'm surprising him," Jane said, and took another sip, a little too big. "Cancer."

"I'm sorry to hear that."

"No, no, I mean it's almost his birthday. I believe in astrology, very strongly. Do you believe in astrology?"

American Astrology, he thought idly.

"What's your birthday?"

The coincidence was discovered, with some squealing. Levine raised her eyebrows at him and finished her drink, and on cue the airplane shifted stiffly downward like a flipped switch. Out the window, the bluey mosaic of swimming pools hadn't started up; they weren't near Los Angeles yet. He looked down at the paper: "Possible Titles," "American," the last words he would ever write?

"Do you think there's a problem?" Jane asked him.

"No, I think we just hit air," Phil Needle said. "So tell me, what kind of music do you like?"

The plane dipped again, right in everyone's stomachs. Jane named an idiot.

"You like him?" I'm going to die next to you?

"You're not going to die," said the crackle on the loudspeaker. Not a word was audible, but the message was clear.

"Did you catch all that?" Levine asked him. Her hand, the one not clutching the cup, reached across the aisle and rested on his shoulder. "Did you catch any of it?"

"No," Phil Needle said, one shrug for his assistant and the other for Jane.

"I really hate flying," Levine said. "I'm scared of it."

Phil Needle watched her suckle spiked ice with new understanding. The flight attendant said something to the business class passengers, too far from poor Phil Needle to be audible, and then walked halfway down the plane to repeat herself.

"As I'm sure you heard from the announcement," she said, "our plane is experiencing electrical problems. They are not dangerous, but as a safety precaution we are landing ahead of schedule. Please put away all your carry-on items, including purses and cell phones."

"We're landing early?" Levine asked.

"I'm sorry," the flight attendant said. "Purses and purses. You may keep your cell phones. I'm sorry, computers."

"But we're not in Los Angeles?" said another passenger two rows up. He looked like a monkey, with a monkey face.

"We're landing early," the flight attendant said, "at San Jose International Airport."

"San Jose?"

"Your luggage will be made available to you if you wish to arrange for alternate transportation," the flight attendant said. "We won't have an accurate assessment of how long repairs will take until we're on the ground."

"You mean it's going to be a long time and we should find another flight to L.A.?" said the angry monkey.

"We won't have an accurate assessment of how long repairs will take until we're on the ground," the flight attendant said, as if she hadn't before.

"What is she saying?" said some poor fool even further back. The flight attendant didn't answer but began dumping everyone's cups into a bag. San Jose veered into the window, an ugly and successful city with several affiliates airing radio shows Phil Needle had produced. Still, no one recognized him as the plane bumped into town. The brakes were loud and rough, and Phil Needle had the feeling the other planes were laughing scornfully at Winter Air as they taxied into a paltry gate. Disembarking Phil Needle realized the page of titles was still crumpled in his mad hand.

"I need to give you this," he told the flight attendant, but she frowned as he pressed it into her hands.

"I'm sorry," she said. "I can't accept this. Winter Air does not allow its crew to accept gratuities."

"It's not money," Phil Needle said, and uncrumpled the paper in front of her. Behind him, passengers wondered what was going on. "I wouldn't tip you, not for this shitty morning. Talk about not meeting my needs!"

He didn't say any of this last half, of course, not out loud, though he reworked several drafts of it as he stalked beside Levine. The airport was skimpy, just a couple of hallways, and everyone in it looked unhappy.

"What shall we do?"

Phil Needle saw that Levine wasn't going to solve this, either.

"Get a rental car," he said. "We can throw our suitcases in the back and floor it down there. It should be quicker than waiting for Winter Air."

"Yeah, Winter Air blows," Levine said. "Okay, a car. Down here, I think."

"I have to get my suitcase first," Phil Needle said.

"Right, I forgot you checked things," Levine said. "I'll find the car."

But she had found this terrible airline. "No, stay with me," Phil Needle said. "I might need you for something."

Levine narrowed her eyes but followed him as he followed the arrows. In this day and age, people's baggage was found on something called a carousel, even though it was nowhere near as elegant or circusy as the term implied. WELCOME TO SAN JOSE, MANY BAGS LOOK ALIKE. The machine whirred into life and, surprisingly, the bags began to appear, just as Winter Air had said they would. Phil Needle watched for his suitcase among the tossed and tumbling bags, but the closest he could find was another suitcase, similar in color, that went unclaimed for lap after lap around the carousel while Phil Needle and Levine stood in silence. He thought he could smell the vodka on her breath, but it was possible he was making that up. He turned on his phone and looked at the names of the people he knew.

It's difficult to make Phil and Marina Needle the heroes of their love story. They had smiled vaguely at each other for a couple of years in New York, whenever Marina came in to do voice work. Through a seedy boyfriend she'd started out dubbing Italian horror movies—you can hear her to this day, badly synchronized with the scarlet lips of vampire victims—and then moved into radio ads, cooing suggestively over nightclubs or with prim anxiety about who to call if you have been in an accident. It was a good voice— you could almost picture the injured husband, wincing behind a shattered windshield. Phil Needle paid no real attention to her, as it was the long story of Eleanor at the time, screaming and lying, and anyway Marina was dating a guy, another seedy boyfriend named Rafael Bligh, who was all wired up with his idea of having Marina record descriptive narration of classic films for the blind. She'd hole up with Rafael in an unused booth for the afternoon, and Phil Needle would walk by and catch a glimpse of her saying "The old man drops the snow globe" or "She slowly picks up the black statuette" while Ray stood behind her offering advice and, Marina told him later, cupping her ass. She'd dated another guy too, who worked there before. Too many boyfriends and you look like a bitch.

The party was on a hot, crappy night in a Brooklyn brownstone with crackly staircases and long, leaning hallways, and inside were people loud and laughing. The hosts were friends Phil Needle had since lost track of, and the room was full of strangers. Reggae loped out of speakers someplace. The ceiling was strung up with too many lights. An inked sign taped to a ceramic bowl read TONIGHT I'M AN ASHTRAY, and there was a tall, skinny boy of no more than twelve sulking in front of the refrigerator where the beer probably was. The drugs had worn off on the subway and Phil Needle's arm still hurt where Eleanor had scratched him. He stepped back out the door and climbed a metal ladder to the roof, where it was cooler and seven or eight stars could be seen. He stood up there for a moment, beneath the stars, and then, without Phil Needle having said a word to anyone, the brittle floor collapsed beneath him, right where he was standing. He fell halfway and then stopped, his legs kicking air beneath him and his hands clawing on the sandpapery surface of the roof. Strangers reached out to him and tried to drag him out; strangers ran up the ladder and pulled at his legs. Tipsily the two strategies were debated, but nobody, Phil Needle noticed, talked to Phil Needle much. At last he was down, and, wiping his plastery pants, he decided to leave. He ran into the twelve-year-old boy on the stairs. It was Marina, with a new haircut. A year later they were married, not at the sort of wedding where all the guests are flush with happiness, believing the couple to be a symbol of all that is right with the world, though neither was it the kind with everyone thinking it wouldn't last. It was just a wedding, memorable to guests only because the rabbi asked for the rings when he already had them himself. They were still married, and it was not a loveless marriage—Phil Needle certainly did not think that, scrolling down the list of names in his cell phone's memory—though something had downshifted. Marina had changed, becoming the sort of woman who bought a bottle of iced tea and stuck a straw in it and walked around all day, sucking, sucking, sucking. More and more, Marina stayed in the room where she did her paintings. Lord knew why she wanted to paint. She couldn't take photographs—many of their vacations, to anyone glancing at the pictures, had been spent in the looming shadows of giant thumbs. There was a shadow over Phil Needle, too. Marina had not erased the girl, Eleanor, who didn't want him anymore, and for these reasons and more Phil Needle didn't want to phone his wife, who had left too many messages, it looked like. He erased them, almost by accident, unheard, and then on impulse he scrolled ahead of Marina's name alphabetically and called his father for the first time in months.

"Hello."

"Hi, Dad."

"Who is this?"

"Your son."

"My son is dead," like always.

"*Dad.*"

"He died of drugs."

"This is your *other* son, Dad. Phil."

"You're dead to me too."

"No," Phil Needle said. "No, I'm not."

"You both did drugs."

"Dad, *please.*"

Alma Levine blinked out of a reverie and frowned at him. Most everybody had their bags, except for whatever schlump hadn't claimed the suitcase similar to Phil Needle's. From the tinny, tiny speaker on the phone came the laughter Phil Needle had never liked.

"How's what's-her-name?"

"Marina's fine, Dad. How are you?"

"Fit as a fiddle. And Gwen?"

Phil Needle knew this conversation like the back of his hand, and looked at it now. The ink was still there. Behind it, the similar suitcase made another lap, and it occurred to Phil Needle that someone had taken his suitcase by mistake and left him with this. "She's fine, too. I'm just calling, Dad, to check up on you, I guess."

"Well, it's the world that's all gone wrong."

That was it, of course. It had come to this. Some passenger— the monkey guy, it came to him—had taken his suitcase and Phil Needle was now alone, standing with Alma Levine in a strange place like Adam and Eve while this voice talked to him, his father, from nowhere. He had nothing to wear, he had nothing for a title, and he stood alone with his head filled with schemes for his own deliverance. And then on the umpteenth lap he saw that it was his baggage after all.

"I tell you," said his father, "black people—"

"Don't start," Phil Needle said.

×

The magazine wanted to know if Gwen knew what all girls had in common. There was a girl on the cover, and the address label for the magazine, DR. DAVID DONNER, DDS, was pasted on the girl's denim thigh, with another sticker on the other leg, DO NOT REMOVE, as if she were prepped for surgery. Gwen picked up the girl. No, she could not imagine what they had in common.

Parental jazz hummed around the waiting room, empty except for another girl, Gwen's age probably, dressed better, with a long chainy necklace, spreading out the magazines like she was tiling a floor and angry about it. The office woman behind the open, sliding window kept frowning behind her headset, deciding whether or not to say anything.

"This is the *worst ever*," the girl said. She was not looking at Gwen. "The *worst ever* selection of magazines I've seen *ever*."

Gwen had been dropped off by her mother for her dental appointment, rather than her mother waiting for her. She wasn't grounded anymore, and Gwen's mother was trusting her to walk herself to her punishment when the dentist was over. Gwen's mother had hardly needed to remind Gwen that she should not screw this up. Gwen was determined to screw it up, but had not yet seen how.

"There is *nothing* worth reading here. This is *atrocious. Verily.*" She slapped down the magazines so hard that the lamp rattled. The woman sighed and leaned through the window, her hand pressed flat against the textured glass.

"Is there a problem?"

"*Yes.*"

"*Amber.*"

"Don't *Amber* me. This waiting room is stupid. *And* I have a nine-thirty appointment and it's nine forty, almost nine forty-five."

"That clock's off," said the woman.

"Well, then that should be fixed too."

"*Amber.* Is there a problem?"

"I just *told* you."

The woman slid the window shut. "*I know you can hear me!*" Amber called, and slapped a magazine down on the table before giving Gwen a sudden grin.

"The magazines do suck," Gwen offered.

"*Verily,*" Amber said again.

"*Verily.* What's *verily?*"

"Like, for real."

"Oh."

Amber snorted and drummed her dirty nails. "I hate coming here. All those fingers in my mouth. *And* my teeth are *fine*, you know?"

"Me too," Gwen said, although she'd never thought to be bothered by the dentist.

"Verily," Amber said with a fiendish grin. Her teeth *were* fine. Dr. Donner walked in and gave them each a sigh.

"Gwen, hello, thanks for waiting. I have you in One, and Amber, you're in Two."

"Aren't you going to thank *me* for waiting?"

"Thank you for waiting, Amber."

The window shuffled open. "I think they were fiddling with the magazines," the woman sang out to Dr. Donner. Amber said nothing, so Gwen looked at the woman, who had never been kind, not since Gwen at seven or eight had thrown up at her first fluoride treatment.

"I fail to see your controversy," Gwen said, something she'd read to Errol just the other day, although Dr. Donner tilted his head a bit, doglike, so maybe she'd said it wrong. Amber smiled behind his back, and Gwen returned the smile and went into Room One and lay down on the daisy yellow chair, squishy and tilted so she had to look at fake duck butts and duck feet they'd attached to the ceiling to create the disquieting illusion that patients were having their teeth cleaned at the bottom of a pond. She was separated from Room Two by half a wall and a large bubbly aquarium filled with very small fish. The aquarium never covered the sound of the drill or even the patients, and Gwen could hear Amber's sour replies to Dr. Donner's muttered questions: "I'm not." "I'm *not.*" "I *said* I'm *not.*" "No, *you* are." "I don't care." "I don't care." "I don't care." Gwen smiled at it. Amber, her name was, but she didn't know anything else. Now they'd never see each other again.

Dr. Donner came in, wiping his hands of Amber. "And how are *you*?" he said.

"Fine," said Gwen.

"I trust you don't have any quibbles about what we'll do today."

"What?"

"I said, I trust you don't have any quibbles—"

"No," said Gwen. Dr. Donner had considerably less hair than last time.

"I'll have my associate clean and polish your teeth," he said, "and then I'll come in to give you a complete checkup and make sure your smile is the kind that all the boys look at." He raised his eyebrows and gave her the smile of the world: *Please let us have a laugh at your expense.* "Is there anything you'd like me to look at?"

"Just that thing," Gwen said.

"What thing?"

"That thing that's on my chart; you never remember it."

Dr. Donner frowned and opened a folder. From the other side of the tank Gwen was pretty sure she heard Amber snort. "Oh yes, that irregularity," he said.

"I always forget what it's called."

"It's an irregularity," he said again, mortifyingly. "After my associate does the polish, I'll come in with the Aquapressure system. You know the drill."

Gwen knew the drill, ruthless, relentless, useless. Dr. Donner's associates were all motherly women who didn't like kids, so Gwen faced the ceiling and closed her eyes. She imagined that she really was underwater, drifting in a thick layer of duck shit and toddler-tossed bread, while the associate put on gloves and began to tramp around Gwen's teeth. *All those fingers in my mouth*, Amber had said, and now it bothered her.

"Don't!" It was loud, on the other side of the tank.

Dr. Donner muttered something.

"I said *don't*!"

The associate sighed. Gwen kept her eyes closed and tried to join up with Amber's fiery anger. "I said *don't*! I don't *care*. I don't *care* who hears me. I don't like it and I'm not going to put up with it."

Gwen grinned, closing her lips around the associate's fingers. "Hey."

"Sorry," Gwen said.

"I *won't*."

Dr. Donner muttered something again, and there was the clink of his poky tools.

"I *won't*."

Mutter-mutter.

"*You* shut up."

Amber, mutter-mutter-mutter.

"*You*."

A great, clinky sigh.

"Then *fuck* you. *Fuck you!*"

The music was turned up, and the rest was lost underwater. The exam took longer than usual—Gwen kept smiling—and Two was empty when Gwen left One, the chair tilted and clean but the paper where Amber had rested her head crumpled like an angry brow. The woman behind the window gave Gwen a little card with the details of her next appointment on it. She agreed to keep an eye on her gums and walked out to find Amber leaning against the far wall of the parking lot, mouthing the words to her music. From the other end of the lot she seemed to be in a steady, angry shiver, as if wearing cold clothes. But when Gwen crossed to her, she could see that Amber had one shoe off and was rubbing it vigorously sideways against the concrete. "Hi," she said to Gwen, too loud.

"Hi," Gwen said, but kept walking so she wouldn't look eager.

Amber scowled and took her music off her ears. Gwen thought she might recognize the tinny, tiny beat. "Fine, don't say hi."

"I said hi."

Amber smiled then. "Maybe," she said, and kept rubbing her shoe.

"What are you doing?"

"My new shoes. Toxes, but I don't want them looking so new."

"Toxes?" Gwen's mother wouldn't buy her Tox.

"Yeah, I know, they look stupid, right? So new like this. You wear Tox?"

"My mom won't buy them."

"Well," Amber said, "your mother's a bitch."

Amber laughed then, loud and hoarse, and Gwen joined in. The laughter could have meant anything on that day, that the *bitch* was a joke or was absolutely true. "Verily," Gwen said, and they laughed again.

"Here, do the other one."

Gwen knelt down beside her and took the shoe off Amber's foot, bruised with broken black polish. "You gotta redo your nails."

"You think it looks stupid?"

"It looks like you did it a long time ago."

"Well, I did," Amber said, squinting at Gwen like she was reconsidering. Gwen smiled, quickly, and started wearing down the shoe. "Relax," Amber said. "What's your name—Gwen? Are people usually mean to you? You act like people are mean to you."

"I guess," Gwen said, rubbing rubbing rubbing. "I don't know." It was a few seconds before it became enormous, the thing Amber had said, a firework that sparked in the dark for a bit before flowering out across her whole body. It was true. Gwen had not thought of it like that.

"At school?" Amber asked.

"Everyplace," Gwen said shakily.

Amber smiled. "How was it in there?"

"Dr. Donner? Okay." Gwen took a breath. "Better than yours."

"Yeah."

"I guess it's not your day," Gwen said, something her father said sometimes.

"It's not my life," Amber said, dropping her music on the ground for drama. "*And* I want to do something else, you know? Different?"

"Yeah," Gwen said, gripping the shoe harder. "I know, I know, exactly."

"Exactly *verily*," Amber said, and put on her shoe. She stood up, and Gwen looked right between her feet, one bare and one shod. "Give me that, it's good enough," Amber said. "You want to go to the bakery? It's stupid, but I need a snack."

"Okay."

"I like to eat sugar right after going in there," she said with a sharky grin at Dr. Donner's door. Gwen nodded. They walked toward a short, depressed neighborhood with a few stores and shops, all crowded in by wires for the streetcar, which at the time this story takes place overhung the streets like a sketch for a claustrophobic dome. Gwen took one last look at the direction she had promised her mother she would walk, and at Dr. Donner's cross office.

"Are you in trouble for that?"

"In there?" Amber sighed. "Probably. Thanks for nothing, *Dr. Donner*. I'll hear about it at home."

"I just got done being grounded."

"For what?"

"I took things at a store," Gwen said.

"Like, stealing?"

"They could have pressed charges."

"Did they tell you that stupid thing? They don't charge girls our age."

"Well, there's punishment. I have to volunteer at this place for old people."

"Today? Can I go with you?"

"What? There?"

"Is that stupid?"

"No, I don't know. It's old people."

"Do you like it?"

Gwen stared out at traffic for a second. "Yes," she said. "One guy, anyway."

"So I'll go with you. Better than no place. What do you do, swim?"

"How did you know?"

Amber pointed at a badge Gwen had forgotten she'd pinned to her bag. It said MARIONETTES and had the silhouette of a slender, graceful woman. "Are you good at it? I can't swim at all."

"I don't know."

"I bet you are." Amber ran her nails through her hair, fingers crossed like she was actually betting on something. None of the cars stopped, each of them with someplace to go, but Gwen couldn't walk, only look right at her. "I bet you're good," Amber said.

Gwen could not believe how easy this was.

Le Bakery, French for "the Bakery," was a place Gwen had never been, and for a moment on arrival she stared with Amber at the window display of cracked, old wedding cakes and cookies misting up under the yellow lights. Then they heard it, faint laughter, and realized two boys had been looking at them from inside the bakery, making faces while they blanked out at the pastries. Gwen didn't recognize them until she clattered open the broken door and entered the place.

What *do* all girls have in common? Nathan and Cody Glasserman were on their way out with a big pink box. Nathan had on a large, billowy shirt, maybe his dad's, unbuttoned enough for a glimpse of his chest, and big ratty shoes with untied laces; Cody blinked underneath a baseball cap and was carrying the box by the string. The boys and girls paused for a moment in virtual voraciousness—the great fierce swath heterosexuality has scorched across the planet—and then the boys smiled.

"Those cakes were hypnotizing you," Nathan said. "Remember: one moment on the lips, forever on the hips."

"Brave words for a guy with a whole cake," Amber said.

"I swim," Nathan said with a shrug. "Eat what I want."

Amber turned to Gwen. "You guys know each other?"

"We all do," Cody said, and Nathan gave him a small shove. A comic book fell out of his pocket—a heroine in flames getting revenge with big boobs. He picked it up with a blush as Amber walked by. Nathan and Gwen were left looking at each other, Gwen remembering the part of the magazine date guide on how to turn a no into a yes. 1. Control your emotions. 2. Decide if you got a mixed message. 3. Understand the other person's motivation. 4. Offer a revised date.

"Who's the cake for?" Gwen tried.

Nathan blinked very slowly, and she had to stop herself from licking her lips.

Cody stood back up and looked at her sympathetically, and his big brother gave him a shove. "Get going, Yankee," Nathan said, and made a motion with his circled hand—just like her father had about Allan, up and down, along an imaginary penis—that ruined the word "Yankee" for Gwen forever. "Hey," he said to her, with bright eyes. His hand was still circled. "I think you're like a pirate treasure."

"What?" she asked. How did he know?

His hand uncurled and pointed right at her. "Sunken chest," he said, and ruffled Cody's hat on his way out. "See ya, Spot." Gwen could not watch them, only the cake in the box, each time it bounced in Cory's hands, like a boat in a storm. Naomi's birthday, she thought with some relief, was not now.

"Who were those guys? I've seen them."

"Nathan Glasserman and Cody Glasserman."

"Jerk."

"Yes."

"But gorge."

"What?"

"Gorgeous."

Gwen felt a jealous shiver. She hunched over so nobody would see her sunken chest and decided to do so every day until she died. This would be our Nathan's legacy.

"What was it you said, though?" Amber said, slipping a pen out of her pocket. "I fail to see the contraband? I prefer older guys, like Tortuga."

"Controversy."

"Piece of paper?"

"What? Yeah." Gwen unzipped her bag. "Tortuga's cool."

"But you like that Glasser guy?"

"Well," Gwen said, and then didn't say anything.

"It's okay to like jerks. I mean, it'd be better to like a nice guy, but there aren't any. Look at them."

Gwen tore out a piece of paper and Amber held it to the wall and started writing on it immediately.

"Don't you wish," Amber started, and then paused to scribble more, "that with guys like that you could just kidnap them? You know, and shut them up somehow?"

"Like, stuff them into a car," Gwen said. She could not tell if she had thought of this before or was just thinking of it now.

"Have our wicked way with them," Amber said. "What do you want?"

"What?"

"Don't get a muffin; they taste like potpourri. You like the almond cookies?"

"I've never been here."

"But you know what cookies are, right? With almonds?"

"Yeah, okay."

"Six almond cookies," she said, and then finished with the paper. "With my ex, it was like that. I hated when he talked most of the time."

Her *ex*. Gwen followed her to the counter. "Amber, my princess," the man said. "What does your father want today?"

Amber frowned at the paper like she couldn't read it. "Two black coffees, two chocolate chip, six almond cookies," she read, and drummed those nails, those nails, on the wall.

"Charge it to his account?" the guy said.

"That's what it says." Amber slid the paper over to him. He turned to get the coffee, and she leaned into Gwen. "I can do anyone's handwriting. Anyone's."

"Wow."

"We don't need a tray," she told the guy, and handed Gwen one of the coffees.

"All right," he said. "Tell your dad to send us more vinegar."

"I will," Amber said with a smile that stayed on until they were back outside.

"Your dad makes vinegar?"

"I know." Amber took out a cookie and broke it in half against her chest, handing one piece to Gwen and opening the lid on her coffee. The steam rose into the air, disappearing before it reached the streetcar lines. "It's stupid. He and another dad bought some land up in Napa and they grow grapes, to make a fortune off wine. *And* the wine was awful. So now they make vinegar, and they named it after me and the other guy's daughter. *Amber Dawn Vinegar*. Can you stand it? Thanks, name me after bad salad dressing, *Dad*."

"He makes vinegar in Napa and gets his cookies here?"

Amber was looking at her. "Vinegar is just on weekends," she said.

"Oh. What's the rest of the time?"

"He's a *dentist*," Amber said, and pointed back toward his office.

"Dr. *Donner*?"

"Yeah, I know, right? Hey, I didn't ask, but you wanted coffee, right? Otherwise pour it out."

"It burned me when I was little."

"What?"

"I was four and I reached up for a doughnut and spilled a carafe of coffee. It was boiling hot. It was a second- and third-degree burn. I ruined my grandmother's birthday, because we all had to leave the hotel and wait in the emergency room. I still have it, the scar of it on my leg. That's what he meant, Nathan, *Spot.*"

But Amber was already outraged. "What? Ruined your grandmother's birthday? Who told you that?"

"Everybody."

"They told you it ruined her birthday? *And* what about your leg? You were *four*?"

"I don't know," Gwen said. "My parents said when I was four I was trouble. They still think it. I'm still trouble."

Amber took a sip of coffee and spat it right back in the cup, shaking her head. "They are wrong," she said. "Gwen, they are wrong, your parents. Let's go to my house."

"I have to be at the Jean Bonnet Living Center later. That's the place I was saying."

"The old people?"

"He's depending on me."

Amber grabbed Gwen's coffee and dropped it into the street in one deft move. "Okay, but my house after, right? We can do, I don't know. TV, but I hate TV. We can listen to music."

"Where do you live?"

It just kept getting bigger, bigger, bigger. Just when Gwen was heart-beaten and all her fortifications down, to have this offered her, this maiden voyage to a new place previously uncharted in the plotted day, made her eyes wet. All of it was thrilling, but the thrill's first swell was there on the corner when Gwen asked this forger and flirt, this fierce battler against fathers, this rogue adventurer with gypsy earrings and embattled nails, where she lived. Where do you hail from, marvelous Amber, who shall expound thee? Whither your three-bedroom, two-bath?

"Octavia," Amber said, just the name of the street, but smiling like she knew all along.

CHAPTER 5

"Radio?" Levine asked.

"Yes, yes." Phil Needle was still furious about the rental car, and the rental car growled on the asphalt like it was mad back. The stupid girl at the stupid airport had given him a car no man should be seen driving, be he even of most humble birth, and she had done her job as if at gunpoint. It made him want to shoot her, but there wasn't much time, still so far from L.A., a drink at the bar, enough sleep for the big pitch in the morning. The way out of the rental lot was long, curving past the strange parts of the airport, the warehouses and private planes, man in a suit—me—looking up hopefully from his cell phone as he waited for his ride. Phil Needle was not it. He turned the knob, and there was the thumping song that his daughter liked so much. "Tortuga," he said.

"Hey," Levine said, "did you go to a club?"

"A club?"

"Yeah, the handstamp."

Phil Needle rubbed his hand. "Yes," he said primly. "I know I probably seem old to you, but I still go hear music. It's how I keep in touch with what's going on."

"Who did you hear?"

"What?"

"Last night."

"Nobody good."

"Nobody good," Levine repeated, and rolled her window down further to stick her hand out into the air, cupping the wind like a breast.

"Can you keep a secret?" Phil Needle asked.

"No," Levine said immediately.

Phil Needle kept his hands on the wheel.

"Yes," she said.

"Well, I think what I'm going to do down here is going to be very big," Phil Needle said. "This is a big show."

"The Belly Jefferson thing?"

"Yes," Phil Needle said, "and just as Belly Jefferson, with just a few short songs, electrified the world of music, I think this show will change everyone who listens to it. And I will be producing it, so I will be listening to it most. It will change me, and all of us, profoundly." He had a lot of interesting things to say, every day, if only somebody would write them down.

"You sound excited," Levine said, and tapped one finger on her window.

"I guess I am," Phil Needle said.

"Ray always said that," she said. "You should have that desire, the desire to do things. He told the whole company, it gets everybody excited. It's like a turn-on. You have the same thing."

They had come to a place where some men were working on the road. No, one of them was a woman. "I mean it. I know I don't sound like I mean anything, but I do."

"Well," Phil Needle said, and then thought he should say "thank you." He did not say it. He thought again, again, again, of the document he had found on Levine's computer, and felt a small flutter between his legs, underneath the seat belt.

"What are you going to call the show?"

"I was going to have you write it down. I have that notebook. I can't think of it. I can't think of what to call it."

"Well, that's what I'm here for," Levine said, briefly hoisting one leg onto the dashboard before sliding it off. "Do you want to do it now?"

"We could stop for lunch," Phil Needle said. "We should stop, at some point."

"I'm a vegetarian," she said, meditatively.

"Really?" Phil Needle said. "Because of the animals, or—"

"The animals, right."

Phil Needle thought about it. It was a shame about the animals, but the other thing was, who cares? "It might be hard to be a vegetarian on this road," he said. "San Francisco's full of vegetables, but they just kill things here in the middle. There's a steak house, I know, a ranch that's still a ranch, I think."

"Well, I just lost my appetite," Levine said. "Actually, I'm starving." She stretched her leg again, her heel rubbing against the plastic or whatever it was that the glove compartment was made of. Her legs could not help but be open, just a bit, while she did this. It had to be plastic. "Now, can *you* keep a secret?"

Phil Needle smiled right away. "No."

"Then I'm not going to tell you," Levine said with a smile for the road.

"I was kidding."

"So was I." She continued to smile out the window rather than at Phil Needle. "Ray Droke?"

"Who?"

"We were just talking about him. Ray Droke. My old boss."

This wasn't going to be exciting. "Yeah. Advertising, you told me."

"You didn't call him?"

"What?"

"Ray Droke."

"No." Phil Needle shook his head, swinging the view in front of him.

"I listed him as a reference. You didn't call him?"

"No," Phil Needle said again, and then added, "Not yet," although he wasn't going to call him, and it was too late now. Alma Levine, with her leg up, her eyes inscrutable behind her sunglasses, reflecting the bright sun and the stupid road, worked for him. She was his, or he was hers: anyhow, they were together already, in the car.

"Remember how I said I had a problem with him?"

"Yeah."

"Well, if you want to know the absolute truth," she said, and then nothing for a minute. The radio stuttered over itself, briefly flirting with some other signal.

"What?"

She sighed, and took off her sunglasses as if she was looking at Phil Needle for the first time. "I fucked him."

The car went faster.

×

They were on top of a wild place, unbuilt and scraggled, with lean-to trees giving way to unexpected slices of vista. From a bench they could see the city tossed out like dice and string, the streetcars ambling out to the Embarcadero, the domino dots of changing traffic lights, the gray grove of downtown skyscrapers—a city where anything might happen, even Gwen.

"Sick, right?"

"Yeah."

"This is our place, you know?"

"I've never been here, though," Gwen said, embarrassed. It was just blocks from the Jean Bonnet Living Center, but it was Amber who showed the new way to go.

"I knew you'd like it, though."

"Yeah, I do."

"Right? I told you it was sick."

Sick meant cool. Having Amber around was like finding a big maze in your backyard. "*Verily,*" Gwen said.

"*And,*" Amber said, but then she just sighed and found a broken branch to play with, waving it in circles around the view of the city like she was designating favorite buildings, or important targets. Gwen sat. In her pocket crinkled another letter to the *San Francisco Chronicle* regarding the unfair treatment an ex–naval officer was receiving. "So good of you," Amber murmured. They both knew what they were talking about. Gwen felt her body warm like a blush and felt so happy for a moment that she did not ask the question.

"*And,*" Amber said, "you were right about him." She swirled the stick in the air. "I mean, verily, he's crazy, but so's everybody, you know?"

"I know," said Gwen. She had an itch on her leg and just moved her pant leg up to scratch it, not caring about the burn.

"What do you call him?"

"Errol."

"No, no, Captain something."

"I just called him my captain that time. It's not something I call him really. I just think it."

Amber laid her hand on Gwen's. She stopped scratching. "I get it."

"Because he seems kinda captainy."

"He *does.* I thought that."

"And he used to be in the Navy." Gwen would never know this was not true.

"Maybe we should start calling him that to his face."

"I guess so. We can call him anything."

"I know, it's cool, because he doesn't remember. You can start over every time with him."

"More than every time."

"*Verily.* Like every five minutes. *Seconds.* I wish I could do that with everyone."

"Yeah."

"Not you. But everyone else."

They sat and stared at the city on the hill. Amber let go her hand. "But the thing is, Gwen," she said, "what are we going to *do?*"

This was the question. It had been the question for lo these three long weeks of friendship. She and Amber had so much in common. Neither of them liked it when people acted like dicks, and when they were alone they liked to eat ice cream and dance. Neither of them needed much light to do anything, and hated it when people turned on the light for them, particularly if they said, "Here, I'll turn on the light for you." Amber's house on Octavia had a neighborhood with free perfume samples, gorgeous boots in the window, a yoga class they might take someday. Gwen had offered her meager Embarcadero in return, but Amber had showed her that if you kept walking, through the farmers' market and past the gleamy hotels, past the hospital where they'd check Gwen for dehydration, shock and exposure, another destination was within their grasp: a pier, tarted up for tourists with expensive ice cream and a body lotion place and piles of sea lions rolled up on the jetties like dead sleeping bags. It was *sick* just how much they could hang out, unseen by the tourists, except the occasional wistful pimpled boy embarrassed with his parents. They tumbled around all day, blitzing on candy, taking pictures of each other, the endless sea as background, the foggy bridge, the island prison, a shiny boat of new wood where every afternoon they put on a show. The best was one Amber rigged so it showed up on the screen whenever they texted: Gwen, looking brave and slim, her hair draped by the wind perfectly across her brow, with the wooden ship, the *Corsair*, behind her with its canvas sails and its tiny little turret on top of the mast.

The picture was so good of Gwen.

But still there was the boring squall of their lives. One thick and drizzly day they waited it out in Gwen's room for once, safe from Marina, who was locked up painting and didn't even come out to see who was raiding the fridge. They watched the rain, leaning backwards off the bed, touching each other's hair. Amber took something out of her purse and uncrumpled it against her thigh.

"Got back my final," she said. "F."

Gwen squinted at a large drop on the glass, one that didn't want to leave. "I'm ashamed of you."

Amber gave her a flick and held the paper up over them like she was signaling to a plane. "I just gave honest answers for each one. Number One, A. Number Two, C. Number Three, False. Number Four, E. Number Five, I Don't Know. Number Six, I Don't Care. Number Seven, Fuck This Class."

They were both kicking with laughter. "And they *flunked* you?" Gwen said, fiercely and kidding.

"The Stepmonster *freaked*," Amber said. "I don't know why. I told her I wouldn't transfer, not to the school she's crazy for me to be at, even if I got the grades."

"Someone was murdered there," Gwen remembered.

"Years ago," Amber said. "I got the grades for it and *still* I can't give honest answers." She sighed deeply on the bed, her hair slumping down to the carpet in a broken fan. "This is what we're up against," she said, and then turned her head to see the stash of books underneath Gwen's bed.

Gwen had not quite been ready to share them. They were a big secret.

"What are these?" Amber asked. Gwen hoped she would not ask if they were dirty, as Naomi would have. "Did you read all these?"

"Um, yeah."

"*Verily?* I couldn't. I have the attention span of a carrot. What are they?"

"Just books."

But Amber was already flat on the floor after a slow-motion tumble and was turning them over like stones. Gwen stayed on the bed, staring at her nothing ceiling, her hands at her chest like she was buried alive, trying to think of something plausible to say.

"Are they all like this? Where did you get them all?"

"I borrowed them," Gwen said. As many as she wanted, for as long as she wanted, Errol had told her. Nine times.

"From Errol," Amber said. "I remember, in his room. What's a privateer?" She was pointing to the gold, double-lined letters but didn't wait for an answer. "It's a pirate?"

"I know."

"You read these? Pirates?"

"I know," Gwen said again.

Amber opened the book and saw the definition Gwen had copied onto the inside cover. "An advocate," she said, "or exponent of private enterprise. Is that a pirate? It's the same thing?"

"Sort of," Gwen said.

"Look at me," Amber said, and at last Gwen turned over and slid off the bed to sit with Amber and the books. Gwen looked at her.

"I know," she said. "It's stupid."

But Amber was already shaking her head. "What does it mean, an exponent of private enterprise?"

"You can do whatever you want, I think," Gwen said, very quietly. "Go anyplace."

Amber looked, just once and just quickly, out the window at the bridge and the sky and the sea. "*And*," she said, "without anybody telling you."

Gwen watched this self-spoken information, engined with shivery wisdom, flow into her friend. Behind her the waves waved.

"What do you know about pirates?" Amber asked.

"They're," Gwen said, "um."

Amber turned a page, and they looked at *A History of Dispossession*. "What's that? It sounds like—"

"It's depriving someone of their possessions," Gwen said. "Taking stuff away."

"It sounded like demons or something," Amber said, and Gwen could see that she was embarrassed for not knowing.

"It's old," Gwen said, touching Amber's hand holding the book. "You have to read it and look up everything almost."

What does anyone know about pirates? At the time this story takes place and for centuries before and afterwards, pirates were not unknown, not to anyone. It was thinking about them that was different. Gwen and Amber thinking about it was like lightning in the room. Everybody knows lightning. Nobody expects it in the room, and the air crackled around the next book Amber overturned.

"Which one should I read?"

Gwen was breathless. "That one."

It will be generally admitted that *Captain Blood* is the most sublime story that has ever penetrated into the human mind. All sorts are satisfied by it. The hero is a physician with a grisly name. He heals soldiers who have been wounded in battle and is arrested, convicted, and banished—*grounded*—whereupon Captain Blood embarks on a career of dispossession in order to restore justice previously hijacked. *Why, first he's a rebel, then an escaped slave, and lastly a bloody pirate.* It is this philosophy that had sent Gwen bolt upright in bed, so late that the sparks of cars across the bridge were scarcely to be seen. One day you have taken enough, and you begin to take it all back.

"Captain Blood is foul-mouthed but plainspoken, superstitious but irreligious, courageous but rowdy, dependable but difficult," Amber read from the flap. "I would get with that in a second."

"You don't think it's stupid?"

Amber shook her head and blinked very quickly. "I do it," she said in a near whisper.

"What?"

Amber reached a hand into the pocket of her sweatshirt, and withdrew it still empty. No, she uncurled two fingers and there was a tube of lip balm.

"From that place," Gwen remembered gradually. Amber had abruptly announced that she was bored and they'd left in a hurry. "Underneath the big billboard, on the pier."

"All the time," Amber said. "All the time I do it and I never knew why." She tapped the book: *This is why.*

Gwen took *Captain Blood* from Amber and then handed it to her with both hands, like this time she was doing it the right way. It was the start of something, although even now, the next day on the top of the hill, they could not quite see what it was. What *were* they going to do? Gwen lit an imaginary cigarette. This was something else they had in common. Amber smiled and took it for a puff. But what else could they dream up?

"What is this pirate stuff?" Amber asked. "Ganging up, right? But what are we doing? It's not just—taking stuff from stores."

"No."

"And it's not just making him your boyfriend, is it? That *guy*, what's-his-name, Cody Glasserman."

"Nathan. *No.*"

"No. Because it's stupid. Like my ex. It's kind of sad how obsessed I became with the idea of being with him."

She seemed to be waiting for something, so Gwen started to agree, but then Amber just tossed the imaginary cigarette away. "I tried to kill myself a little over it," she said, and reached down to show Gwen a tiny, tiny scar on her ankle. "Bled like crazy."

"I thought it was, the wrists."

"Yeah, well, I said it was a little," Amber said with an almost grin. "Anyway, that's the end with boys. Too stupid. You can make out with him if you want to, but I'm not ganging up just to get you Cody."

It would spoil it to correct her again, although his name, *Nathan Glasserman*, still rolled in her mouth when she thought of him. But that wasn't what they were going to do. "It's got to be like that day," Gwen said. She could practically taste the sting of the salt of the sea.

"That was so good of you," Amber said again. "Tell me something."

"What?"

"No, I mean like I told you. About my ex, and the razor. Tell me something. We need to know each other the most of *anything.*"

"I'm a mistake," Gwen said, before she could change her mind.

"What?"

"I am," Gwen said. "They didn't tell me, my mom and dad, but they lived in New York forever and wanted to be, I don't know, big radio stars."

Amber snorted.

"Yeah, well, they didn't want me." Gwen felt another sting, tense under one eye, like the tip of a blade.

"They might say things," Amber said, "but they don't mean them."

"They *don't* say them," Gwen said. "That's the thing, is what I mean. I had to figure it out all by myself. They watch me and they watch me, and I can't take the bus alone, and we practically have to steal time to be together. I'm supposed to be a good sport. I'm not, though. I quit swimming."

"Stop," Amber said, and put her head down on Gwen's shoulder.

"I don't want to," she said, "*keep up the good work.*" Gwen felt so fierce she could picture the cigarette starting a fire that would scorch the hill. Amber's breath warmed her sweater. "I'm tired of keeping up the good work."

"Let's tell today," Amber said. "Let's do something like we said, let's tell him."

She was already standing, and so, Gwen realized, was Gwen. They strode down to where they were going, both thinking of the photograph again. They did not need to look at it to look it over. They could look elsewhere, Gwen thought, not at the girl but at the ship waiting in the background. What does *Corsair* mean, anyway? It was an old word. Old people would know it.

Errol had good days, Gwen had learned quickly. In his room, she hoped this was one. But "I worry about it" was what he was saying now, and Gwen sighed and looked at her hand. *Memory* was the word he was looking for. "There's something on your hand, Vera."

"*Gwen*," Gwen said.

"I know! What is it?"

Gwen and Amber were standing up. Perhaps that was the problem. Gwen knelt down close to him, taking a tissue from his lap and gently wiping the drip off his nose. It was very hot in the room. Always. "Hi," she said.

"I remember you," Errol said.

"I'm glad."

"You come here all the time."

"Yes."

"Because you stole things."

"Yes."

"And you read to me."

"Yes. Today I wanted to talk to you," she started again, "about something, okay?"

"I have a problem with my memory."

"It's okay."

"I worry about it, though. What's that river?"

Gwen knew this part of the territory. "The Nile. But it's okay. My friend and I wanted to talk to you about something."

"*Senile*, that's it. Who's she?"

His finger pointed at Amber, Gwen was pretty sure, although

he was looking straight at Gwen. His eyes were hungry and angry, not cloudy at all. They looked, Gwen thought, like Gwen's.

"I'm Amber."

"Nice to meet you, milady."

"I come here all the time too." She said this every time.

"No."

"Yes, several times."

"Quiet, wench!" Errol shouted, and then immediately burst into laughter. Gwen and Amber laughed too. Gwen could see that this would be something they'd keep saying: "Quiet, wench!" She could even hear it over the roar of the wind sweeping across the sea.

"That's from what you read to me, right?" Errol said. "Sometimes I remember everything fine."

"Yes," Gwen said. It was true. "Amber and I wanted to talk to you about something."

"A parley, eh? You'll find me willing."

"We want to do it."

"*And*," Amber said, "for real."

"What for real?"

"Pirates," Gwen said steadily. Errol waved in her face, indicating his disgust with her kneeling. She stood up.

"You already steal things," Errol said. "That's why you're here. Otherwise you would be with your friends."

"I am with my friends," Gwen said. Amber put her hand on Gwen's shoulder.

"You have something on your hand, too," Errol said. "What is it?"

Gwen and Amber held their hands together, fist against fist, for Errol to read. He read the words. "We want to do it for real," Amber said. "We're summed for something else."

"*Summoned*," Gwen said.

Amber grinned. "Quiet, wench!"

"Did you tell me that already?"

"Yes."

"What's that river?"

"Not the river," Gwen tried, "the sea. We would take to the sea."

"Pirates," Errol said uncertainly.

"Brethren," Amber had learned, "of the coast."

"You can't do that," Errol said. "Not anymore."

"Yes," Gwen said. "You can do it in the present day. There's an equivalent."

"It can't be the same thing."

"It is too. It *is*."

Amber was nodding beside her, but Gwen knew she was the one who had to talk. She had a better grasp on it. She knelt again and put her hand on Errol's hand. He read it again: the word HO. They had made them yesterday, with their hands so close together Gwen didn't realize how stupid it looked when it was away from TALLY. Now it didn't make any sense, just when she was trying to make it clear. She looked into Errol's eyes.

"We'll do everything," she said. "We have a boat. We have supplies or we can get them."

"At the drugstore," Amber said.

"We have maps. We have knives. And we have the spirit of rebellion." Gwen looked down and then up again to see if that had worked. It was from a book, of course, but it sounded right. It sounded true. She *did* have the spirit of rebellion, even if "spirit of rebellion" was not something that was said, not at the time this story takes place. "But we'd not stand a chance without you on the open sea. We don't know how to sail. You've been in the Navy. I think we can get you out if you will come with us."

"And be pirates," Errol said. His hands were moving on his knees, shaking back and forth in a tremolo Gwen had never seen on him. He also, for a minute at least, did not say he was worried about his memory. "Where are we?"

"The Jean," Gwen started, "Bonnet—"

"No, no," Errol said. "San Francisco, right? San Francisco?"

"Yes."

"I *knew* it!" He slapped his own knees. "This whole town is at sea level."

"What does that mean?" Gwen said. *Sea level* made it sound flat, and the city was entirely peaks and valleys.

"The time to start is *now*!" Errol sort of roared. "If I am crazy enough to listen to you, milady, you'll find me willing."

"*Really?*" Maybe it was the good day they had hoped for.

But then Errol frowned suddenly. "Your parents," he said. "Your father surely would not let his two daughters do such a reckless thing." His shoulders shook a little, a flick of aggression, or a shrug.

"Our parents aren't here," Amber said, and this was when it happened. Before, even with the plan in their heads and the ink on their hands, everything was still intact. Nothing had ruptured. Nothing had happened. Smooth as glass. But now there was movement, and it was all because there was no one there to say it could not be so.

Errol stood up. This was always a gamble, and Amber and Gwen waited for him to find his sea legs. One shaky hand grasped the end of his metal, medicinal bed and the other stretched off uncertainly toward the window until Gwen took his hand in hers.

"What are you doing?" she asked gently.

Errol smiled a big smile. "Do you know what I like about the idea?"

"What idea?"

"Pirates!" Errol shouted. "It's a life of adventure, grommets."

Gwen blushed. *Grommets* were apprentice sailors. But Errol was shaking her hand off and heading for the door.

"There's a map!" he said. "I know there is!"

Gwen watched him get, lose, get, lose, sort of get back his balance. "A map of what?"

"I see it every day during chair dancing!"

"Chair dancing?" Amber asked.

"Chair cha-cha-cha," he snarled, and led the stumbly way out. The way down the halls was a trail that still lost Gwen sometimes, but the captain was out front and proud and got them all there in one piece. The *solarium* was the word for it, like a birdcage with panes of glass where fresh air should be, bad furniture and plants laid out for the residents and a real birdcage in the corner. The sun shone through too hot, and there were famous paintings chopped up on the tables, for people to fit together, as was the elderly custom at this point in history. Just one woman was trying. Errol wrinkled his nose and pointed to a garden by the wall.

"Look," he said, "at all these." Gwen followed his finger to some large flappy flowers, lined up in pots. "A beautiful semaphore, the fat lady says. What is it?"

For a moment Gwen could not remember the word either. "Orchid," she said finally, but Errol was already nodding.

"The worst gift in the world. Someone gives you an orchid, and then what? You have an orchid. It is an insult."

Gwen nodded in fierce agreement. She also was pretty sure that *semaphore* was not the name of a plant. "I see your controversy," she said.

"It is all an insult," Errol said. To shake his head he had to steady himself on a table, and a few pieces of Mona Lisa fell to the floor.

"Hey," the old woman said, but calmly.

"You said there was a map," Amber said.

Errol lit up. "So I did! So I did! So I did! So I did!" He reached through the orchids and took something off the wall, flat and large, that sent an orchid crashing. He banged it down on the puzzle and the woman took off her glasses.

"I was working on this puzzle," she said. "Put that somewhere else."

Gwen knew what Errol would say, and like a prophecy he said it. "Quiet, wench!"

"We've all had enough of your nonsense," the woman said and stood up. She had a little bell tied to her walker, though the birds in danger would have to be flightless and slow. Errol fluttered a hand at her and stared down into the reflective glass. Gwen and Amber appeared on either side, their faces floating over a hand-drawn world. Errol stared and stared, and then looked around quickly as if he'd been asleep.

"Girls," he said, "what is this?"

"It's a map," Gwen said. It was the yellowed kind, with serpents in the corners and words spelled with the *A* and the *E* Siamese-twinned. Her stomach dipped, but then, to her amazement, she recognized the shape of the shore. She was, she thought, a good grommet. "It's California."

"From the Navy, I remember this," Errol said, nodding very seriously. The old woman muttered something and rang her way out. "Before the fandle-dandle you have now. Phones that tell you where the car goes. We used this map to cover every last place."

"Everything's in Spanish," Amber said.

"Used to be," Errol agreed. "Unless it's a forgery."

Amber brushed some dust off the glass and then looked at Gwen uncertainly. "It looks like it just came with the place."

"That's it," Errol said. "Falsity on paper, to lure enemies into open water."

"It's true," Gwen said, from one of the books. "The pirates made fake maps sometimes. Ships would think it was a shortcut, when it was a lagoon."

"An ambush," Amber said.

"Leave them stricken on the deck," Errol said. "Weaklings and fools bother me everywhere. I have a problem with my memory."

"No," Gwen said, looking at California, "you don't. You're vital to the success of the venture."

Amber rattled her fingernails on the map. "*And*, what about me? Am *I* vital to the success of the what's-it?"

"Of course you are."

"I don't know anything. They wouldn't let me in the lamest navy."

"You are a forger," Gwen reminded her. "Not of maps but of scrawl."

"I can do anyone's handwriting," Amber admitted, and Errol gave her a captain's smile before glaring at the doorway.

"Don't interrupt!" he growled. "We are in conference!"

"I hear your conference is disturbing Mrs. Hinterman," Manny said calmly, and reached out with a palm surprisingly pale. "Give me the map."

"I'll fight to the eyeteeth for it!"

Gwen blinked. Combat she was sure would happen eventually, bloodshed inevitable, but maybe right here in the solarium was not the best idea.

"You cannot take things off the wall," Manny said.

"Every penny I've had was stolen from me," Errol said, his knuckles tightening on the frame. Gwen looked at it again, the corny fake-old gilted curlicues. "Every penny."

"You're in a nice room," Manny said, grabbing the other end. Errol tugged but then surrendered at once.

"I don't like you," he said, but mildly, and slumped down into a chair.

"I know," Manny said, and tucked the map under his arm.

"I have a problem," Errol said wistfully, "with my memory. What's that river?"

Everyone said the name of the river. "Let me help you settle down," Manny said, and gave a deep, quaking sigh. "I'm, how do you say it? Too old for this shit."

"This is Manny," Errol said, his manners reconvening. "He is a man, which is why I call him Manny. And I don't like him."

"Let's settle down," Manny said. "Tea?"

"*Tea*," Errol said, giving an order.

"Tea," Manny agreed wearily, and left. Errol flicked more pieces of the puzzle to the floor. Gwen helped him. She learned in fifth grade that nobody knew what the woman was smiling about, and that was in, what, 15-something? Spanish Armada days. If nobody knew then, they wouldn't know now.

"What's the level of peril?" Errol asked.

Gwen dropped a border piece. "What?"

"We are plotting piracy, are we not?"

"We *are*," Gwen said, relieved he was still on the subject.

"Well, what is the level of peril? Compared to the expected gain?"

Gwen recognized this one, from the story that ended with nothing but corpses on the deck. "Compare it not to expected gain," she said. "Compare it to what paucity you have."

"What's paucity?" Amber asked.

"Nothing," Gwen said, with a look at the orchids. "Everything's been stolen from us, too."

"We have nothing," Amber agreed, "and nobody will leave us alone."

Errol kept flicking. "So you have a score to settle?" Gwen thought of Nathan Glasserman, wet from the pool. He'd called her Spot.

"*She* has a boy she wants to steal," Amber said. "A captive, like."

"Some well-rigged young man?" Errol said, and gave a shouty little laugh.

"He wouldn't get this," Gwen said.

"He doesn't have to," Amber said. "He'll be there anyway." She held out her hand—TALLY—and knocked it against Gwen's HO. "Tell you later."

Gwen put her hand on Errol's, which had a fistful of Italian landscape. "Captain, is this enough crew?"

"How many is it?" Errol asked.

"One," Gwen said, pointing at herself, "two, three."

"Four with Cody," Amber said.

"*Nathan*," Gwen said.

"Not enough," Errol said, shaking his head. "Impossible, impossible!"

"It's not a big boat," Gwen said, although they hadn't really checked out the boat.

"Quiet, wench," Amber said.

"Ha!" Errol said, and Manny returned with the steaming pot. On the tray were four small cups, rounded like urns, and he placed them all over the hand-wrecked puzzle and poured odd, weak tea.

"What is this?" Errol asked.

"The same tea I make always," Manny said.

"Catmint," Gwen remembered.

"Catmint," Errol repeated. "Maybe I do like him."

Everyone sipped. To Gwen it tasted almost like nothing, and then, softly, she felt something woozy on her tongue, and grinned at Amber, who was blinking down into her cup. Manny was able-bodied, Gwen thought. Strong. She caught Amber's eye.

"Is this Haitian?" she asked Manny.

Manny nodded and sipped his own tea. "There is no place to make it here, not the right way. So what are you planning?"

"Who says we're planning anything?" Amber said quickly.

"A little bird told me," he said, and gestured around the room with a thick, thick arm. "What are you up to, little girls in this room?"

"We're not little," Gwen said, but she was grinning. "Pirates."

Manny laughed. "Pirates!" he said. "You say it so strong for such a thing. *Pirates*, with a capital *P*?"

"With a capital everything," Gwen said.

"What do you mean, *pirates*? There's no pirates now."

"There's an equivalent," Amber said. "We have it in our heads."

"We want to get out of here," Gwen said, "and take back what's taken."

"What the hell are you talking about?" Manny said. "This is an old-age home. You are girls."

Gwen felt very fierce, and held Manny in her fierce gaze. Her brain sloshed with catmint, and she thought of something she had read, hidden under the bed. "We want to forge a social order," she said, "beyond the realm of traditional authority."

"Traditional authority," Manny repeated, and scratched his big, flat ear. "That actually sounds pretty cool."

"We will set the world afear'd," Errol said.

Manny chuckled. "Every fear hides a wish," he recited, maybe, "and vice versa. Why don't you tell me what you are the hell talking about?"

They told him. Gwen thought she was better at it this time. Errol was looking deep into space, lost in thought, or just lost, but Amber was smiling almost proudly at Gwen as she talked of pirates of old and then, slowly, with help from Amber, moved the plan into what was then, for a few days at least, called the present, and when Gwen was done, Manny had put his cup down and looked around the table like everyone was capable.

"Pirates," he said finally.

"Yes!" Amber said. "Gwen and I've already stolen, so we have a taste of the life."

"What did you steal?" Manny asked, and then put up his chalky hand. "Don't tell me. Enough troubles. But there is a difference, yes, between pirates and thieves?"

"Pirates have a reason," Amber said. "For, I don't know, glory. Glory and justice."

"And what is your reason? Why are you girls doing this thing?"

"We can't just," Gwen said, gesturing around the cagey room, "*sit here*. We have to get away."

"From what?"

"From the whole thing," Amber said, and to Gwen's surprise, Manny nodded.

"I know what that is," he said. "It is why I am here, cleaning up after grandfathers and grandmothers miles from my home."

"What's Haiti like?" Gwen said.

"Terrible," Manny said with a shake of his head. "I miss it so."

"The whole world's terrible," Errol said moodily. He was holding his tea but wasn't sipping it. Gwen thought maybe he'd forgotten it was to drink, and sipped hers obviously, to help him.

"The whole world?" Manny said. "That's all we have, man. Besides the whole world, there's not much."

"Exactly," Gwen said, and knocked her hand against Amber's again, spilling a little tea onto the fancy rug. "We are leaving it. We are doing it. It's the right thing to do."

"If it's the right thing, you should do it," Manny said. "That's what they say in my church. Even if they say it's wrong, and you know it's right."

"Beyond the realm of traditional authority," Amber said.

"Tallyho," Errol said.

Manny nodded. "And good luck on it."

"You don't want to join us?" Amber asked, and Manny chuckled again.

"No, no. No, no, no."

"But you just said you *hated* it," Amber said, amazed and loud. "You said it was *terrible*!"

"I'm still," Manny said, "not going to hop on a boat with you little ducks. That far I have not fallen."

"I see I'm interrupting a tea party," cooed Peggy from the French doors, and then folded her arms in front of her chest, too high, like she needed a shelf for her chin. "Mrs. Hinterman was complaining."

"Just a little incident," Manny said. "A ripple on the water."

"It didn't sound little," Peggy said.

"I gave the map to Grounds," Manny said. "It needs a stronger bolt."

"I'm not talking about Grounds' job," Peggy said. "I'm talking about yours."

One narrative, about the hated people in our lands, is that eventually they get what is coming to them. This is what prisoners have told themselves, the afflicted and the fallen, since the first asshole walked amongst us, kicking infants and click-click-clicking a ballpoint pen. But Peggy did not fall into a vat of anything ravenous or burning, not then and not ever.

"I made tea for everybody," Manny said. "We seem to be calming down."

"I see a fallen orchid," Peggy said, pointing, and Gwen remembered that she had called him *invaluable*. He certainly looked invalued. "Cleaning it up would go a long way, Manny. A *long* way."

"Yes," Manny said.

"Perhaps dirt floors are de rigueur in Jamaica," Peggy said, "but working here, let alone if you want to start your own business, you have to clean it up. *Now*."

Terrible Peggy stopped talking. Manny nodded and gave his frown to his tea. Just about everybody else, by the way, in this book is white. He stood up to the fall of more puzzle pieces, and looked down at Gwen blinking slowly. "Yes," he said. "I will go."

"*Verily?*" Amber said, and plunked down her empty teacup. Errol shouted a laugh, and Peggy, stupid, kept frowning.

"He's not from Jamaica," Gwen said of her newest crewman. "He's from Haiti."

Manny whistled something and opened the broom closet. "Where am I from?" he asked. "Where am I from, Jean-Robert? Where am I from?"

The closet was in the corner, and Gwen craned to see. It was the little bird he had mentioned, although it was big and bright, scuffling in the cage in the corner where the sun razored in. It was a parrot, its jerky eyes moving from the seed in its claw to all the staring eyes in the room. Gwen thought a parrot was too perfect almost, but why not? Why not a perfect plan, with a perfect crew? Why not pirates?

"Tortuga!" the parrot cawked. *Perfect.*

CHAPTER 6

They could not hear each other over the music, but it was no fun talking on the phone if you weren't playing music, and it was ridiculous to text if you were reading something out loud. Gwen liked to lie on her stomach, looking out at the bridge and the sparkling sea, with one leg stretched out—the one with the burn—with her toe on the volume knob. Synchronized swimming had finally paid off. It was her right leg—or *starboard*, she was trying to learn to remember to think.

"Listen to this," Amber said on the other end. "There is never a boredom. There is always plenty to occupy the mind of a watch-keeper on the bridge at sea. But there is a restlessness. A man realizes many things on deck, and can find his eye clouded with a yen for home and other matters of seeming urgency. But what of the future? What's yen?"

"I'm not sure," Gwen said. "Chinese money, I think, or Japanese."

"Oh, yeah, Japanese money. I learned about it in Global. That doesn't make sense."

"Maybe they fenced something in a Japanese port," Gwen said, "and then they wanted to bring it home. A yen for home?" Gwen was still proud of knowing *fenced*.

"Okay," Amber said uncertainly. "But what of the future? Even the most vibrant of adventures requires the safest of passages. The vision of the watchkeeper should be the triumphant arrival and not one other thing on God's earth."

Sometimes it was hard. Gwen and Amber had been doing this for days. Or *nights*, really, because their days were spent prowling the docks, looting the drugstore—Amber did this alone, while Gwen served as watchkeeper outside, so as not to be recognized from her first caper and thus have all their plans undone—and generally battening down the hatches. They stared at satellite photographs of the Glasserman home, which at this point in history were glittering prizes ripe for the plucking on any computer screen. "Click ZOOM," Amber would say, and they would get closer to the roof of the house. They would imagine the well-rigged young man following the false map that would make him irretrievable to the civilized world. But at night they kept reading the logs and the lores, frowning at slippery vocabulary, the thorny, gendered nouns of untranslated Romance languages, the frustrating lack of imagination of town names in the New World, New York, New Orleans, New everything. Would they need a victualler? Should the *Corsair* prove to be a frigatoon, would Errol's naval training be sufficient? How heavy is a cat-o'-nine-tails, and how easily can it repel the strong arm of the law?

"*And*," Amber said, "it says a man realizes many things on deck, but they must mean women too, right?"

"I hope so," Gwen said. The monsoons of men in the books, and the tiny drizzles of women, were a problem they didn't want to admit. There is a slender, secret history of female pirates, but it was nowhere in the private library of their captain. Promising names would be dashed by a pronoun in the next sentence. Jan Janssen was a man. Jean Laffite was a man. Andrea de Lomellini was a man. Jean Rose was a man. Adrian Jansz Pater was a man. Countless Turkish pirates, all men, were named Kara. Sandra, queen of the pirates, dressed as a man. Anne Bonny not only disguised herself as a man but a gay man, a man who liked men, which is why her mother had a heart attack. (That part was good.) Alwilda just became a pirate to escape marrying a man. Arabella Bishop was a woman, but she wasn't a real pirate, more of an enabler. Elizabeth Killigrew was more of a pirate patron. Rachel Wall was more of a pirate wife. Ruby of Kishmoor was more of a pirate's daughter. Lydia Bailey was simply captured by pirates—the Nathan Glasserman of the Old World. There was Grace O'Malley, although she was trained by her father, and there was Maria Lindsey, who committed suicide by taking poison *and* by jumping off a cliff, and there was the troubling entry in Errol's *Compleat Pirate Dictionary*: "Rape: see WOMEN, TREATMENT OF." She lay flat on the bed.

"You *hope* so?"

"Quiet, wench. Of course there are risks. We'll be on the high sea. It's not, I don't know. It's something."

"*It's something.* Verily. It's like, in science class? There's, you know, control and experiment. This is an experiment. But there's no, if you know what I mean, control."

From where Gwen lay the rest of the bed was flat and continuous with the horizon of the water. But it was all control, was what she felt. She was a hockey puck—people hit her with sticks and sent her places, but who cares, even when she scored a goal? The goal wasn't hers. It belonged to the people who hit her.

"We just have to," Gwen said. She said it like it was the beginning of the sentence, but then she said nothing at the end. Amber said nothing too, probably nodding, and the beat of the same song kept nodding too.

"*And,* I was thinking," Amber said. "I probably won't do it, but I should get a tattoo."

"Shouldn't we both?" Gwen said. "But I probably wouldn't either."

"On my leg," Amber continued, "in the same shape as your burn. You know, like sisters."

"Mates."

"Mates," Amber agreed. Naomi would have made some big lesbian deal of it. "And an ivory dress with a long train."

They laughed. This was a slap at Amber's stepsister, a blonde with flat teeth grinning on the refrigerator in Amber's kitchen. She sold real estate, which was so stupid, in Denver, and was getting married and had sent Amber a frilly book with ribbons on the edges and a tiny lock with a key on a chain to wear around your neck. Or, you could tear the lock off the cardboard of the cover and open it that way. Inside Amber was supposed to write down her dreams for her own wedding, so she could look at it when she found the guy and pick the right flowers. There were some girls who did this, planned their weddings. The other girls planned their funerals, and Gwen and Amber had already talked one night, late late, about burial at sea. The death part was in the books, too. "The captain," read a caption under a ghastly etching, "hanged in chains. Like a ruin he looks." That was where it ended, they knew. You went off the map and they found you anyway, go figure. Or you ended it yourself. "The mates toss themselves off the ramparts into the raging sea rather than face certain brutal justice." Either way, it was finished deep down in, you couldn't help giggling, Davy Jones's locker.

"I'm doing it tonight," Amber said quietly.

"What? Where?"

"Not the tattoo," she said. "The note."

Gwen looked at her desk, where an envelope gaped open, as if it had been ransacked by her mother. "G" was scrawled on the outside of it, just "G," which at a different point in her life Gwen had found endearing. Now it just looked like Naomi had been too lazy to write out Gwen's whole name.

"How long will it take?" Gwen asked. Gwen had already seen Amber's handiwork. It was perfect. It fooled everybody.

"Not long. An album, probably."

"Tortuga?"

"Can you believe that, where he's from? And the parrot?"

"I know."

"This is really happening."

"Verily."

"I'm nervous about it, though."

"Yeah."

"Goodnight, Gwen."

"Goodnight, wench."

Gwen hung up on Amber's laugh and glared back at the envelope in the fading light. Among the many things she remembered was the phone number of the girl she used to call when she was *naive*. She stretched out her starboard leg, the burn like a badge of honor—*mates*—and turned the other knob on the radio, to find a station. Something she'd never listen to, loud and scraggly. Then she blocked her number and punched in her call.

"Hello?"

Gwen used a new voice. "I'm going to fuck you up," she said.

"Who is this?" came the instant answer, shrill and scared like a little girl. "Who are you?"

"You fucking bitch cunt," Gwen snarled. "I'm going to fuck you up, Naomi."

It was dead in the earpiece. Naomi would never guess who it was. When she was an adult, this voice would come to her sometimes, her silver pen tapping on the documents she was supposed to work on, but she'd never figure it out. She had made so many people hate her, the suspects were endless.

Gwen let the phone drop to the carpet. She wondered—she was sure there must be—if there was a bottle of rum in the house. This was really happening. This was going to start; it was starting already. Look at her swearing like a sailor.

×

This year's hotel looked shabby. Phil Needle got out of the car like he was bad on stilts, one leg sore and jerky from the gas pedal. He still had no title, and it was getting late. Or it was late already. But he was here, he had to remind himself. In front of the hotel, too large for the space, was a fountain tinkling water into its own pool. He was not like one of those drops, creating a tiny circle gone and unmissed.

"Make yourself useful," he said to Alma Levine, who was blinking at the fountain. "Please," he added. "Go in and see about our rooms."

"Right," Levine said and slouched through the doors, which slid open as she stepped near them. Phil Needle retrieved his little suitcase and stepped out of the way of a van marked COURTESY. The doors opened for him, too.

The lobby was empty but full of laughter somehow, broadcast from around the corner. The bar, surely, full of the conference. Soon he would go, batten down the hatches with a drink, with luck run into Leonard Steed. Or call him. Have Levine call him. Something. He strode hopefully purposefully across the lobby, past a painting of squares and foil with a plaque saying it had been donated by the artist. Thanks a lot, pal. Levine was talking to a man behind a desk, and behind the man was a ficus, a sort of plant, at this point in history, that needed hardly any care at all.

Levine had her frown on. "There's a problem, Phil."

No, Phil Needle was not surprised.

"What?"

"No room at the inn."

Phil Needle decided to check with the man directly. "Are you," look at the name tag, "Florio, going to honor our reservation?"

"I didn't," Levine said, "make a reservation, actually."

Phil Needle blinked. Fuck that ficus.

"You didn't actually tell me you needed a reservation," Levine said. She looked not even apologetic about not being apologetic. "Just for the plane."

"Winter Air," Phil Needle said coldly, but no, he should be staying mad about the hotel.

The man was typing into his computer and then changed his mind and looked at a clipboard. Nobody spoke. Then he slowly, slowly put the clipboard on the counter and pointed to something with his pen. It was a mess of squares and ink, with numbers crossed out and circled, and then, suddenly, below it, an empty oasis of blanks for his name and address. "A suite," the guy said.

"What?"

"I have a suite," he said. "Two bedrooms with a shitty view. Separate baths, but you'll have to share a sitting room."

He quoted a large, laughable price, without laughing, and on the clipboard Phil Needle saw that Florio was the name of the hotel. *City* view, he must have said, and the rest was like the setup of a dirty joke. Wasn't it? He handed over his credit card thinking of it, the shared part of the shared room. "Is it okay with you?" he thought to ask Levine.

She shrugged, her shirt moving a little bit. "Yes," she said. "I guess it was my fault."

Phil Needle thought that was a good guess.

"Do you need validation?"

"Yes," Phil Needle said. "I have a car outside."

"You can give the key to—"

But Phil Needle, the American outlaw, just put his keys down on the counter, at the price he was paying. "You can give it to them," he said to the man, and began to walk away. Levine, unintentionally or perhaps humbled, wheeled his suitcase behind him. He thought that Alma Levine would say something about his getting them a room, as they elevatored up to the twentieth floor. It wouldn't have to be "Oh, Phil Needle, you're so wonderful," but surely *something*. But Levine didn't say a word until Phil Needle had the door to the room unlocked, and then she said, "Phew," and quickly traipsed ahead of him into the room.

Here they were. In the sitting part, two couches sat, and the curtains were open at the big window. Outside it was dark, with lights here and there tilted at warehouses. Phil Needle had been right the first time: it was a shitty view, particularly with his large, disappointed face reflected in the middle of it. It looked funny-looking. The ends of Levine's legs were visible, kicking off their shoes on a bed in a doorway, her feet arching on the ugly bedspread, and then scratching at each other.

"Would it be okay to order food up?" she called to him.

"Sure," he said.

"I'm going to take a shower," she said, but she did not rise and close the door.

Phil Needle took his own suitcase to his own separate room and lay it down on an identical bedspread, right where Levine's legs were now. He unzipped and looked at everything his wife had put in his baggage. She had put in an extra shirt, as she had promised, one of those shirts that makes you remember the time you were in a gift shop of a fancy hotel buying it from a girl in a cowboy hat while your wife and daughter napped upstairs. That journey was another adventure, not the journey he was on now. The view looked worse from his room. Tomorrow he hoped he would be flush with victory, or maybe even tonight when he went downstairs, ran into Steed and sealed the deal. He thought umpteenthly of the document in Personal: *I ask what you want to do. You unzip your pants.* And of course her legs on the dashboard of his car, while she talked about desire and excitement, and now on the bed, identical to the one he was sitting on.

"Levine?" he called.

"Yeah" came faintly.

"What if I told you there was no conference?" he asked.

There was a pause, with the hum of something, maybe faint traffic outside, or something in the room adjusting the temperature. Then he heard the *pad, pad, pad, pad* of feet, unmistakably bare, and then Levine's head appeared in the doorway. He could not see the rest of her. Was she in a towel?

"What?" she said.

"I thought you were going to take a shower," he said.

"Yes," she said.

Yes.

"I'm just going to wash my face," Phil Needle said, "and get a drink downstairs with the people from the conference."

She watched him but did not step further into the room. She was waiting for something. She wanted something.

"I want you," he said, "to wait upstairs."

"Okay," she said. "Can I still order food?"

"Yes," he said. "I'll be up later."

"Did you need me for something?" she asked. "Otherwise I'll probably be in bed before long. It's late."

He was her boss. There was nobody else the document could have been about. If he'd had a drink already, he told himself, he'd have the resolution to unzip his pants, right there on the bed. Then she would walk into the room, if that was what she was waiting for. But he hadn't had a drink, and he was not quite so foolhardy to think he couldn't be wrong. So he took his hand and waved at Alma Levine, just a little wave. She smiled and waved back, and then there was the *pad, pad, pad, pad* of her retreat. He let himself lean back on the bed and stare at the ceiling with the blinking smoke detector ready to scream if the building caught fire, or if it just malfunctioned. He tried again to think of a title, but it was just Levine's legs on the bed, all the way down the elevator.

It was not a piano bar, but the bar had a piano in it, shiny on a small round stage with a plaque where the man playing it should have been. The plaque advised guests of the Florio that they had an opportunity to win a piano actually used in the movie *Mississippi Marvel*, the word "actually" more or less admitting that the entire statement was a lie. *Mississippi Marvel* was the biography of another American bluesman, of higher stature than Belly Jefferson, because the Mississippi Marvel had a movie made of his life. The Belly Jefferson people hated him. Phil Needle caught his own nervous reflection in the side of the piano, and checked in with his doubts and fears. They were doing fine, thanks. *American* something. The face of Leonard Steed appeared next to him. Phil Needle did not shriek.

"You're here," Steed said.

"Of course I'm here," Phil Needle said. Leonard Steed had told him to come. And so what if maybe he had, a little shriek.

"I told you to come and you came. I like that. I've been looking. We're all at the bar thinking you were going to come in. Everyone you need to meet."

"Yes, the bar."

Leonard Steed put one hand on Phil Needle, somewhere between paternal and bouncer. "We're in the *other* bar," he said. "Come on."

Phil Needle followed Leonard Steed down another turn and past a podium where the man grinned at Steed, who said gently, "Thanks for your help, Jeffrey," as they walked through an empty restaurant. The walls were red, with light fixtures here and there pretending to be candles. At the back was an enormous table, black and high, and everyone was sitting at it. They were all there, and they were all the same type, and Phil Needle's distance from that type was off the map. But everyone smiled.

"Ten bells and all's well," Leonard Steed said. "Everyone, this is Phil Needle."

"*The* Phil Needle?" asked one of them.

"No," Phil Needle said, because it couldn't be so.

"Of course!" Leonard Steed said. "Phil Needle of Phil Needle

Productions. From San Francisco he comes to you, having fled New York City to reinvent himself. Tall, handsome, married, Jewish, hobbies include kicking your ass at the big presentation tomorrow."

"Is that so?" said one of them.

"That is so," Steed said. "Tell them, Needle."

"I'm giving out ass whoopings and lollipops," Phil Needle said, as heartily as he could muster, "and I'm fresh out of lollipops."

The men roared, calamitous in the echoey room. One man pointed a tut-tutting finger, shaky like a nervous gun. "First thing in the morning, Phil Needle," he said. "Maybe you should go to bed."

"Fuck you," one of them said. "Get yourself a fucking beverage, Needle!"

"The good stuff," Leonard Steed said, and lifted a bottle like a magic trick, a decanter half-empty, or, Phil Needle supposed you could say, half-full. He poured a bolt of it into a glass that fit in Phil Needle's hands not at all, poking and biting like a living skull.

"Sit with us," said one of the men, his face in an eerie shadow. Phil Needle started to slide into the booth, but Steed blocked him on the chest with the decanter.

"No," he said. "We've got to hole up for a little bit, gentlemen. We'll see you tomorrow morning."

"At least tell us the title," said one of the guys. "The name of this famed entertainment. Wet our whistles."

Steed moved his eyes to Phil Needle, but then someone's phone rang, a jumpy song that made everybody laugh. Tortuga. The drinks arrived. Thank you, powerful angels, et cetera. "See you in the morning, gentlemen," Leonard Steed said, and tugged Phil Needle across the shadowy room.

"Watch him closely, Needle," one of them said. "Don't let him give you that nonsense from Socrates."

"Steed tells that to everyone!" cried another one, but they were already far enough to fade away. This part of the room felt hotter, or perhaps that was the sip of fiery drink that felt to Phil Needle like it must be lighting him from the inside. Then he was sitting down, beneath the fluttering electric flame casting streaks of light across Leonard Steed's face.

"How are you, Needle?"

"I think I'm all right," Phil Needle said and then took a large gulp, so as to be able to say, "I should say I don't have a title."

Leonard Steed blinked for a second that made Phil Needle's stomach sink. Then he smiled. "I've been reading," he said, with a pause for the listener to appreciate that. "It's this book about futile times. What do you know about them?"

"I don't know."

"The prevailing wisdom is that the peasants were working all the time," he said with a sigh. *Feudal*, he must have said. "But there were always holidays, Needle. Lots of time to drink mead, roll around in the hay, what have you." He opened his hands like something was simple.

"Oh."

"I'm trying to follow their example," he said. "Abandon the striving for wealth and embrace the striving for joy."

"Peasants?" Phil Needle was nervous. He had no wealth, so he did not want to abandon it.

"Peasants," Leonard Steed laughed, his eyes bright and focused just above Phil Needle's head. The room was not spinning, but nevertheless Phil Needle felt spun. He could not help but think of the receipt for the rental car, the piece of Florio paper he had signed indicating that he knew what the rate for the room was. "Tomorrow we're going to change radio. Do you feel eager?"

"Yes."

"Of course!" Leonard Steed said. "Eager, but not desperate. The thing is not to be desperate. I mean, sound desperate. They like you already, Needle. I told you it's a downhill battle, and you just slid further down the hill. Ass whoopings and lollipops—where'd you get that?"

"You told it to me," Phil Needle said. "Two years ago."

Leonard Steed opened his mouth wide to laugh at the ceiling. Two glints of light from the fixtures, curvy and sharp like tusks, framed his head. Shadows at the big table swiveled to listen to him. "No wonder I liked it. Now let's stop talking about it. How's tricks?"

"What?"

"How are you?"

Phil Needle finished his drink and commenced an abbreviated history of his day: Winter Air, Pennies Rental Car, Florio Hotel, Alma Levine.

Steed refilled him. "So your assistant is upstairs sharing a room with you now?"

"A suite."

"To the victor go the spoils, eh?"

"What?"

"It sounds like this will be an exciting time for you. I expect to see you refreshed and delighted in the morning."

"Steed—"

"*Needle—*"

"I'm a married man."

"Nobody is denying that. Send an orchid to your wife."

"And she's young."

"Too young?"

Phil Needle felt the flutter he had felt in the car all day. Leonard Steed reached under the table and patted his knee. For a sickly, jazzy moment, Phil Needle thought he might touch him between the legs, but the moment disappeared, and so did the hand.

"I don't know," Phil Needle said, putting more liquor in his mouth.

"Levine told me she mostly went to girls' schools," Leonard Steed said.

"When did she tell you this?"

"I talk to all of your staff, Needle," Leonard Steed said. "You know that."

"Yes, when they answer the phone, but—"

"Of course. I was touched on the phone with her," he said, and drank from the decanter with his eyes closed. "Mmm. By something she said, Needle. She felt that a part of her was unfulfilled because of that school. Access to boys. She has a real candor, Needle. I like it. It has a sexual energy."

It had taken Phil Needle this long to realize Leonard Steed was drunk. "I think I'm going to go to bed," he said. "Long day."

"And a long night waiting," Leonard Steed said. "Or do you think she's too young?"

"I'll see you in the morning," Phil Needle said. "I want to be ready."

"Yes, yes," Leonard Steed said. "Venture out to get what you want, tonight and tomorrow. Learned that studying the classics at Harvard. *He who wants the world must first escape from it.*"

He did not say this quotation was from Socrates, and indeed it isn't. It's something Leonard Steed invented, and then reinvented as a remark of Socrates's, for mutual authenticity. Phil Needle stood up to escape, deserting his drink and walking through the restaurant like he did not know where he was, which he didn't quite. He slipped his key out of his pocket and tried to remember the number of his room, turning it over to see if the number was printed on the card—it never is—and then the world went blurry, visible only if he winked. For an instant he saw the tiny circle in space like a drop of water, and then it slipped to the floor: his contact lens. It had fallen away from him. He knelt down and felt along the floor for it, carefully and quickly. He could not feel it. He spread out further, although it couldn't have gone far. Still, it was gone. *Did you need me for something?* his assistant had asked. On the bed. He moved his hands farther out, grabbing for it, then farther on all fours. Farther still. He would find it, goddammit, this thing he wanted. It was his. If he could not walk, he would crawl.

×

Where is she going? Gwen imagined them thinking it. Her coopera-tion was requested in reserving these seats for elderly and handicapped passengers, but she was not cooperating. The seats were in front, nearest the driver, not a great place to sit if you were out committing a crime. Still, Gwen felt safer there, from the rattling wheels of the 38 and the total strangers in the other seats. She kept her eyes up. She was sure everyone wanted to know where she was going. It was none of their goddamn business. She put the bag down between her legs but kept gripping the paper handles. TODAY, it said on her hand.

It was the big night. She was taking the bus by herself.

The 38 was the bus's name and number, swaying down San Francisco's longest street, a straight, wide river passing banks alter-nately bustling and seedy. Out the window the city kept changing its mind in the night, with big department stores and then, suddenly, boarded storefronts, a strange, helmeted cathedral with a shiny plaza spread in front and then nothing but shifty apartment buildings and a bruised mall with a crumbly pagoda. And then it was Gwen's stop, just as they had practiced. *Keep moving, wench,* she thought to herself, and lugged herself and her bag out the front door and down the stairs. Inside the bag was a can of gasoline, purchased at a faraway station with a story Gwen and Amber had invented and practiced about a breakdown and a pregnant mother, and a box of matches— the two items it seemed risky for the taxi driver to see, stacked up with the other provisions. And, squished in on top, a blanket, to cover the gasoline can and to throw over Nathan Glasserman, if necessary. If the bus driver heard the faint *slosh* inside the bag, he did not indicate it as the doors hissed closed, and if he had indicated it Gwen decided she wouldn't care. The night air was so cool and smooth she wanted to marry it. It was the most pernicious secret weapon: Gwen was hooded in a sweatshirt she'd taken from her father. It hung a little loose, but she. Did. Not. Care. Anymore.

Hey,

I got tix to Tortuga tonite at the Fillmore!! I want you to be my date. My parents took my phone :(so don't text just meet me here where it says on the map, so we can spend some time alone before the show . . .

Naomi

The letter had been drafted and redrafted at an emergency meeting. Her father giving her the tickets had changed everything. She'd texted Amber right quick and then held her father's money in her damp fist in the taxi's backseat, hoping it was enough to cover what was already on the meter from her dad's stupid assistant and this journey too, from the condo to Octavia Boulevard. It wasn't. She'd had to jump out at the corner of Market, throwing the bills into the front seat and sprinting out of view, her breath in her ears, rounding a corner and pressing flat against graffiti on a dirty brick wall. *U.S. Out Of This Alley.* They'd rethought the whole strategy, holed up in Amber's room, where the other equipment was hidden.

The tickets seemed a better inducement. The original had only promised sex. Nathan was to meet Gwen at the bench, the wild place, and she would use her wiles on him until he was convinced or otherwise beaten into joining the others in the taxi. But Nathan played bass in a band: they couldn't be sure what he'd been offered before. "This is better," Amber had said to her, ripping the tickets to shreds and flushing them to sea so not one speck would be found.

Gwen had closed her eyes. "It's tricky, though."

"Verily," Amber had said. "Tricky. Tricky and better."

It *was* tricky, what they were doing. In pirate history, kidnappings are mostly a matter of ransom: what we can get for who we have. And there are rescues, young lads snatched from the streets who didn't even know they wanted the pirate life until they were unchained and allowed on deck. But the plot for Nathan Glasserman was somewhere between these two opposite poles of being taken and being rescued. Gwen wanted him to be joined to her, but also to whisk him away. It was shanghaiing, what they were doing, with the drugged ale and the bright coin at the bottom of the glass. In *The Raid upon the Waves* the captain shanghaied an entire crew this way, hosting a party on his boat and putting up anchor when the last man had passed out. When they awoke they were a day toward Shanghai, but there was the coin as payment: both proof that they had agreed to such an arrangement, in the blur of ale and song, and the glittering first installment of the treasures promised them. Amber thought the map was the ale, and Gwen the coin, so that he might agree, in the blur of meeting someone in the dark, to come aboard. Amber redrafted the letter—one that would mislead the authorities when they ransacked his room, as Gwen was sure they would—and drew a new map. The arrow pointed to a dark park, just blocks away from the show. Nathan would approach from the southeast most likely and take the map with him. But the law, finding only the note, would scour the Fillmore audience and find nothing.

Gwen was early. She paced for a minute, afraid to be witnessed, then entered the glowing cube of the only open business on the block, a coffee shop that had nearly surrendered. A short guy with bloodshot eyes mutely handed her an empty cup and her change. You had to get it yourself, pump it out of a black plastic urn. She'd had little besides coffee all day. Gwen lugged her dangerous bag to the only table and huddled over it, still hooded. She would always remember this, she thought—her last coffee on land. Even if it all went wrong, she would remember the cheap steam that rose to the stained ceiling while she blinked and stared and gathered her nerve. (And Nathan Glasserman, the one responsible and maybe even to blame for all this? No Davy Jones's locker for him. He would be scared with a good scare, but there would be nothing that would stop him from being a successful entertainment lawyer in fifteen years flat. Cody Glasserman, the younger brother, would be a different story.)

The bloodshot guy shuffled through a door marked PRIVATE, leaving Gwen alone. Next to her table was a stack of cardboard trays holding bottles of water, all covered in tight clear plastic, a dusty accumulation of rations. They would have to steal water. Amber was only bringing one case.

The door opened. Gwen did not look. Two figures passed in front of her narrowed, hooded view: a guy and a girl with their backs to Gwen and their hands wrapped around each other.

"Hello?" the guy said.

Nobody answered, and after a pause the guy took his hands off the girl and cupped them to his mouth. He took a deep breath and then, earsplittingly loud, did a very good imitation of a monkey. "*Eep! Eep! Eepeepeep eep!*"

The girl laughed and Gwen froze and lowered her head.

"Oh, no," groaned an invisible voice. "Monkeys."

Everyone—not Gwen—laughed. The guy with bloodshot eyes returned and stretched his hand across the counter to greet the other guy in a knocking, clasping ritual believed at the time to be favored by black people. The guy introduced the girl, and the three of them laughed about a couple of things while Gwen's teeth ached. They asked what time the bloodshot guy was closing up the place, and Gwen moved her hands below the table, knowing they would turn to stare at her. Inside the pocket of her sweatshirt was one of the two knives she had taken from her parents' kitchen, the only two good ones, and it had been further sharpened with a stone she and Amber had found on the beach. The whole crew was in agreement, that in case of danger it was better to leave blood than wish it had been spilt. Should she, Gwen Needle, wait until they looked at her or knife them all now? Her brain rattled and jittered with the question, and her shivery hand reached into her pants pockets and pulled out one coin, a penny. She held it over the table. When the penny drops I will make my decision, when the penny drops I will make my decision . . . drop.

Heads.

But it was too late. Without a glance at her, they just laughed again, at something Gwen hadn't heard, and then the guy, who was some asshole, kissed the girl, who was Naomi Wise, right on the sunglasses, and they went back out into the dark. Gwen stood up, pushed her chair back.

"You scared me," said the bloodshot guy. "I forgot about you."

"Keep it that way," Gwen said, and she left. Her feet hurt a little in her new boots. Amber had bought them for her with the Stepmonster's credit card, a crime that would not surface until the bill came at the end of the month—June—and they were long gone. They were perfect, the zippers smooth as an expensive automobile, the leather crackly like a man snapping a whip. Or, a woman.

Outside, the block was empty all the way to the park. The bag sloshed against her knee. The dark sky lasted all the way down, stopping at the tips of stretched trees and a cement overpass allowing pedestrians to move over the traffic. Gwen could only see a few figures in the park, two men stepping around a whisked-out shrub and a woman, her head swiveling every which way for trouble, walking a spiky and unidentifiable dog. Gwen reached the bad grass. The men kept walking and the woman got nervous.

"Come on, Barky," she said, and Gwen realized she would never see Toby II again. Another dead dog. It said it on the door of the Fillmore: ALL EXITS ARE FINAL. The park was empty now, just stilled swing sets and their scrawny shadows. The taxi was coming soon, but there was only so long she could wait before arousing suspicion. *And* the bag was heavy. It was like a football game she'd watched with her dad, waiting for it to end so that he might sigh and go in and apologize to Marina for throwing a bowl at her. Thirty-seven seconds left, but they kept stopping the clock.

At the edge, one of the scrawny shadows moved smoothly toward her. "You're not Naomi," he said. "It's okay. I knew."

Gwen stared at him.

"It's okay," he said.

Gwen felt an anger that had no name, it was so gigantic and without border.

"I knew," he said. "It's okay."

"*You*," Gwen managed to snarl, "did *not know*." It was Cody Glasserman. The name and number of everything changed. The younger brother, skinny in a hooded sweatshirt and black jeans, with shoes, new and clean, the brightest thing in the park. And his nervous eyes, his mouth trying not to smile.

"It's okay," he said. "I thought it would be you."

Gwen was going to kill him if he did not stop talking. She could not say anything herself.

"It's okay."

"How—? Did—?"

"They broke up last week," Cody said. "Naomi and my brother. She gave him back his picture. He says he dumped her, but . . ." He shook his head. "I know you guys aren't friends anymore, or something. You used to be together at swimming. So I thought it was revenge."

Gwen just looked at him. The bag was going *slosh, slosh, slosh,* so she must have been trembling.

"Or something, a joke on her, to—to fuck her up."

The curse made her blink finally. "It's not revenge," she said.

"Like, now she's dating the younger brother."

"No."

"I hate her," he said. "Everyone hates Naomi." He took paper from his pockets, and Gwen saw that the police wouldn't find the note because it was right goddamn there.

"Why do you have that?"

Cody frowned. "It was addressed to me. It had my name on it."

He tilted the envelope so she could see, and Gwen tried furiously to stalk away but got only one step. There was nothing else but Cody Glasserman standing in front of her, hysterically wrong. He looked cold. It was the only thing, Cody Glasserman lured here, never a possibility of anything else. It was already going to be Cody Glasserman when she had her last cup of coffee, when she got on the bus. TODAY on her hand. Every answer was Cody Glasserman now, instead of what she had asked for. The younger brother, fuck fuck fuck.

"It's okay," he said. "It's okay. I—I really like you, Gwen. And Tortuga's awesome. I know it's not what you thought, but we could—"

"We're not fucking going to a Tortuga show," she spat.

But Cody was holding the note that said so. Gwen put the bag down and felt the tears sparking at her eyes. It was wrong, but it was still happening. She remembered, from nowhere, that her father liked him.

"Please," he said. "I—I've always liked you."

She was just remembering the knife when the taxi pulled up at the corner, a yellow van, just as Amber had ordered. Gwen could see Errol and Manny in the back, behind the sliding door but looking out at her, and Amber was already getting out of the passenger side, saying something to the driver and walking quickly toward them.

"What—who are they?" Cody had followed her gaze.

Gwen picked the bag back up. No, the knife, then she couldn't—

But Amber was already here. "*And?*" she said.

"It's not," Gwen said, and pointed at him. But everything was crumpled and tripping in her head. It couldn't be, could it, that Amber had always thought something this wrong?

"You haven't told him, have you?" Amber said.

"What is this?" Cody had already backed up a step. "You're from, I know you."

"Yeah, we've met," Amber said. "You're coming with us, Cody."

"It was *Nathan*," Gwen said.

Amber narrowed her eyes. "Are you Nathan?" she asked him.

"*Cody*," Cody said. "Where are we going?"

"*No*," Gwen said.

"Errol will explain it," Amber said. "He's in rare form." Amber put a dark-nailed hand on Cody's back and pushed him in the direction of the van. The window was already rolling down and Errol leaned out with a wide, gray smile.

Cody turned back to Gwen in confusion. "Who are they?"

Perfectly, this was a question that had been put in chapter three of *Seaward Sinister*, which Errol knew practically by heart. "We are *pirates!*" he crowed. "We are men, men and women, without a country. We are outlaws in our lives and outcasts in our families. We are desperate, and so we seek a desperate fortune. We band ourselves together now to practice the trade of piracy on the high seas."

"For real?" Cody asked.

"Most certainly yes," Errol said. Amber must have given him coffee, or maybe he was better in the nighttime, or simply with something to do. He was more like a captain than he'd ever been. Gwen stepped closer to the proceedings, walking so near Amber they kept brushing arms.

"This isn't him," Gwen said.

"Why not?" Errol asked. "There's always room for honorable people and those who are not welcome elsewhere. My first mate thought you'd be of suitable employ."

"We're not taking him," Gwen said. "He's a kid! We're not cradle robbers."

Cody stepped closer to her and, for the first time, touched Gwen, on the shoulder. Gwen could see Errol's foggy smile. "Nuh-uh," he said. "Everybody says that because of how I'm short. But Gwen, we have the exact same birthday."

She would not be moved until later that he would know such a thing. Now she was just racing to go, to maroon this first mistake before it became an omen. Cody took the bag from her, wincing a little at the weight.

"What's in here?" he asked, and moved the blanket. Even the cabdriver looked down to see.

"Are you—burning something down?"

"Not unless absolutely necessary," Errol said, his eyes looking off at chapter four. "There are rules. You must pledge to be together in a life-and-death bind. Breakfast will be had in silence. All valuables which may come into our possession shall be held together in a common fund used first to fit, rig and provision the ship, and then to recompense any who have lost a limb in armed combat. No cellular phones."

"What?" Manny said.

"They can use them to trace us," Amber said.

"What the hell is all this?" the cabdriver said.

"Close your ears and leave the meter running," Amber said, and touched her belt so Gwen would see the knife there. "We are paying you twice, once for transport and once again for your silence."

"Cocktail hour will be strictly observed," Errol kept going. "Everyone will stand, will stand, will stand a watch at night. Entertainment," and here he looked at his shoe for a few blank seconds, "will largely be confined to storytelling. Keep orderly storerooms. All of us, is the word, will know every knot."

"Do we have to wear special things?" Cody said. "I had to wear tights once for a school play."

"There is no dress code, but there are restrictions on language. You may say *God*. You may say *Christ*. You may say *Goddamn* or *Christ on a stick*. *Shit, fuck, bullshit, motherfucking cock, cunt, asshole*. But you may not take to task a member of anyone's family, as we are all family now, and the people who raised us are left on land to rot away."

"I'll do it," Cody said.

"You will *not* do it," Gwen said. "This is wrong."

"It sounds fun," Cody said.

"Those who would go to the sea for pleasure," Errol said sternly, beginning a slogan Gwen remembered from *Mutiny!*, "would go to hell for pastime."

"And I'm tired of them," Cody said.

"Who?" Amber asked.

"Everybody," Cody said.

"Everybody," said the parrot, its cage in the back someplace, but Cody nodded like it was a person who'd agreed with him.

"Every-stupid-body," he said. "I'm—I guess I was happy. Or I thought so, for a long time, but lately, with my *brother*. My *dad*. My *mom*. It's all of them hemming me in, you know? Watching and *talking* and telling me all of the things to do."

To Gwen it was like the handle on the door of the drugstore. Push or pull, in or out. "Pop the trunk," she said finally.

"Whatever you say," the cabdriver said. The trunk hinged open, and Cody knew without being told to stow Gwen's bag. Everyone crowded into the taxi.

"If you hadn't let me," Cody said, when they were inside, "I would have told."

"None of that," Errol growled. "We are together now and have each other's backs. Understood?"

He nudged Gwen, who swallowed and then turned to look at him. It wasn't that they looked alike, but something was alike about them. They had each other's backs. She steeled herself. "Yes," she said.

"Yes?"

"Yes *what?*"

"Yes *what?*" said the parrot, and Gwen grinned fierce at her whole crew.

"Yes, *Captain*," she said, and felt herself breathe. Cody breathed beside her, and Manny and their captain, while Amber leaned over in front to give the driver further instructions. It was true. They were together now. Cody Glasserman had been shanghaied—not quite rescued, but neither could it be said, as it *was* said, over and over for years, that he was kidnapped, brutally snatched from a playground. Those reading this history can at least have the satisfaction that such a horrible piece of villainy has not been committed. They were pirates, a band of them. The taxi began to move and they all went forward with their eyes open.

CHAPTER 7

CAPTAIN SCROD:

All hands are the wrong hands when they clutch what is not theirs. I
learned this from the words of Socrates, and all my life I believed it like
my given name, until the day everything was taken from me by the
treacherous hands of the crown. So now I swear it, by this drawn cutlass,
that on every civilized shore the most feared name will be—

(offstage: cannon fx)

And so on. The drama ran just over an hour, scripted, as with so
much of pirate lore, by a variety of hands, passed on mostly via
computer to hirelings at a large entertainment company that had nine
Pirates! going in port cities across America and Canada, with scarcely
any supervision save a week of unpaid rehearsals for the company of
nine actors and one stagehand, plus the driver of the *Corsair*, who took
the boat out on the same short loop with a coffee mug in his hand,
filled with beer. Performances were at noon, three, five and seven, and
tickets were fifty-five dollars for adults and thirty-five for children,
because at this point in history everything cost less for children, on the
grounds that they didn't take up as much room. The stage was

everywhere people weren't standing, the lights were the fogged-out sun, and the music was a little prerecorded deckwork piped through speakers on the masts. San Francisco was a new port for *Pirates!* and despite a rich pirate history the city had not made the show a success. The boat was usually half-empty, the tourists cold in shorts and taking halfhearted pictures of the boys in tights and poor Sophia, about to abandon her theater major at the state university, in a prickly hoop skirt and her own makeup. A poster called it a one-hour ride that would last a lifetime. Even from shore, the only way Gwen had seen it, you could see it sucked, with flouncy boys shouting to be heard over the *Corsair*'s motor and the cap pistol often as not failing to fire. In the mornings the actors were required to pass out *Pirates!* flyers in targeted areas where rich people might take children.

The Savoy was the fanciest supermarket, with food shipped ethically from faraway ports. Gwen's mother had already ordered the food from their catering department for the barbecue with the invitations leaving out Gwen's name because she was a mistake. Near the entrance was a boy with an arrogant chin passing out flyers for something or other. Gwen's mother sighed past him and rolled several shopping carts a few inches before choosing one, sighing again, and leading Gwen toward sparkly produce.

"So," she said finally, "do you have anything to tell me?"

What had Gwen's mother spotted? "What?" she asked.

"You heard me," Gwen's mother said, and took a list out of her pocket. "You've been distant."

"No, I haven't."

"Well, I thought so."

"I was *grounded.* I couldn't go *anywhere* until a little while ago."

"Let's put that behind us," Gwen's mother said, and put lettuce in a bag. She ate a lot of lettuce, which Gwen found embarrassing.

"Then, what?"

"Gwen," Gwen's mother said. "I'm just asking you if there's something on your mind."

"I want a folding knife," Gwen said, because why not try.

"Do your apple thing," Gwen's mother said, and then "What?"

"A folding knife," Gwen said, going over to the apples as instructed. Soon she would be released, she thought, from all bossy people. She was very good at finding the ones without bruises. "I think they have them here, near the cheese graters and stuff."

"A weapon?" Gwen's mother asked.

"It's for picnics," Gwen said. "I was thinking, you wanted me to use the Embarcadero."

"Well—"

"That's what you *said*," Gwen insisted. "Anyway I thought I could have a picnic with some friends."

"Well, we have cheese knives at home."

"But those are *yours*. This would be my *own*."

"Gwen, you get every single thing you want, and you are *still* demanding."

"Don't *yell* at me!"

"Gwen, I know you're having a hard, I don't know, something is hard for you. But expand your horizons."

"I *am*."

"Look around the world."

"I *do*."

"Interesting things happen every day," she said, gesturing up and down the boxes of crackers. "You can find the out-of-the-ordinary everywhere."

"Then it's *not*," Gwen growled, "out of the ordinary."

But Gwen's mother wasn't listening. Her eyes were blinky and angled above the highest shelves. "It will happen to you," she said. "It's like when I went to France, although of course I was much older. I've told you that, I know. It will happen to you too, Gwen."

Gwen knew this wasn't the case. They had agreed that they would have to stick to the Pacific coast, heading south probably, to

Mexican ports and South America. She would never get to France. A consequence of the life she had chosen.

(It was not true. Gwen would go to France and find it beautiful.)

They were silent through checkout, while the clerk pawed through their items and an old man, too old to be working, put them in bags. It was another injustice, Gwen thought. Her mother said something to the clerk Gwen didn't hear, but the old man snorted, so she knew it must have been stupid. She stood on tiptoe and pretended to look into one of the bags so she could whisper to him, "My mother's a bitch."

The old man snorted again.

"I'm out of here tomorrow."

The old man nodded. "I know what you mean," he said.

"Fourteen?" Gwen heard the cashier say. "That's a hard age."

Gwen and the old man glared at her until the bags were finished.

"Have a good today and a good tomorrow," the old man said to her. Gwen noticed that he had a hearing aid, the pink color an indignity, an outrage. "Don't be a stranger."

Gwen's mother smiled nervously and pushed the cart away. "You really shouldn't talk to strangers," she said when they were outside.

"*Mother*, he was an old man."

"The old men are the worst," Gwen's mother said, although she was smiling a little. "Anyway, I would think you'd had enough time like that, with your punishment. Where are the keys? I think the car's over there."

"I *see* the car, Mom." Gwen was yearning to be reprimanded, so she could walk away. But Gwen's mother was unfolding a triangle of paper she had found in her pocket. Gwen looked elsewhere and then back again. Her mother was reading it with a tiny smile, and— *perfect*—Amber was walking straight toward them. They pretended not to recognize each other, which was sexy, but Amber gave her a secret wave, her hand fluttering at her hair and clutching, Gwen knew, two hundred forty dollars in filched twenties from their dads. Amber's ex worked at the Savoy making sandwiches. He was going to see to ordering and delivery, as Gwen and Amber had learned that liquor stores would not leap to believe they were of legal age, let alone deliver a case of alcohol to the Barbary Coast Hotel.

"What if he says he won't do it?" Gwen had said on the phone a few nights earlier. "He could be fired for that, making up an order that he took on the phone."

"I'll tell him that if he does it I'll give him a blow job."

"*Amber!*"

"And I will, too."

"You told me you guys never even kissed."

"Yeah, well, that wasn't my idea. I'll do it if I have to. Everybody does it sometime."

Gwen had never thought about it but realized it was true, at least for all girls, pretty much. Blow jobs weren't out of the ordinary. She was realizing it that evening when she slunk down the staircase at the instructions of her mother, who was in the living room switching purses. Everything was out on the table like evidence, and, to Gwen's embarrassment, her mother was sucking thickly on a straw dipped in a bottle of iced tea. She had noticed the missing money, must be what this was about. If only she would stop sucking.

"What?"

Gwen's mother put the bottle down. "I asked this morning if you had anything to tell me."

Gwen looked at her carefully. "What?"

"Don't *what* me."

Gwen scratched her ear and felt her hair. Where was the haircut she'd meant to get? There wasn't time now.

Gwen's mother shouldn't have sighed again, but she did, and reached down past her legs to the floor, as if looking for lost feet.

But then she brought out a box from underneath the sofa. "I found these in your room," she said, not even trying to sound anything but triumphant. "Hidden behind a bunch of books I know you're not reading."

Gwen felt all possible fury. It was an injustice, a grave injustice, that she had a knife but it was upstairs in the sweatshirt she'd wear tomorrow. It was in case blood had to be spilt. Her fingers were wide open, down at her sides like two splayed-out stars.

"You're stealing again."

"Those were a *present*."

It was her boots, her unworn secret. Their ownership was not in dispute, as it had passed down without incident, to Gwen from Amber, to Amber from the boutique and the credit card, to the boutique from the factory, to the factory from the tanner from the cow. They were aboveboard, and almost tall enough to cover the burn.

"Do you know how much these cost?"

Three hundred fifty dollars. "*No!*" Gwen said. "I said they were a *present!*"

"I don't know what to do with you!" cried her mother.

"You don't get to *do* anything with me," Gwen said with scorn.

Gwen's mother rose up with both her hands in the air. She had never laid a hand on Gwen, and she didn't now. But what?

"I'm serious," her mother said, in a hoarse and desperate voice.

"So am I."

"This is *it*. If I weren't your mother . . ."

She stopped talking, or anyway Gwen stopped listening. If Gwen's mother weren't her mother, she'd just be some lady. And beautiful, too. It was true. Gwen looked at her mother and thought, I'll never see you again, Mom. Like her mom was a candy bar. But she had a hot feeling, down in her throat.

"Give me those," Gwen said wearily. "They're mine. You have no right to take them."

"I'm not *naive*," Gwen's mother said, but then she reached

down and threw the box in Gwen's direction. It opened midair and the boots stepped out, beautiful and empty. "Take them, then. I wash my hands of it. *Take them!*"

"I *will* take them," said Gwen, although she let them spill on the floor. "I'll take them and walk out of here," and this is the part of this history with much shouting. *Guttersnipe! Cow! Scum! Ingrate! Galley slave! Sea hag! Fiend in human shape!* It was an uproar, the last of many, and Gwen knew even when she stalked upstairs and burst in on her father, who was hiding in the bathroom trimming his nails, to scrawl I HATE HER on his hand, that it didn't matter. The liquor would be delivered no matter what Amber had to do. It was why she'd written it on her father's hand and not her own, so she wouldn't have to scrub it off in the morning like a fool. Tomorrow she would write TODAY. The ship was almost already sailed. It was all about to be water that was about to be under the bridge, and when Gwen screamed at her mother, raged at her downstairs and upstairs, all the while she was doing a kindness, for never did it escape her mouth that the note Marina found in her pocket, the one that made her smile, was Amber's handiwork.

Dear Marina,

This is just a note to say I was thinking of you, and that I will love you always.

Love, Phil

PS Don't worry about our daughter. She's beautiful.

There was no strategy to this. It was something she had asked Amber to do, just for a kindness. Just because she knew her mother would worry, as the mothers of all rapscallions have worried, gazing at the sea and wondering if they would ever return. Gwen's mother deserved to worry, but still Gwen gave her this as the ship pulled away, a last call, just as the bartender called last call at the Pisco, the bar where the *Pirates!* cast went after the last performance of the day. Amber and Gwen had tailed them there at a discreet distance, and then convinced Manny to go in to watch the end of it, stone sober, as drinking was against his religion. "They drink up their pay until closing," he'd reported over catmint tea. *Last call*, the bartender calls it. And then he says, *you don't have to go home, but you can't stay here.*

It was exactly how Gwen felt, almost the very same thing. She wasn't going home and she couldn't stay here. That night she slept deep and long, her heart pounding the whole time but her head empty as the night sky. It would be how *Pirates!* would sleep, the entire crew.

Normally the crew of the *Corsair* rose early, to make sure the costumes and props were in order for the first show of the day. Gwen and Amber had seen them working with false, forced cheer on the otherwise empty pier, and they saw the hook on board, where they left the keys careless and easy because who would take them. But Friday night the crew would be made to sleep late. After the Pisco turned them out, a crate of liquor would turn up, left for them at their inexpensive, shoddy lodgings. The Barbary Coast. They would not ask questions, but pass the night in drunken revels, noticing not that one bottle was spiked with the sleeping dosage of a stepmonster. Saturday morning the actors would awaken, their heads splitting, but it would be too late. The real pirates would sneak in the night and larder the *Corsair* with new equipment, a new crew, and a truer calling. They would come in the night and take what was rightfully theirs.

Gwen hadn't made this up. This was history. It was

happening. She wasn't thinking about it, imagining the boxes and duffels on the deck. She was really leaving. She and her captain, her fellow belligerents, strode through the patches of tourists leaving restaurants, smoking in silent pairs, or glowering silent in families. Her crew was carrying clothing, water, some food, gasoline, miscellany, Jean-Robert in his cage, rustling and covered in a towel, and weapons. It felt real. The pier felt solid. The railing felt metal. The boat looked like an actual, genuine pirate vessel. The sky was the limit. Their lives were now disengaged from all control and drifting out of bounds.

On board were benches with hinged tops for emergency storage, and they threw the life vests overboard. They had decided to jettison these, as no such things could be found in the books they had read. Gwen grabbed two, reading what was written on the inside of the bench:

LIFE PRESERVER INSTRUCTIONS:

1. Put on as a vest.

2. Tie strips tightly to hold jacket against body.

3. Clip the hook into the ring.

4. Pull strap tight to hold jacket close.

5. Ready to go.

Ready to go.

"Manny." Errol's voice was loud on the deck.

"I'm just getting my act together," Manny said. Gwen watched him gaze at the screen of his cell phone one last time, scrolling through something before turning it off and tossing it onto the pier, where it scuttled next to the one dropped by Cody, who was already down below looking through the costumes, not having brought a change of clothes when he was shanghaied. Manny heaved the cage aboard and then pulled something out of the pocket of his seaman's coat. This, too, he gazed at, and scrolled through. This, too, he tossed away. It was his Bible, black and worn as the heavens. He did not have to abandon it, but Gwen had showed him a captioned drawing. Captain Nebekenezer, known to his men as Neb, burying his Bible. Its divine precepts being so at variance with the wicked course of his life that he did not choose to keep a book that condemned him in his lawless career.

"Come along," called Errol. As they had suspected, the captain's wheel was not how the boat was actually steered, but the captain stood by the wheel nonetheless. "Too late to die young, Manny."

Manny's eyes were on the Bible, invisible on the pier. "I don't know. I was raised it was wrong to live without rules or punishments."

"They already told us the rules," Cody said, coming up the wooden stairs.

"There's punishments too," Errol said, and Gwen watched him rack his brain for the list of punishments he liked so much in *Captain Blood*. "Any pirate who conceals, conceals, conceals captured treasure shall be set ashore on . . . I forget the word."

"Island," Gwen said.

"Island," Errol agreed, "and there left with a single bottle of water, a single loaf of bread and a single bullet in a single pistol."

"Assuming we find one," Amber said. She was unwinding a thick rope, tied in a showy knot to a cleat on the pier with *Pirates!* painted on it in gold script, and Manny leaned in to help her. Gwen could see the crumply bulge in his shirt pocket, the packet of tea he had brought along, catmint likely being irreplaceable on the high seas.

"Your parents are worried already, you know," Manny said. "They probably haven't started dinner. It's bad luck to start dinner, my mama always told me, before your children are home. Please God let this not be the meal I cooked, they will say, when I found out she's gone."

(But it was. Chicken.)

"We will be the scourge of the San Francisco Bay Area," Amber said, "dedicated to the egalitarian and comely—no, shit."

Gwen and Amber had texted this back and forth to each other, polishing and sloganeering when the world thought they were safe in bed asleep. "*Comradely*," Gwen said. "Dedicated to the egalitarian and *comradely* distribution of life chances."

Amber grinned and got back on track. "And all the happiness in the world shall tumble into—"

"*All* the happiness?' Manny asked from the pier. "That's a lot. How about just an unfair amount of happiness?"

"Treat reluctance like seasickness," Errol said, picking something off his sleeve. "If you feel it, focus on the horizon."

"On the boat, I thought," Gwen said. "For seasickness."

Errol's eyes got uncertain. "Well," he said, "focus on *something*."

Manny laughed and in one fat swoop leapt aboard. It was not wise, now that the history is known, to do so. Given the madness ahead, it was madness to join. But all occupations and philosophies are to some extent foolhardy. His bulk upon landing briefly unsettled the ship, but then it righted. Time to get the show on the road. Gwen would stand at the front of this stolen ship, facing out and proud like a figurehead. She would feel her own cells dividing, growing and dreaming of growing at the same time. It was going to be easy. Tallyho and hallelujah! Exodus and excelsior! Avast! Here goes!

Errol looked out from the wheel at the dark, untamable water, his face as open and bright as the moon. "Off we go," the captain said.

"Off we go," the parrot squawked. It's so easy to steal things.

Part Two

CHAPTER *8*

O the morning, this morning, early and sunny through the window, halcyon until the wind blew it all to sea. The drapes hadn't worked at their job, which was keeping the room dark for their occupant, Phil Needle. His body was long and sore, stretched out like a limousine across the bad bed, naked and blinking, parts of him damp in hot sheets. The room was loud with an old song. Belly Jefferson, deep and scratchy, pouring water through his phone, ringing by his bed, next to a glass of water, scarcely full, and his wallet and a magazine about Los Angeles the hotel had left for him. The headline said, LOS ANGELES. He picked up.

"Yes?"

"Is this Phil Needle?"

"Yes."

"Phil Needle of Phil Needle Productions?"

"Yes." The room, and its carpet, discredited him.

"I have Leonard Steed on the line."

"Hold on." Phil Needle used one of his stiff elbows to prop himself up. The phone rubbed against his ear, and with his other hand he quickly reached out, grabbed the glass of water, and splashed some of it in his face. There was a lot more water than he thought, and it slapped itself onto his sticky chin and ran down his neck and chest. "I'm ready," he said into the phone, dripping. But Leonard Steed was already there.

"Glad to hear it, Needle," he said.

"Who was that? Where are you?"

"Downstairs with coffee. I had my assistant patch you in." At this time in our history, satellites in outer space were often used this way, to connect people who were almost within touching distance on earth. Phil Needle put the glass back, knocking his wallet open. Something was gone.

"How are you, Steed?"

"The normal nonsense," Leonard Steed said. "It's the morrow, though. I'm having coffee and I wanted to check. Good to go in half an hour?"

"Yes," Phil Needle said. "What time is it?"

"Tell me I didn't wake you up."

"No, no," Phil Needle said, and swung his legs out to the fluffy floor. His shadow looked gaunt and crappy on the wall, and the sheets were wet in patches.

"Good, good. I want to conference before the powwow."

"Yes, a half hour," Phil Needle said. "Thirty minutes."

"Make it twenty," Leonard Steed said.

"Okay," Phil Needle said.

"*Okay*, you mean *yes?*"

"*Yes*," Phil Needle said.

"What, you're not dressed?"

"What? Yes."

"You want to fuck her again?"

"What?"

"To the victors, yes? How was it? Tell me something about it."

Phil Needle sat up and looked out the window. His legs were too close together for his penis to get comfortable. "I'll see you downstairs."

"Come *on.*" His voice got closer to the earpiece. "Is she a moaner? All quiet? She seems like a moaner. Come on, tell me something that'll give me a buzz with my coffee."

"Leonard—"

"Did she suck it first?"

"I'm not—"

"Tell me. It will bring us closer together."

"No."

"Is she right there? She wants to do it again."

"No."

"Okay, then tell me something else. What's the name of this show we're going to pitch together?"

"I told you before, I don't have a title."

"Surprise, surprise. Okay, well, say nothing to the king's men. Make them guess, maybe. *What do you think it's called?* Will that work, Needle?"

"I don't know."

"We'll need strong arms and strong backs. Now it's eighteen minutes, so I'll let you go. You're not going to tell me, I know. You fucked her on my say-so and you're being a gentleman?"

"Leonard," Phil Needle said. "How much did you drink last night?"

"Felt great on the treadmill this morning," Leonard Steed said. "Seventeen minutes."

He hung up. *Strong arms and strong backs.* But Phil Needle stood up brittle, everything creaking with nothing to offer. On a chair, upholstered too fancy for the room, was last night's discarded clothing. He looked closer. What was it that was missing? There was a slot for something in his open wallet, a tiny plastic rectangle behind which a photograph of his wife and daughter smiled. They were two different photographs, as it seemed impossible to get both of them to smile in the same room. But the photograph of his daughter was gone. It was just his wife, and a blank leather rectangle. He tapped the space, and spread his legs further. What time was it?

Belly Jefferson sang again.

Phil Needle picked it up. "What?" he said, but there was just empty humming and nothing on the screen. The satellite had spun away from Leonard Steed's assistant, probably, and Phil Needle waited, nude, for it to return to orbit. Then he heard, dimly over the hum, a man saying, "We've got the father."

Phil Needle stood there, like a picture of a snowman. Dripping water. A man came on the phone and asked him if he was himself and he said he was. There was another muttering over the hum. He remembered, from something someplace sometime, that when someone calls for an emergency, the first thing they say, if the person is alive, is "She's alive."

"*What?*" Phil Needle shouted. "*What?*"

"I'm sorry," said the man. "There's an emergency. It was difficult to find you."

So it *was* an emergency. "What's the emergency?"

"I don't know. We're trying to get your wife on the phone."

"What is it?"

"I don't know."

"If you know," Phil Needle said, "and you're not telling me, then you are—"

"Your daughter's missing."

Phil Needle would never remember how his eye fell on the blank rectangle in his wallet, only that his first thought, nonsensical and guilty, was *How'd they know?*

"Missing," he said finally, or right away. He was cold now, and grabbed the blanket from the bed, tugging it, tugging it, tugging it harder from the corners of the mattress and wrapping it around all of him. He saw his underpants on the chair. When he'd taken those off, he'd been happy.

"We're trying to get your wife," the man said, "to the phone."

His wife, his nearest and dearest. And his daughter, someplace else.

"Marina?" he said.

But there was nobody on the phone, just the same hum and a new, tappy sound: *hic-hic-hic.* He remembered the phone call from the drugstore, the man who told him he had a daughter named Octavia. That had been wrong. Surely that was the case now: that some other girl—maybe that girl Octavia—was missing. Where was she?

Hic-hic-hic. "Phil-*hic?*"

It was Marina, crying. "Honey?"

"Where are you, Phil?" *Hic-hic.*

What? "I'm here, Marina. I'm here at the hotel."

"They couldn't find you," she wailed, "and you didn't answer your cell. You didn't call. I didn't know where you were."

"I called you when the plane landed. There was a plane problem."

"No," hic-hic-hic, "you didn't, Phil."

It was his *father* he had called. The world, he'd said, had gone wrong.

"Gwen's missing, Phil. She didn't come home last night. I haven't seen her since she ran to pay the taxi."

"What? She took a taxi?"

"She didn't *take a taxi*, Phil. Remember that girl of yours lost her purse."

By magic Alma Levine entered the room. She was wearing a robe, and her lips were freshly red with hip, wet lipstick. She had something in her hand that looked folded up. Phil Needle pulled the blanket tighter around himself and shooed her away.

"I have to talk to you," Levine said.

Phil Needle felt that his wife could see into the room, and he stared back into the phone's little screen. He lurched one step toward Levine, his body warm in the blanket, hot even in one place, a place Levine had touched him. It felt like a burn. He covered the phone.

"I'm on with Marina," he told Levine. "It's an emergency."

"I really have to talk to you," she said.

"Not now."

"Yes."

"In a second, in a minute. This is an emergency. Go to the bathroom."

"What?"

"The bathroom, get out of here."

"I don't have to use the bathroom."

Hic-hic-hic. Who cannot at any time force a little urine out of them? "*Go.*"

Levine stalked past the bed and slammed the bathroom door. "What was that?" Marina asked.

"Nothing," Phil Needle said. "I'm sorry. I'm just learning this."

"I left like ten messages," Marina said. "Even the hotel couldn't find you."

"I was in the bar."

"The *bar*," Marina said angrily.

"Tell me what happened."

"I don't *know*," she said. "She went out this morning and never came back."

"But it *is* morning."

"*Yesterday*," Marina wailed. "I've been up all night."

"Did you call—"

"I called, of course I called, and her phone rang in her *room*, Phil. She abandoned it, her phone is in her room but where is she? I called *everyone. Everyone* from school and everyone on the swim roster."

"But she quit swimming."

"I called Naomi Wise and Wendy, but she said they weren't *friends* anymore. But she's been out all the time."

"Doesn't she have a new friend?"

"Who?"

"I don't know, maybe I'm wrong."

"Who, Phil? Who are her friends?"

Phil Needle looked at his clothes on the chair, flat and wrinkled and shameful. There was a man missing from them. Missing, Phil Needle thought, was better than dead, although Gwen could be dead too, dead and also missing. *Hic-hic-hic.* He did not know who his daughter's friends were. Once, when she was four years old, she ran around their old house in the Sunset, shouting "Six ears! Six ears!" Phil Needle had never understood a word she said.

"Swimming," he said. "That Glasserman kid from swimming."

"*You're* the one," Marina said, "who likes him. Even *I* know that."

Phil Needle was thrown by the "Even *I*," as if his wife were the out-of-touch parent, when he thought all along that was his role. "Marina, what happened?"

"I don't *know*," she said. "She told me she was playing with Naomi."

"She doesn't *play*," Phil Needle said. "She's fourteen."

"Something with her, a movie maybe, I don't know," Marina said. "She never came back upstairs from the taxi. Something's *happened*, Phil."

"Have you called the police?"

"Of course I called the police. And *they* called the police."

"Who?"

"The people here. A guy, I don't know."

"Where are you?"

"I'm at the morgue."

The rebel in Phil Needle departed. The earth split, too. *Dead,* he thought. *So it feels like this.*

"It's not the morgue," he heard clearly in the background.

"I was here as soon as it opened," Marina said. "They didn't even believe I *have* a daughter. Oh, God, Phil."

"Where are you?"

"I thought the morgue was in the basement of City Hall."

"What?"

"You did a show about it once."

Phil Needle thought and then found it: some mixing, a few years ago, on a spot for somebody else's program. Marina had stopped in before the doctor's and he had her listen to it. "That was the tiniest town in Texas," he said. "Did she call you? Have you heard from her?"

"I was painting all day," Marina said, "but no."

Painting, he thought, unable to picture what her painting looked like. "Okay, I'm coming home," he said. "I'm coming home right now, Marina."

"I don't know what to do," Marina said. "They won't help me here."

"It doesn't sound like you're anywhere."

"I'm in the basement of City Hall!"

There was a staticky scuffle and *hic-hic-hic,* fainter and fainter, until Phil Needle heard the man's voice again.

"We've called the police," he said. "I'm sorry for the confusion. That is your wife?"

"Yes, Marina."

"She was so disoriented when she came here. She was looking for your daughter—you have a daughter?"

"Yes, Gwen."

"Because she showed us a picture on her phone, then one in her wallet. Otherwise we might have thought, I mean, nothing personal."

"No."

"It's just that this isn't where you go. She was upset."

"Who are you?"

"I'm on the janitorial staff. We're getting her a taxi home. She doesn't know where she left her car."

Marina grabbed back the phone. "I never should have come here," she said.

"Yes," Phil Needle said.

"Gwen, I mean. Never should have left."

"I'm coming home," Phil Needle said.

"Leave your phone on," she said. "*Leave it on, goddammit!*"

"I'm coming home," Phil Needle said helplessly. "You come home too."

"Where is she?"

"I'm coming home."

"*Where is she?*" She sounded so much like Gwen, furious Gwen, that Phil Needle remembered how much they had been fighting. She was probably fine—stalked away from her mother, but fine. Still, though, where? Where was she fine?

"I'm leaving now," Phil Needle said. "I'm coming home."

He hung up the phone and held it in his blanketed lap. What had happened? He felt he should call somebody else, as it was an emergency, somebody else right away. But instead he stood up with the blanket, let the phone topple, and walked into the bathroom to take a shower. He should shower. He smelled of last night, and his own panic.

Levine was standing there, right in the center of the tiny room, still in a robe and holding the object, which turned out to be a newspaper in the stupid bag they hang on the door. Phil Needle held his blanket tighter. Her robe had the name of the hotel, on her breast, or on a fold of the robe. Phil Needle could not think of what her breasts looked like.

"You told me to go in here," she said, as if in reply. "Can I talk to you now?"

"Something has happened," Phil Needle said. "I need to take a shower."

In the small room they were startlingly close to each other, considering the size of the hotel suite or the damn world. Levine handed him the newspaper.

"I quit, Phil," she said. "I thought about it, and I can't work for you anymore."

"Something has happened," he said. "That was my wife on the phone."

"You didn't tell her," she said.

"My daughter is missing," he said, unfolding the newspaper absently. Gwen's disappearance was not in the papers yet, he thought. It was just everything else, alphabetically listed in a box in the corner: Advice, Business, California, Classified, Crossword, Editorial, Legal Notices, Life, Lottery, Movies, National, Obituaries, People, Sports, Television, with Gwen nowhere to be found. "She's not at home," he said. "Nobody knows where she is. My wife is very upset. I need to get home as quickly as possible, and I need to take a shower."

"Did you hear what I said?" Levine asked.

"Leonard Steed," he said out loud. That was who. "He's having coffee downstairs. You need to cancel the pitch."

"You're not listening to me," Levine said.

"I'm listening, I'm listening," Phil Needle said. "I've spent this whole time listening. Go downstairs right now and tell Leonard—"

"I'm not dressed," she said.

"Get dressed if you're not dressed. I need to shower, shower and shave."

"Phil, I'm quitting. I'm done."

"Levine, if you don't get the fuck out of the bathroom, I'm going to I don't know what. *Get out. Go downstairs.*"

"I *quit.*"

"I *know.*"

"Then *why*—"

"How are you planning to get home?" he asked. "Without a purse, by the way." They were in Los Angeles right now. The magazine.

Levine scowled but nudged past him. Phil Needle shut the door and tossed the newspaper into the sink. He dropped his blanket. His body looked rancid in the jaundicey light of the bathroom, his thighs shaky and wide, his feet too curly and too yellow. His penis was half-hard—*Did she suck it first?*—and Phil Needle grabbed it for a second in guilt before stepping in and turning the faucet. The shower was spiny, but it barely touched him. Hot felt the same as cold. On a tiny shelf were three bottles in a tight row, and he put something in his hair, which used to be thicker, not so long ago even, when Marina was pregnant. Phil Needle said something out loud, realizing that Marina had been pregnant with Gwen, who was now nobody knew where. He turned the water right off. This was not a way to broadcast a hero, to do something selfish like bathe, while his child was missing. He wiped his face with his hands and hunch-backed over to the towels. He dried himself. There was lint on his legs. He would not shave, not just because heroes were unshaven at the time this story takes place, but because he was trembling and would likely slice open his throat. Phil Needle could almost feel the blood running down his neck, but it was the water, from the shower. He had to get home. He sat on the bed again and put on his unhappy underpants, but halfway up his legs he stopped.

"God," he said. His voice sounded too mean in the room. "God," he said again, more politely, the way God probably preferred. But then what? He prayed probably once a month but never knew how he did it. He sat on the bed, impure and desperate. *Find my daughter*, or something. But God could find anyone. It was unthinkable, even naked, with Levine stomping around outside his door, that he, Phil Needle, did not deserve to know where his daughter was. Who would think that? Nobody would think that. Phil Needle supposed what he meant was that he wanted to *be* God, just long enough to find his daughter. It was not a prayer but a promotion. This was why nobody liked God: they wanted his job. "God," he said, one more time, and shook his head mightily, like a dog, water everywhere, until a new sound came to his ears.

It was Belly Jefferson. His phone.

Phil Needle stood up with underwear around his ankles,

pulling it up and grabbing the phone. The screen told him who was calling, and he pressed the button indicating he would not answer, and sat down again, this time on the chair, on top of the clothes he had to put on. Shirt, with buttons. Pants first, one leg at a time. He had to go. He couldn't stay here.

Phil Needle put the phone down. It was not Marina. It was not Gwen. It was nobody he wanted to talk to.

×

Who does not see rich people on a boat and want to destroy them? A ship is a wooden world, with invisible delights below deck and vain displays above. But past the boundaries of land, just as the boat in storms is subject to the blue whip of the sea, the treasure is anyone's game. Those in yachts are powerful, but their disputants also have a power granted in oppositional culture. They have *contempt*, utter and irrevocable, rage produced even in the gentlest. It must, this thing, lead to brutality. Gwen was ravenous to prove these ideas true. She was certain about it, as certain as the circles around each view of her prey, the limits of the binoculars they had found on board.

Over Paradise Bay a tiny rain was stopping and starting and the sun blinked indecisively in the air. The water was so cold, your favorite ring could slip off your finger, making identification much more difficult. Catherine Vogel was standing at the back of the boat, with her hands visored over her eyes in the shape of a heart. She had a beautiful body and a frown. She was looking out at Tiburon, a wealthy peninsula three miles away and Spanish for "shark," and thinking, it appeared to Gwen, *When I put on this bikini I was happy.* She'd covered herself in a short, thin robe that belonged in a closet, two flights down, by a dark bed in a low room. You could see a loop of ink around her thigh, a few lines of French. She did not belong on board. She was twenty-three and just figuring this out. It was stupid, to be on a yacht, and she was not stupid. With a clear head she could see, Gwen could see, that she wouldn't be caught dead here.

Her boyfriend was inside checking a piece of equipment. He was older. His name was Roger Cuff. He had been dressed in a buttoned shirt and a windbreaker, like a political candidate at a disaster, but he had just shucked his clothes and was now wearing only the hair on his body and his big, worried head. Roger Cuff had just had a big project canceled by his producing partner, who was also his consultant. This yacht, *Outside the Box*, a forty-footer with full detailing and a top dry ride up to twenty-six knots he co-owned with his last remaining friends, was no longer affordable for Roger Cuff. Yesterday his girlfriend had returned from a vague trip—a friend's wedding, she'd murmured—on a later flight than she'd originally said, and had been quiet and cold on the boat. They hadn't made love last night, and the removal of Roger Cuff's clothes was a rash, hopeful gesture, although more than sex he wanted to lie around afterwards and talk of the other men who had, if you looked at it as Roger Cuff did, stolen his success. If Cath had come inside at that moment, he would have started to talk about it, naked or not, so prickly and immediate was it in his mind. (How many people have died thinking of such cheap things?) But Cath was looking at the approach of another boat.

The *Corsair* sailed under the gray sky, the whole crew openly bent on plunder. Errol was at the wheel, and Manny had found the controls for the ship down below and through tinted portholes was guiding the boat with ease and fire. Cody was bringing up mugs of coffee—nobody had slept yet—and Amber was untangling some netting, if it ever came down to fishing. And Gwen was staring down hard at the boat they would soon attack. The water was a large, wide noise, and the Golden Gate Bridge, improbable and orange, looked like it had been stuck into the sea just seconds ago. Out here they could do anything, and nobody could do anything about it. Gwen lit an imaginary cigarette, her courage and determination gathered tight. The knife was in her hands, and she was breathing smoke.

"*Sick*," Amber said beside her. "I've never seen water so blue."

"Sunglasses," Gwen said, without turning around.

"Quiet, wench," Amber said, but she took off the sunglasses that had been left absently on a shelf below, blue and angular, belonging to an actor waking up just now with a splitting head. "Oh," she said. "Now it just looks like normal water. But it's okay. It's better that it looks more real."

"Getting close," Gwen said, and looked up at the flag flying over the mast. She had always wondered about the pirate flag, as it announced from afar intentions that seemed better kept secret. Only now, at this time in our nation's history, did she see why it worked: people thought it was a joke. The woman now, in the robe on the deck, must have been thinking so. Soon they would be close enough to see her smile.

"Heaven in a handbasket!" cried Errol. "I see great success for us in this our first venture! Treasure—and a treasure map!"

"Treasure map," Amber repeated quietly, and Gwen finally turned because she had to see her face. A treasure map was unlikely—they weren't stupid—but still Amber smiled like it could be true, the reluctant sunlight turning enthusiastic in her bared eyes and on the blade of the other sharp knife of Gwen's. Amber's knives had been distributed—a long, rusty saw for Errol, two small blades for Manny and a meat cleaver for Cody Glasserman, very sharp and wide as a woman's thigh. Gwen raised and lowered herself on her toes and handed the binoculars to Amber.

"Looks like just two of them."

"Yeah," Amber said. "Ew, the guy's naked."

"What?" Cody said, trading coffee for the binoculars. "Let me see."

"Steady now," Errol said, adjusting the wheel. "Arm yourselves, grommets."

"Armed," Gwen said.

"Armed," Amber said.

"Armed," said the parrot.

"I'll do the talking," Gwen announced, and everyone nodded. How did she live, she wondered, or any of them? How did we live before this?

"Hey," said the woman on the boat. "Be careful, you're close on that end."

"The starboard end," Gwen corrected.

"Uh-huh," she said. "What are you guys—"

Errol interrupted her with a shout from the wheel, with the words comprising the title of the present volume.

"Okay," she said, and then "Hey!" to the crackle of wood as the *Corsair* pulled up to their side. Cody unswung a hinged plank and rested it just inches from the woman's bare feet.

Gwen put her coffee cup down, cold and coldly. "We are boarding," she said. "You will give us food, water, and everything of value this sorry vessel is holding. And then, perhaps, we will let you live."

"What?" the woman said. "Is this some kind of joke?"

"No," Gwen said, and felt the fury surge into her heart, just as promised. They had never been kidding. They had been serious the whole time. In quick, quick steps, she boarded *Outside the Box*, her boots loudly clacky on the wood.

"No, no, no," the woman said, waving her hands in front of Gwen. Gwen thought she probably hadn't seen the knife yet. "Roger!"

The man—Roger, it must have been—stepped out of the door and then doubled back down the stairs when he saw they weren't alone. Gwen's cohorts hooted with laughter at his nakedness as they followed her onto the boat.

"Surprise, surprise!" Errol called. Amber stood at Gwen's side and Cody helped the captain aboard. Roger leaned out of the door-frame again, with his quizzical hairy chest.

"What is this?" he said.

"Food," Gwen said again, "water, and everything of value on this boat."

"What?" the man said with a chuckle. "Hold on, let me get dressed."

Gwen shook her head, and then in one fast movement, as if she had done it before, jabbed the knife in an arc and left a thin red line on the woman's arm. The woman shrieked, and the man stepped back out.

"What?" he said. The woman was holding her arm and sat down as the blood moved past her fingers. "What?"

"She *cut* me, Roger," the woman said, in a tone of voice that could not quite decide to be alarmed.

"Seriously?" Roger said.

Errol clumped heavily toward him, his saw out and toothy.

"What is this?" Roger said.

"We told you," Errol said. "Get us what we demanded and you will consider yourselves lucky for the rest of your lives. Resist and you will see us rip her open with a cutlass, tear the living heart out of the body, gnaw at it, and hurl it in your face!"

Roger blinked and then laughed a little, but the woman raised her arm. "She really cut me," she said. "Do something."

"I don't know what to do," Roger said, with a graying shrug Gwen knew from her father. "I've never had this happen."

"You're not *having it happen*," Gwen said. She took her imaginary cigarette out of her mouth and threw it into the sea, rather than on deck, where it might start fires. "It's just *happening*."

"Look, get out of here," Roger said. "Away with you. I don't have time for whatever it is that—"

"*Water!*" Amber cried. "*Food! Everything of value! On the deck right now or we'll keelhaul the both of you!*"

The woman blinked. "What?" she said, all anybody said. "What's *keelhaul*, again?"

"Dragging a person over the keel," Gwen said quickly.

"And what's the keel?"

Why wasn't this working? Everyone was on deck, brandishing knives, and still these two were just looking at them curiously, as if there was nothing that could hold them, as if pirates were so out of bounds as to actually be unimaginable. But Gwen had imagined this for years! For a long time, anyway. Weeks! She pushed herself past the woman and led Amber toward the door where Roger was standing. His body was thick but halfhearted, sickly in the gray light, and Gwen could see that his penis was not quite soft. Ew.

"Look," he said, and took a step backwards on the stairs. "Get out of here. There's a radio. I'll call—"

Gwen reached forward with both hands and shoved him, hard. He fell on his ass and bounced down the other three stairs, landing loudly on the floor of the cabin. The woman made a noise, rough and gaspy. "*What?*" Roger said. "What the hell?"

"*I told you!*" Gwen screamed. She followed him down the stairs and looked at the controls of the boat, metal and mechanical like science fiction. How difficult could this be, that nobody could understand it? There was a small box that looked like a speaker, with a curled cord and a brown mouthpiece and several buttons: this was obviously the radio. It should all be like this. She pulled the mouthpiece until the cord was in reach of the knife and in two cuts it was done.

The woman screamed behind Gwen. Roger rubbed his shoulder and stared warily at the cut, limp cord. "Manny!" Errol called up on deck. "Come up and fetch that rescue boat! It's better than ours."

"We have no rescue boat," Amber said from the top of the stairs.

"We do now," Gwen said, and they both smiled.

"Get the hell out of here," Roger said, pushing himself backwards along the cabin. His naked body wiped against the floor, and pushed up a corner of a small carpet held down by a table. There were cabinets everywhere. "Get out! This is my boat!"

"No peace beyond the line," Gwen said. "No law and no property neither."

"Fuck," the man said, backing up further, "you. This is ridiculous. You're a little girl and you don't know what you're doing. Be reasonable."

Where does trouble come from? There was a huge *clump* on deck, the whole boat shaking as Manny came on board. The woman screamed, one more time, the way the appearance of a black man makes everything suddenly scary, and Errol came down the stairs as Roger reached the back wall, clawing at cabinets of wood that was either fake or made to look fake. Past him was one more staircase, where the bedroom was, and the mess, full of snacks maybe. Gwen was hungry.

Errol's breath came in heaves, from effort or perhaps mirth. "D'ye hear?" he asked the two girls. "D'ye hear? *Reasonable.* What have we to do with reason? I'll have you know, rascal, we don't sit here to hear reason. We go according to justice."

"Listen to this," Roger said, and slammed the cabinet door. Gwen had never seen a gun before except in the holsters of cops. One cop had held one up at an assembly. *If you ever see this, don't pick it up. Tell an adult.* Roger did something with the gun, something that clicked, and then he turned the gun not at her but at Errol.

"Put that down," Amber said, and Gwen was *so* proud of her. "Put that down and give everything to us."

But Roger Cuff was too happy with his line. He said it again. "Listen to this."

"Give it all to us," Amber said again, coming down the stairs to take Gwen's side.

Roger Cuff sneered at her. "Get off the boat now or I will shoot your grandpa here dead. I don't know what you think you're doing, girlie, but this is my property."

Girlie? Property? Gwen shared a look with Amber at all this nonsense. "Better to leave blood," Amber reminded her.

"Than wish it had been spilt," Gwen finished, and they stepped to him.

"We are warning you for the last time," Amber said.

"Over my dead body," the man sneered, and Gwen just stared at him, this flabby heap of a man, his eyes nasty and his legs open. "You're playing with danger," he said. "*Fire*, I mean," and now with his grabby hand, the one empty of weapons, he touched Amber right below the knee, where she had offered to ink herself in sisterhood.

"Take your hands off me," Amber said, standing steadfast.

"And now you'll get burned," said Roger Cuff, and he turned the gun to Amber. He was still on the floor, so she, Gwen Needle, was taller than he was. With sharp, blue fierceness, Gwen kept her eyes right where they were, staring and thinking one thing.

What would Octavia do?

"We will fight any man with any weapon," she said, and plunged her knife deep into his chest.

There hadn't been much choice. With the weather, there were not too many boats on the water.

The sound Roger made was raw, with his mouth open. He let go of Amber, and the gun fell straight down onto his leg. Whatever it was he had said he said again, and Gwen pulled the knife out, easily, and easily made another hole in him even as the first spouted. The third she made higher up, right next to his shoulder bone, so deep it took a few seconds to slide it out again. He kicked, but by now she was sitting on his knees. He gave up on words and just screamed, but his eyes were asking a question that surely has been asked since piracy first darkened the seas. She stabbed him again, and the question bleeded out to her.

"Why—?"

She was prepared for this. She leaned forward and said it to his gaping face, paling and sweaty. "She who wants the world . . ." she said.

He frowned and his hands both fluttered on the floor.

". . . must first escape from it."

He shook his head, which rattled against the cabinets. They would have to move him to see what was inside. "About," he said, maybe, "about time," and she gifted him three more stabs, *quick* and *quick* in both arms and then *deep* in his stomach, and he died in a bloody mess. The clot thickened. She stood up with blood on her hands and arms. Errol was looking at her, but he didn't look alarmed. Amber's eyes were wide, terrorized or delighted or, Gwen thought, both. It was the reason they were here, that teetering boundary that had sliced their lives to shreds. She had sliced back.

"Are you all right?" Amber asked her.

She actually felt as if she had something in her mouth, something about the size of something large, but soft, and watery. Amber held her shoulder, and Cody stood halfway down the stairs, looking at them both.

"I've never seen that before," Cody said quietly.

"*Sick*," Amber whispered.

Errol had leaned down to put his fingers on Roger's neck, silent for a minute before shaking his head, like doctors did in movies. They never nodded yes. They were always, whoever they were, dead after they were stabbed.

The woman clattered past Cody, all the way down the stairs, and then stopped short with a cry like she'd run into a glass wall, invisible between herself and the pirates. "*Oh my God!*" she screamed, and then turned to the controls. "*Oh my God!*" she screamed at the ruined radio. It sounded exactly the same, as if she were equally horrified at the two crimes. "You're gonna," she said, and closed her eyes. "I'm gonna," she said. "What—"

Cody turned to her. Even those few, at this point in history, who had never heard the phrase "Dead men tell no tales"—well, everyone knew what it meant. Gwen watched the woman realize it herself and try to stumble back up the stairs. But Cody was there, right where she wanted to go. Across the starboard windows of the cabin was a plastic *squeal* as the rescue boat was dragged to the pirate ship. It was time to go. They would leave her, Gwen decided, let her howls, like a ghost, warn other sailors away. Let her scream away to nothing, clutching her paramour fallen in battle. It was what pirates would do.

But Cody, brand-new to this, was an amateur. He'd never even read *The Sea-Wolf.* Without permission or preparation, he raised his cleaver and struck it down on Cath's bare thigh, right above the tattoo. It went deep and she screamed. Amber gave Gwen a look, but even the look was unnecessary. It was a mistake, Cody's bloody deed, but mistake or not, they would have to finish it off. Amber's knife moved in her hands, and so did Gwen's. They all did. *Countless dead*, said some of the former ridiculous and extravagant accounts, but it was nonsense. You could count them, of course you could count them. So far it was two. The woman was quaking frantically as if something were infested with spiders on her lap. *Get them away! Get them off me!* Her leg was already ruined with blood, covering skin and ink as she fell.

N'importe où! n'importe où! pourvu que ce soit hors de ce monde! It was from a piece of French literature, which called for adventure when Cath was younger and more reckless. But she was learning now. Now she was figuring it out. *No matter where! No matter where! As long as it's out of the world!*

Gwen stepped forward and they scattered her all over the boat.

CHAPTER 9

Levine was laughing in the lobby. Hard. She had a hand on Leonard Steed's knee to steady herself. Phil Needle exited the elevator and went to them, dragging his suitcase, which felt lighter, probably from things he had been too panicked to repack. Gone forever.

"Your messenger," Leonard Steed said in a mean playground voice, "has brought your news, as what I understand is her last duty."

"I'm sorry, Leonard," Phil Needle said. "Obviously it's an emergency."

"Obviously it is."

"I need to get out of here."

Leonard Steed held up one finger and a surprisingly long nail. "I moved mountains to make this happen, and now you slink away."

"Then she didn't tell you," Phil Needle said. The silvery painting sat disinterested on the wall.

"You can't let me down. This has been brewing for *months*."

"You *just* called me about it."

Leonard Steed sighed, and only then, Phil Needle noticed, did Levine take her hand off him. "As your producing partner, yes," he said. "But as your consultant—"

"My daughter is missing," Phil Needle said. He looked at

Leonard Steed, but Leonard Steed's eyes were too scary to look at, so he looked elsewhere. He hated that fucking painting of squares.

"Wait," Levine said. "Missing? What, is she really?"

"Nobody knows," Phil Needle said, "where she is. Could you go get the car."

"Really?"

"Yes, *really*," Phil Needle spat. "*Really!* Get the car!"

"She told me she quit," Leonard Steed said evenly. At the end of the sentence he left his lips slightly open, and Phil Needle could not help but feel a good-sized chunk of sexual shame.

"She can't quit here," Phil Needle said.

"She could work for me," Leonard Steed said and then turned to her. "I may have use for you."

"Phil's right," Levine said tiredly. "I forgot where we were."

"What's this? Are we ready?"

Phil Needle looked elsewhere, at this new voice. It was one of the men from last night. He couldn't remember his name, if he had known it, if he had a name. "Phil here was just giving us the disappointing news that he has to cancel the pitch," Leonard Steed said.

The man frowned. "Oh?"

"I'm afraid," Phil Needle said, "I have a family emergency."

"Oh," said whoever it was. "I'm sorry to hear that, Phil. I'm sure we can do this on the phone sometime soon. I think I have a Friday next week. Go take care of your family, Needle."

"Yes," Leonard Steed said. "Take care of your people. I'm saying that from here." He was pointing at his heart, so that it would be clear that what he had said was meant from the heart. The executive nodded and also touched his heart, or at least the pocket of his shirt. "Shall we count on that Friday then?"

"I don't know," Phil Needle said. "I don't know where she is."

"Give us a guesstimate," Steed said, folding his arms.

"Let me get back to you on that," Phil Needle said. He was not talking frantically, as far as he could see, or moving frantically, but everything was frantic anyway, a frantic, unconcerned lobby. "Let me get back to you."

The doors opened for Phil Needle. Outside, the morning was stale and windy. His glasses sweated on the bridge of his nose. He had never found his contact lens. Where was his daughter, that he could find her? He checked his phone. It was on. Nobody wanted him. He could not call his daughter, only her phone, abandoned useless in the condo. The company that sold him the cell phone said he could call anyone, anywhere, anytime, and he wanted Gwen, right now, wherever she was. But the phone company had lied. Liars, all of them.

Levine was next to him with a phone to her ear. "Flights will be tricky," she said. "We're actually closer to the Burbank airport, but they're smaller."

"What?"

"I'm trying to get you a flight." She was staring at him, her face shuffling like a deck of cards: helpful, worried, confused and, somewhere in there, something else.

"Winter Air?"

"Whatever we can get, I thought."

"Not Winter Air."

"Okay."

"That was a mistake."

"Okay."

"You're saying you know it's a mistake?"

"I'm saying that we all made mistakes yesterday."

Phil Needle looked at her face and hated it. "What airline were you calling?"

She didn't answer right away, or apologetically. "Winter Air."

"We'll drive," he decided instead. "It's quicker to go fast. Where's the car?"

"Phil—"

But Phil Needle found himself making a noise. He checked his phone again, but the noise was him.

"Maybe we should fly," she said. "Why aren't we flying?"

"I don't need any more of your help," he said.

She scowled at him. "I'm still quitting," she said. "I realize it's an emergency, but—"

"It *is*. This is really happening, with my daughter." He thought of something. "It was probably happening last night."

"You didn't know that," she said.

He told her then how sorry he was for last night, but not out loud. Never out loud. Just a sigh, outside a hotel. "Are you coming with me?"

"No," Levine said, but she said it the same way she had said it before: not firmly enough. Phil Needle's phone rang, and he looked at the screen. He still would not answer.

"This man," Levine was saying, and for a moment Phil Needle thought she was reporting him to the authorities. But the uniform was not that of the law. "This man needs his car."

"Do you have your ticket?" the attendant asked.

Levine did not have to look at Phil Needle for him to remember slamming down his keys in the lobby. She *was* looking at him, though. Yes, he remembered.

"Make and model?"

"Rental," Phil Needle said. "Small. Help."

The kid sighed and opened a little wooden box with hooks inside. On the hooks were keys. On the keys were tickets. On the tickets were numbers. In this day and age, such a system looked ancient and wrongheaded, leeches to cure, pigeons delivering news, celestial navigation instead of an arrow on a screen on a phone in your hand. But it worked, didn't it? The attendant pawed through keys like checking which fish smelled fresh. It didn't matter how ugly his windbreaker was. Did it? Wasn't the key there, the right one just right there?

"I'll go with you," Levine said.

"What?"

"You shouldn't do this alone," she said. "You shouldn't drive, probably, but—"

"I'm driving," Phil Needle said.

"I'll go too." She was looking at the fountain, not beautiful, and Phil Needle could not decide whether to be grateful or keep feeling this fury. The fury might propel him. If the attendant, this little boy in a wooden box, were furious, he'd have the key now. Right? Yes? While destiny cooled its heels in the lobby, while Levine turned back to fetch her things? Wouldn't it be right here, wherever it was, wouldn't it be goddamn handed to him?

×

Someone might ask what all this was for. Gwen could picture someone asking. "What is all this for?" And in reply she would spill everything out.

"Look at this," she would say, in the upstairs cabin. "Cashews, toasted almonds, smoked almonds, raw almonds. Peanuts, Spanish and unsalted. Oriental mix with rice crackers and wasabi peas. Spicy bridge mix. Two whole cabinets of this stuff, within reach of the captain's chair on the bridge. Fantastic!"

"For cocktails at sunset," they might reply. "The orange glare of the setting sun behind the Golden Gate Bridge, yes, that would be fantastic. And to stand on the deck of *Outside the Box*, or even lounge on these slick, blue couches, tucked like window seats underneath the portholes, and stare out at the flickering water, yes. All the liquor, awaiting in half-full bottles behind the rolled-up maps, closest to the captain's chair. Individual bottles of club soda, tonic water, ginger ale, all above a special ice maker making ice, letting it melt back into the machine and freezing it again, in an endless cycle of unearned luxury. A few free napkins, flowered and purple, scattered out when you got the door open, one sticking in a pool of blood and a few others tumbling down the woven blanket that you found in another cabinet and used to cover dead Roger Cuff."

"It was Amber who remembered the gun, and found it between his bloody legs," Gwen would say. "We had nothing on board the *Corsair*, only what we brought ourselves, and a lousy, malfunctioning coffeemaker with a few packs of coffee. We would have starved had not our better fortune provided otherwise for us. Manny had garbage bags with him, he'd learned from his own prior journeys, and went down as soon as Amber had the news. They had two pounds of coffee and two pounds of espresso, all crammed into the tiny freezer along with a packet of frozen shrimp dumplings and one of tiny cinnamon rolls for breakfast. In the fridge, smoked salmon. Cream for the coffee. And then two planned meals. I guess he and the girl were going to be on the boat all weekend. Two steaks bundled in butcher paper and a bag of greens for salad. In a brown sack, a small pile of scallion pancakes, probably from the farmers' market, where I've seen them sell them. A cardboard box of black bean sauce. And, wrapped in plastic, pre-broken with a little hammer like they do it, *bang bang bang* like we had done, a chilled, cracked crab. They would have it, licking the sauce off their fingers, with one of the chardonnays tucked into the bottom shelf. You have to admit, that sounds fantastic."

"It does," they would admit. "But you'll pardon me my opinion, that there must be more to a journey than the foodstuffs acquired."

"When you're at sea," Gwen would probably reply, "it's not food. It's *fuel*, for further exploits."

"So the exploit fuels the next exploit, and the next the next, and so on? Is there nothing more, nothing else?"

"Is there ever?"

"Well, I—"

Here Gwen was quoting from a tense bout in a late chapter of *Marauders*. "What have you chosen for your life, that it is more than a stepping-stone thrown into the water? And is even this meager step-step-step, this precarious way to stay above the churning chill, not done without theft and even bloodshed of those less fortunate?"

"Even if that were worthy of some consideration," they would likely sputter—

"In France there were riots over bread," Gwen would reply calmly. "Here on the counter were two baguettes and a stick of unsalted butter. All the cupboards above opened up and with sweeps of Manny's huge arm it was all bagged away. Sugar cubes and tiny squares of chocolate, jars of roasted peppers and smaller jars of olives. Sea salt, which I thought was funny. Get it? Olive oil, sesame oil, dipping oil, drizzling oil, and then Amber began to laugh. Manny didn't know what was funny, but Amber bounded back up the shiny wood ramp to show me. Then I started laughing too."

"What was it?"

"Vinegar. *Amber Dawn Vinegar.* The vinegar her dad makes. She brandished it over her head, and the two of us ran back up the stairs to get on deck. She had the idea to crack it over the helm of the boat, like champagne in old movies."

"A christening."

"Yeah, I guess, I'm Jewish. We were laughing so hard. But when we got to the deck it was slippery."

"From rain."

"No, the storm hadn't started yet. From the blood of her, the gore of how we did it."

"This is what I mean."

"I was laughing too hard to stop. Amber dropped the bottle and it bounced on the railing and fell into the sea. It didn't break, I think. *Amber Dawn Vinegar!*"

"I see."

"It was funny."

"I have to go," they would say. "Thank you. Good luck. Goodbye."

Gwen found herself laughing so hard on deck that even Amber looked a little nervous. Otherwise she was alone, although it seemed that she had been *reasoning* with someone, not simply arguing alone and shivering. Gwen shook her head but kept laughing. There was a joke so vicious and funny she could not say it: *All hands on deck.*

There was a hand on deck.

Manny came up the stairs with a white envelope sticking out of his pocket and a garbage bag, clanking and bulging, over his shoulder. He handed the bag to Amber and then picked up Gwen the same way, her view of the world hilariously upside down, her legs kicking with how funny it was all the way across the plank. From a distance she must have looked like a struggling captive. He laid her down on the deck of the *Corsair*, starboard side, no, wait, port. The wood felt solid on her trembling leg, and she breathed and watched the others. Cody, the amateur, was walking like a tightroper across the plank with a case of wine. The sunlight flickered like a bad bulb, and Gwen turned to watch some roiling clouds, out past the bridge.

"Monster storm," Manny said, standing over her. "No skin off our backs, though." He took the envelope out of his pocket and opened it for her. Inside was made of money, bills crammed into a reluctant, creased stack. "Haven't told the others," he said. "Twenty-five thousand dollars I counted, just shoved into the back of a drawer. We could buy a clear blue sky."

Gwen felt laughter in her throat like a chained dog, and only trusted herself to nod. Manny tucked it away.

"What's next?" Cody said, plunking the box down with a glass rattle. He had killed, without orders to do so, and still he did not know what to do.

"Next, I saw a fire ax down there," Manny said. "I'm going back to bash holes in the bottom when everyone's off. We need her sunk without a trace."

Gwen could not imagine how an ax could help with a fire, not at sea. She gripped the *Corsair*'s side and noticed for the first time a tiny metal loop on the side of the boat, attached to a rope that dangled down into the water. There had been no mention of such a thing in *The Sea-Wolf*. Cody moved the box across the deck, for no reason except not to meet Gwen's eyes, the disobedient wretch.

Amber's shadow fell over her. "Are you—" She couldn't finish it.

"Yeah." Gwen decided to try to shrug. "Are you?"

"Yeah. I don't know."

"Cody shouldn't have—"

"Yeah. But we did it too."

"We did," Gwen said, her eyes full of the mayhem.

"Water, I guess," Amber said, "under the bridge."

Gwen shrugged or something, and began to pull up the rope.

"And you forgot this." Amber handed down the knife, which had been wiped nearly clean.

"Thanks."

"I'll keep the gun."

"Okay."

"Okay."

"Manny said there's a storm," Gwen said. "He said he's going to chop holes in the boat so it will sink."

"That seems like a lot of work."

"Yeah."

"Verily." Amber sat down next to her. It seemed to Gwen she had something behind her back. "*And*, he's not in charge. Errol's the captain."

"Is he coming?"

"He found a closet, it'll be a minute. *And*, it was our idea."

"I know." Out of the water rose a bucket, yellow and badly cracked, at the end of the rope, dribbling seawater down into the splashes.

"So we knew," Amber tried, "that people could, that it would get violent."

"We must have known," Gwen said.

"Well, we know now. *Wench.*"

"*You're* a wench."

"It's the life we chose. Right? Isn't it?"

"It is," Gwen said. "It must be."

"They'll call it a spree, I was thinking. You know? When something like death keeps happening? A spree."

This word had not been in their books. "Sounds like perfume. A pirate spree."

"A murder spree."

"Yeah. What's behind your back?"

"You will not believe it."

"Believe it," the parrot echoed.

Errol came across the plank, dragging a garbage bag behind him and holding a bouquet of rolled-up maps. He was wearing a new hat. Gwen smiled at him, a real smile unruined by laughter. "I like this hat," he said.

"I like it too."

"I know you."

"Yes, Gwen."

"Part of the crew."

"Yes."

"You like my hat?"

"We all like it," Amber said.

"I found it."

"I found a bucket of water," Gwen said, hoisting it on deck.

"I win," Amber said, and produced a wooden box. It was about the size of a bread box, which at the time was a standard of measurement, and had a long key with a silly tassel stuck in the lock.

Errol pointed at it as if it were long lost. "What in the name of seven red devils?"

"Rummaged for it in the bedroom," Amber said.

"But what is it?" Gwen put the bucket down. "What's inside?"

Amber frowned for a second at Gwen's hands but then gave her a crooked, crooked smile. "Would you believe? Would you even believe it?"

"Open it," Gwen said.

Amber opened the box. "There's a lot of other stuff too," she said, rifling around. "It's like any box. Somebody's watch. Bikini photo. Coins from someplace. But then look at this." Her hand emerged triumphantly with a square of gray folded paper, about the size of a magazine, a little tattered and covered in blue lines.

"What?"

"Fucking treasure map," Amber said with deep joy. "Look at it. Unravel it."

It was. The world opened up for Gwen to see. The whole crew gathered over, Manny even hoisting the birdcage like a lantern. It was sketchy, as parts of the world still were. There was nowhere that was truly off the map, as the world, all of it, had been mapped, but there were still patches here and there, like a little park near the Fillmore, that were not quite fleshed out on the globe but were built and maintained in schemes and imagination. The treasure map was a map of Treasure Island, man-made across the bay, and an architect had pitched the story of this adventurous place and what it could look like. The lines on the paper dreamed of a hotel, with gambling if they could circumnavigate the law, or at least spa treatments and entertainment, reachable by boat or from the exit off the Bay Bridge, identified on the paper with two broad lines in an *X*, marking the spot.

"No way," Gwen said, with her hands on it.

"No way," squawked the parrot.

"Way," Amber said. "Look, it's a hotel."

"But there's no hotel on Treasure Island," Manny said. "I pass there every morning."

"Maybe it's not finished yet," Amber said. "Look, on the side here." Someone sometime had written OPENING NIGHT BEACH PARTY!! across the shoreline.

"It's a secret hotel, I bet." Amber said. Gwen blinked at the glimmer of it, a shiny palace obscured on an island. "It's not open yet, and when it is it's a big splash."

"But in the meantime something's hidden," Gwen said.

Amber leaned over Gwen's shoulder. Gwen wanted to keep her there forever. "Our next exploit," she said.

"Look," Manny said, "I'm very tired. We haven't slept in forever. Let me sink this boat and we'll all get some rest."

"Won't they see *our* boat?" Cody asked. Gwen couldn't help it and wanted to hit him. The bloody mess they had to sink, the misdeeds of impulse from this wrong boy, this stowaway almost, amidst their numbers. She had planned everything but him. She started to snarl something, but Manny patted her silent. "Take it slow," he said. "Slow and steady wins the race."

Gwen knew this was not so. In swimming competitions the winners were very fast. "No," she said. "We should go now. Beat the storm. The hotel would be a good place. We could even dock the boat there and wait it out."

"What about me?" Errol demanded, and Gwen put her hand on his shaky shoulder.

"You're the captain," she said.

"That's right," Errol said. "I have a problem sometimes with my memory."

"We raided a boat," she said.

Errol's eyes sparked up. "Then I want a complete account," he said. "A complete account of all the treasure. What did we steal?"

"Food, mostly," Gwen said.

"That's just what I'd steal," Errol said, with gusty relish. A drop of rain fell on his nose. "What's that river?"

Everyone said the name of the river, and Errol looked sadly at the sky. The captain was thinking. He thought awhile.

"Should we vote?" Amber said finally.

"A show of hands?" Gwen said, but at this Cody got panicky. Even Manny said "*No.*"

Amber knelt down to Gwen, her eyes shiny. "Your plan," she said. "We'll do that."

"It's all mapped out," Gwen said. "In my head anyway."

"Mine too," Amber nodded gently. "And . . ."

"And?"

"*And,*" she said, "you have blood on you."

Gwen looked down at her hands, which she had thought were sweaty. It had not been meant metaphorically. The bucket was half-full of water, and she dipped her hands in it. The blood fled into it. She did not know what the bucket was for (the cast of *Pirates!* used it to chill beer, and the map was a tipsy fantasy of Roger Cuff's college buddy, scribbled out over manhattans while the women got bored), but she would use it to wash up and get clean. In a minute she would pour it overboard into the sea and then it would be gone without a trace. The blood had escaped someone's body and now it would escape further, into unmapped territory. Her hands would be clean. Her hands *were* clean, now, at this point in history. She dumped the bucket and the blood vanished.

Hadn't it?

Wasn't it gone forever?

CHAPTER *10*

And here is another little incident. Whenever Gwen heard announcements on the radio, she always thought it was actually happening, not in her room where she was listening, of course, but someplace. She knew that Tortuga had made "You Ain't Hittin'" some months ago and that it was a recording of Tortuga, and not Tortuga himself, shouting while she showered in the condo she'd never see again. But when a politician made his dull case, a satisfied customer rehashed her shopping trip, a smooth voice offered a rare bargain, she could not help but picture the speaker in a booth with a microphone. Nobody had ever reminded her of the very simple fact of recording and duplication. Possibly this was because of old, dumb pictures of her father, on the less popular walls of the condo, smiling promotionally with his hair goofier and more numerous. So when Amber turned on the tiny transistor radio, hanging by a plastic strap from the ceiling of the bridge, and an advertisement began for Lifeline Cruises, and a Lifeline Cruise ship was spotted off the starboard side maybe a half-mile away, Gwen had the thought that the fervent tones of the woman-owned business were being broadcast from the boat itself.

History is written by the winners, and although Lifeline Cruises seemed like a bunch of losers, even at a distance, they would in fact win the day. Within weeks, Lifeline would be purchased by a much larger entity, and the people who had the idea would end up very wealthy, which was how winning was gauged during this era of American history.

The idea was women on boats. Lifeline Cruises pitched itself to women seeking adventure, whether a daylong adventure in the waters of the San Francisco Bay or a twelve-day adventure from San Francisco to Alaska and back. Passengers did not have to be survivors of breast cancer or domestic abuse, nor was any of the profit of Lifeline Cruises given to such causes, but the language of its radio ads, slippery and clear, managed to convey that this might be so. "Empowerment" was one of the words. Its daylong cruise boat was named *The Wild Lady*, from a poem by Emily Dickinson that Lifeline Cruises had made up. Tote bags sold on board broadcast the words of the ad—

> *The wild lady may seem—*
> *adrift to those who cannot dream—*
> *but within her uncharted wand'ring eyes—*
> *a heart beats healthy, strong and wise!*

—and below this were the words "Emily Dickinson."

They had also changed the name of the boat, which was bad luck, and sure enough this boat was now being preyed upon, by individuals with a different idea. The idea, Gwen's idea, was the just and righteous indignation of all her crew against the sordid and vicious disposition of the world. Cody passed around another tray of coffee and peered doubtfully out the porthole.

"Too big," he said, amateurishly.

"Nothing's too big for us," Amber said. "The sailor inhabits a world huge, boundless, and I can't remember."

"International," Gwen said.

"Don't delay," the radio pitched.

Cody put the tray down to scratch his ear, but his worried eyes stayed at the porthole. "Some weather's coming up, right?"

"There's always some weather coming up," Manny said, and reached around Gwen to turn the radio off. It swung silent. "Don't listen to that. Listen to your heart."

"My heart's had like ten cups of coffee," Cody said.

Manny laughed and put the binoculars down. "I could make us some tea," he said. "The real catmint."

"No," Gwen said firmly. "Tea and rest when we get to the island. First we take *The Wild Lady*."

"Very big," Cody said.

"Very big," said the parrot in the corner.

"We can take them," Amber said. "In *Sea Eagle* they cut off a lifeline to the Spanish whatever."

"*Sea Hawk*," Gwen said tiredly. "Armada. You really need to read more carefully, wench."

"I'm trying to learn. I know fifteen men on a dead man's chest."

"Everybody knows that," Cody said. "It's a song, yo ho ho and a bottle of rum."

Manny snapped his fingers. "Take the wheel," he said to Gwen and walked quickly across the cabin, where the crates of liquors were stacked. "Alcohol's flammable. That's how they did it in Port-au-Prince."

"Where's that?" Cody asked.

"*Haiti*," Gwen said. He didn't know anything, this idiot rascal. "How does this work, Manny?"

"Like a car."

"I'm fourteen."

Manny chuckled. "I keep forgetting that. They'll probably try you as an adult, you know. That's what they do for crimes like this."

"But she's not an *adult*," Amber said, helping Gwen with one of the levers. "She's a *wench*."

"*You're* a wench," Gwen said.

"You're lucky they won't try you as a black adult," Manny said. "Then you'd never get free."

"Oh, they'll have me swing for it," Gwen said.

"That's probably a fact," Manny agreed. "When they find them dead, it'll be a piece of news."

"But you sunk the boat," Cody said. "You sunk it, right?"

Nobody answered. Manny had chopped holes in *Outside the Box* but they couldn't stick around to watch it sink, if it were sinking, if it had sunk. With the stealthy windows belowdecks, they could not move forward and look back at their crimes simultaneously.

"They won't catch any of us," Amber said. "We're from an age where all gentlemen are known by their swords."

"And wenches," Gwen said. She took out her knife and pointed it out the porthole. "Straight for it," she said, and spun the wheel to follow her own order.

Cody frowned. "Isn't the captain the captain?"

"Stop questioning us. You're bugging me."

"I'm just *saying*."

"Take him up some coffee," Gwen ordered, "and see if you can get him to come downstairs."

Cody hurried to obey. Errol was the only one on deck in the rain, standing at his wheel and tossing orders into the air. "Please, sir," Gwen heard Cody say, and she wondered if Errol would remember him.

"Are you okay?" Amber said quietly to Gwen. She leaned in like they were alone.

"Fine," Gwen said, but then, "can I ask you—"

"Yes," Amber said.

"What were you thinking? I mean when we had to finish her, after Cody, with the cleaver. What was inside your—"

"The awful howl of vengeance," Amber said.

"Not from a book," Gwen said. "Tell me really."

Amber turned and Gwen saw her beautiful, beautiful friend. "The awful howl," she said, "of vengeance."

The wind howled, too. Errol came soaking wet down the

stairs, with Cody afterwards, looking nervous. "We lost our coffee," he said.

"The wind has risen," Errol said.

"The wind has risen," said the parrot.

The captain held out a battered document. The treasure map, ragged with rain. "I can't fold it," he said. "I was looking at it to steer our course, but I can't fold it up anymore."

"It's okay," Gwen said, and took it from him. She flattened it out as best she could while Errol stood there frowning.

"I used to be able to."

"It's okay, Errol."

Errol looked at her. "I know you."

"Yes, Gwen."

"My grommet."

"Yes."

"If I could fold the map," he said, "we could get there quicker."

"It's okay."

"I have some trouble," Errol said, "with my memory. There was an uproar on deck."

"The wind," Cody said to Gwen. "I told you about it."

Errol said nothing, just leaned against the wall, his eyes gray and wet as everything else.

"Errol," she said hesitantly, "*Captain*, look out yonder window."

Errol pressed his face to the porthole. "A bridge," he said.

"Before that a boat," Amber said. "It's called *The Wild Lady*, something from a poem."

"We're going to crimp them," Gwen said. "One more caper before we rest and regain our strength on the island."

"It's a large craft," Amber said, "but we can take them."

"I never thought I'd live to see the day. Two successful ventures in one afternoon."

"So you remember the first one?" Gwen said.

"Of course I remember," Errol said. He tapped his finger on

the porthole. "They remember too, or they wouldn't be sailing away from us. They've heard such formidable things about us, they'll fight like a demon to get away."

They were getting close. Manny came forward holding two bottles of gin. "How much time do we have?" he asked.

"A few minutes maybe," Amber said. "What are those?"

"Gin's the highest proof," he said.

"That doesn't explain it to me," Amber said. "What are we doing?"

"Something new," Manny said, although this wasn't true. In the late nineteenth century, some histories have it, a man named Cod Wilcox, improbably, also stole a boat and engaged in piracy in the San Francisco Bay. It is possible that his real name was altered by those who caught and imprisoned him, for the purpose of mockery, much like the Finns' theft of the name of the Russian foreign minister in 1939, derisive slang for primitive handmade explosives used by rascals and rogues rather than bona fide soldiers. His name, so they said, was Molotov.

"*Cool*," Cody said.

"*Cool*," said the parrot.

Amber glared out the porthole. "Their days are fucking numbered."

"All our days are numbered," said Manny. "We just don't know what the number is."

"Can I do them?" Cody asked. "I want to do them. I didn't get to do enough last time."

"You did too much," Gwen said sternly. "We all had to clean up your mess."

"Murder is catching," Manny said. "I remember that too."

They were quite close now, close enough to see Lifeline Cruises' logo on the side of the ship, a woman's profile drawn in one wavy line of aquamarine. The face loomed large. She looked calm and smug, not unlike Gwen's mother. Gwen adjusted the wheel so the tip of the *Corsair* might ram the woman in her willowy nose. She could picture the radio announcer inside, the microphone chipping her tooth as the cabin rolled. Her stomach shivered a bit, and Cody clambered up on deck with two of the Molotov cocktails in his hands, followed by Manny lugging his. The wind whipped above. The awful howl of vengeance. Gwen was ready to shout it.

"Bullhorn," she said. They'd found one, and Amber slipped it into her hands. "Take the wheel," Gwen said to her, and then she went up the stairs into the coming storm. The rain was everyplace around her, as if she were being attacked by angry, harmless fish. Manny and Cody looked uncertain, trying to clutch railings and each other and their weaponry all at once. "Not yet!" she called to them. "Not yet!" and she raised the bullhorn to her lips.

"*Ahoy!*"

There was a crackle, audible even over the wind, and then a voice called out, "You're too close! Turn around!"

It sounded just like the woman on the stupid radio. Errol came up the stairs behind her and put his hand around her waist. "Tell them what you are," he said to her.

"We demand everything of value on board!" Gwen called instead. Her voice was broadcasting crackly, too. Boarding was going to be a problem. *The Wild Lady* was much taller.

"Turn around," answered the ship. "There is already an alert for you and the stolen boat."

"Surrender now!" Gwen ordered. "You are being attacked by pi—"

A dull, heavy blow cut short these words. Amber had driven the boat straight into the Lifeline logo's face, and both boats toppled back and then forth. Pieces of something—wood—fell into the churning water. The rain slapped at Gwen's face.

"Stay back!" cried *The Wild Lady*, although it was not a voice of authority. It was prattling on, also like Gwen's mother, nothing but orders that nobody cared about. "We have notified the police!"

"Stop broadcasting! Surrender now!"

"You will be arrested within the hour!"

"You will not survive that hour!" Gwen vowed, and the *Corsair* struck them again. She held on to Errol, but the bullhorn skittered out of her hand. She slid after it, closing her fist around its handle just before it could leap overboard. Her fingers hit a new button, the red one, and a ghastly loud noise shouted at *The Wild Lady*. Cody and Manny covered their ears, and when Gwen stood up, she caught a rainy glimpse of Amber inside, grinning heartlessly and turning the wheel again.

"You're criminals! Stay back!"

"Don't disparage my crew!" Gwen returned. "I'm giving out ass whoopings and lollipops and I'm fresh out of lollipops!"

Errol gave a mighty cackle. "Where did you hear that?"

Gwen grinned, her hair slack on her head, the sleeves of her sweatshirt heavy on her arms. She felt cleaner than she had in a long time. "From some asshole," she told him, and they both laughed as she swiveled to face her armed crew. "Light them up!"

The wind rose, but they lit them up, crowding around a lighter in Manny's hand so the flame might be lit and free, tilting the fuses into the fire. This would be hard in the storm, Gwen knew, but there was always some weather coming up. The rain now was so loud that she had to use the bullhorn to talk to her crew.

"*When you're ready!*"

The pirates threw their primitive handmades at the legitimate boat. It looked like lit matches in the gray void, one landing on deck, one right on the name of the boat, one into the sea and one no place. They actually exploded, just as they were supposed to, and there was a shower of sparks on the deck and a brief black scar on the side of the boat, before the storm washed it out. Cody hooted with joy and then quickly stopped and narrowed his eyes into nonchalance, in imitation of heroes in movies too cool to look back and watch the explosions they've caused.

"How many of those do we have?" Gwen asked.

Manny shook his head.

Amber rammed the boat again, and for a second everything was full tilt. A wide, wicked crack crept down the deck almost to Gwen's feet. It was bad to see. The crack was black inside, and Gwen was so surprised at the dark in front of her eyes that she dropped the bullhorn. This time it was gone. The *Corsair* righted itself and there was a low, throaty yell, or a scream, from somebody near her. A mighty spray, from a wave or from *The Wild Lady* rocking, hit everyone on deck. Errol fell and Gwen clung to his fallen arms, trying to drag him up, while the wind rose again, higher, higher, with a crackly voice from above the fray.

"Leave now!" it said. "Save yourselves!" and then it was upon them. It was all water, from the sky and from below, and several things happened in the storm that bore heavily on the future of the *Corsair's* crew. A monster wave spouted over the crack and slapped down everyone on deck, and *The Wild Lady* leaned sharply away, vanishing quickly into the curtain of rain. The wind had no one in charge of it, roiling the sails and stretching the black flag above them until it seemed the skull would scream. Or maybe that was Gwen, leading the others down the slippery steps. Amber was crying at the wheel.

"What can we do?" she asked.

"Stop crying," Manny said.

"Stop crying," said the parrot.

"We need to get out of here," Cody said, like he was begging.

"There is no *out of here*," Amber said, wiping at her eyes. "The storm is here. We're in it."

"I can navigate us out," Errol said. "I just have to look at the sun for a second."

Manny could not help laughing. He pointed a dripping finger at the treasure map Gwen had thumbtacked to the wall, over a calendar of scheduled performances. "Head for that," he said.

"I can't *head for that*!" Amber pointed out the porthole. "We're nowhere! I don't know where we are! I was just driving toward the ship, and the ship is gone!"

"*Misericordia!*" Errol cried to the ceiling.

"Let's not go overboard," Manny said.

"No," Gwen said. "Let's not."

"Good thinking," Cody said, and rested his forehead against the wall. Gwen watched his blinking eyes. He wanted to go home, probably. *Oh, my boy, my little boy, we are so happy to see you. Come in for blankets and cookies and leave this rebellious day behind you.* No, they could not navigate away. They could not be numbered with the living nor the dead until this storm was no longer over them. But still there must be some bright something. In the navigating in the books, there was always some heavenly orb, appearing brightest and clearest and nearest for the first time in thousands of years. This would be the story of their lives, as long as they didn't die in it.

"Stop crying," the parrot said again.

"We should move," Manny agreed. "Better to go somewhere slow than nowhere fast."

Gwen looked out and saw the towers of the Bay Bridge, sharp gray shapes in and out of the gray of the turbulent afternoon. Last time she had driven across it was for Marionettes. About halfway across the bridge was one small exit nobody took. The sign for it had always promised excitement, although nobody ever went there.

Treasure Island.

"Straight for the bridge," she said to Amber. "We'll see the island when we get close enough."

"*If,*" Amber said. "*And,* how?"

"Cody will help," she said. "He'll navigate through the window."

"God help us all," Manny said.

"Him, too," Gwen said, "and you secure the supplies. Let's break as little as possible."

Manny nodded and moved back to the pile of supplies, which had already toppled in the storm. "And you?"

"I'm going above deck," Gwen said.

"What? Why?" Amber took a hand off the wheel to hold Gwen's shoulder, but then the sea veered out the window and she had to yank it back to the wheel.

"I belong there," Gwen said.

"The *captain* belongs there," Errol corrected. "I will bring us to this hovel."

"Yes," Gwen said. "Come with me. Sing and keep my bravery unquenchable."

Errol gave her a slow, slow smile. "I know you."

"Yes."

"Gwen."

"Yes."

"It's a pleasure, Gwen."

In the cabin the weather broke. Everyone stepped closer to everyone else. A creak came from the ceiling, but for a moment the ship was settled. Such was the calm that came in the storm, and then Gwen and Errol trooped back up to the deck. The rain was so thick it was everything, and the sky was still colicky and gritting its teeth, but the *Corsair* moved quickly, proudly, toward the bridge. There was no sun, and no other boats as far as the eye could see. But the *Corsair* still ran. It would run on, Gwen vowed, as Errol began to sing. It would run on until they ran aground.

> *Fifteen men on a dead man's chest*
> *Yo-ho-ho and a bottle of rum*
> *Drink and the devil had done for something*
> *Fifteen men on a dead man's chest*
> *Fifteen men on a dead man's chest*
> *Yo-ho-ho and a bottle of rum*

Something something on a dead man's chest
Yo-ho something something

and this is why history is written by the winners. Those stuck in the storm are too shaken to remember every detail, but *The Wild Lady* turned around well before Alcatraz, an island prison not in use at the time of this narrative, and was back at the pier before the storm trapped passengers on the Bay Bridge, looking idly through rain-spattered windows while the drivers screeched and cursed. Every Lifeline passenger dined out on the story for years to come, recounting it as a narrow escape and a lark both. As with the pirate flag, it was almost a joke.

Gwen, though, never got to tell, at least not all of it, at least not to everyone. She did not recount the sound of the boat scraping against the shallowing water and the cement shore of their destination, Errol's faltering arm around her, or the useless wooden wheel in her hands, spinning like a prop whenever she let it go. The rain on her face, or if she was crying. With the accounts of the winners so proud and prevalent, bright and showy as fireworks in the sky, the pirate history is a secret one, its treasures buried and only the wreckage left to any wandering guest looking to piece things together. Broken glass in the sea. Bobbing wood in pieces, jostling one another like traffic. All these items, all stolen and all from someplace, appearing in no account but this one, misplaced and forgotten as the items in a shark's stomach, split open when it's caught and dragged somewhere safe.

"Treasure Island," repeated the parrot as the cage broke wide open.

×

You should not put a bumper sticker on your car, thought Phil Needle in the storm. This had not been the wise way to go. The traffic penned in Phil Needle around the middle of the bridge, where there was just one exit, which nobody took. In the rain the eye might be drawn to its green sign, its white arrow, its promise of escape. Phil Needle wasn't looking at it. He was looking straight ahead at the bumper of the car in front of him. What if you had to drive in a funeral procession, for instance, with your snappy phrase forced at the eyes of mourners?

His phone rang in the place for beverages. Levine didn't look up. Belly Jefferson had been another passenger all the bad day.

"Marina?"

"Where are you?"

"Almost home, Marina. No word, I take it."

"Why didn't you fly?" she asked, as she had asked all day.

"The airports are probably delayed anyway," Phil Needle told her once more. "The storm."

"Our little girl is *out* in the storm, Phil."

"Okay," Phil Needle said. "I'm almost there." It was true. Ahead and below, he could see a cruise ship, almost at the pier. Who would be out in weather like this? He could not see it, but not far was his condo, where Marina was on the phone; he could see the clock tower, which was close. It was late in the day, the metal hands told him. Nobody expects outdoor clocks to work.

"The police have been here already. They looked in her room. They want to know what she was wearing, and her activities. They have an alert at the North Point Station, and we're supposed to go there when you get here."

She had told him this already, and again when he'd been speeding through the desert out the windows. "Okay."

Her sigh clattered out of the phone. "Phil, have you thought of anything?"

A truck slid by the window: Impressive Plumbing. He looked ahead. "No," he said.

Pause.

"I've tried," he said. "Marina, she's probably fine. She wants us to be angry. She wants us to be upset."

Hic-hic.

"Marina."

She said it again. "Why didn't you fly?"

Perhaps it had always been this way, a mistake of some kind. Certainly mistakes had been made. At their wedding, Marina's father had announced, "You two have done nothing," and then taken a long sip of champagne before finishing, "but make us proud." There was a sex act, a particular sex act Marina would not do. It seemed shallow to brood about it, but let's face it, Phil Needle thought as he switched the phone to his other ear, the list of sex acts you are going to do if you don't want to be in pain or wearing a costume, despite the boundless horizon promised in dirty books, is quite short. So it was a sizable fraction that she would not do, and she had been painting now for nearly two years and not shown him anything! He had averted his eyes from her bloody tampons in the bathroom garbage, without ever a comment, and still she had never opened her studio door to him to show him what she was making.

"Oh my God, did you hear that?"

"What?"

"Someone's calling on the other line. Hold on, hold on, oh my God! Hello?"

"It's still me."

"Hello?"

"Still me."

"Mother*fucker!*" she screamed. "Hello?"

It was still Phil Needle. They hadn't moved.

"Hello! Hello!"

Phil Needle had no choice but to surrender and hang up, hoping that would help. "Disconnected," he excused himself, to Levine.

"Disconnected," she repeated. She'd been zonked the whole

ride, just the occasional echo like a wet, weary parrot. "I want that," she said now. "I don't want to be connected, you know? I don't want to be part of a team. I don't want to be in your crew. I don't want a network. I don't want to pitch a story and have somebody buy it in a hotel room." She blinked at him, Alma Levine, almost in time with the wipers. "I'm sorry," she said, "and I know it's an emergency for you right now, but it's an emergency for me, too. I look at you and I don't want to be it. Everything in me says, you know, I'm out of here." She blinked and blinked and blinked. "I just sit wondering," she said, "where there is someplace I can go that isn't this."

Phil Needle hated, just *hated*, how familiar it was, the blinking and the desperation both. It was him in New York again, sad and hopeless with drugs and the small, stuffy microphone booth. "Is it that you're drunk?" he said. "A good deal of the time?"

Levine sighed and reached into a pocket in her dress. Out came a tiny and empty bottle of vodka.

"Did you take that from the plane?"

"The hotel," she said. She tipped the bottle over, but it stayed right in her hands and didn't go anywhere. Maybe he could be a resource for her, he thought, instead of whatever it was he was.

"Look, let me tell you a story."

"You're pitching me something?" Levine asked, with a small smile.

"Right," Phil Needle said. "Take our minds off."

Levine closed her eyes. It was a story he told a lot, and it had all the outlaw elements that made a story great, or so said Leonard Steed, who had told it to him. The elements included Leonard Steed, a train, a blues artist, and a cotton gin that journeyed at the end to the big city. The story was authentic, and not just because it was true. It was a story that began with a chance sighting of an item that forged a link with the American past and carried it forward into an outlaw future. But in this stormy weather, the story didn't stay on course, or the course turned out to be drawn wrong and unworkable.

Levine kept frowning and asking questions, and soon the story didn't seem like anything at all.

"So it wasn't the cotton gin in 'Cotton Gin Blues'?"

"Well, nobody knows. It could have been."

"But there's no reason to think so."

"Leonard Steed thought so."

"But why did he think so?"

"Look, he always loved Belly Jefferson, and he turned his love of that kind of music into the kind of radio professional that he is. And not just radio. The label, the franchise—"

"But he just *took* a cotton gin from a field and put it in a building in Los Angeles."

"You don't have to say *took* like that."

She took another empty bottle from her pocket and leaned it against the first one so they were praying together in her lap. "It doesn't make any sense."

"He had a plan and moved forward. The story is that you move forward with a plan and—"

"But the plan is bullshit."

"It's not *bullshit*!" Phil Needle cried, and the steering wheel rattled. "It's a different plan! It's off the map! Outside the box!"

"It must be," Levine said, "because I don't understand it at all."

Phil Needle took his eyes off the road. She blinked back. Maybe that was the story: that all errands, every noble voyage, are ridiculous and impossible. He vowed he would never talk about the cotton gin again. "Levine, you have a problem."

She looked at him, with a cold, cold heart. "Look at you," she said, and look at Phil Needle, look at himself! He was so meager, he thought. He tried, he really tried, to count his blessings, but he always lost track after things like health. It was easier to catalog his wrongs and broken promises, promises Phil Needle had often made only to shut people up. Occasionally Phil Needle thought God was watching him, but it was always when he was alone and nearly always when he was high. This time he knew. God had put Gwen someplace in order to slap him, Phil Needle, around. Phil Needle wasn't a good person, in a what-a-good-person-you-are sort of way, but he was good, somehow, surely. He was merciful. He stepped on wounded bees. He did good, and when he did bad it wasn't his fault. It was a mistake. He was *so sorry*, behind the bumper sticker, for whatever and everything it was he had done.

HATE TRAFFIC? was what the bumper sticker said. It was illustrated with pictures of bicycles. YOU ARE TRAFFIC. And the exit was Treasure Island, where no one would go. The cars were so slow that Phil Needle could get out and walk, the road rivering and pedestrianless, and hunch over to peer into every window and check. Every driver dim through the wet glass, in the same traffic, connected on the bridge like listeners to a show, and *not one of them would be Gwen.*

Someone blew a horn, and then everyone did, hideous racket, like a crowd's loud ovation. Levine stared drowsily away from the window. "Oh," she sighed, "I hate this."

You *are* this, Phil Needle wanted to say, but instead went with "*Just wait a fucking goddamn minute!*" He screamed the last of this behind him, in reply to the mad horns. "*I'm fucking trying you fucking assholes! Go around me if you can find a fucking way you fucks! Think for a fucking minute about why I'm fucking stopped in the middle of this asshole bridge! Do you fucking idiots think I'm goddamn here for a fucking picnic on Treasure Island?*"

"I quit," Levine said.

Phil Needle's fists hurt from pounding on the dashboard. "What?"

"It was wrong what you did. You took advantage."

"You're fucking lying."

"I've been thinking about it *this whole time* and it's true."

"You fucked your other boss, Levine. You don't know when to stop, do you? You should absolutely be at my fucking service."

Alma Levine was crying. Phil Needle had never thought such a thing was possible to see. In some versions of this history he was crying himself. He could not look at her, and so out the window was where he looked instead. "I didn't mean that," he said. "I don't know what I mean."

Belly Jefferson interrupted in the raining car.

"I'm out of here," she said. She opened the door and walked right out into the noise and rain, squeezing by the car and going back the way they had come. Phil Needle would think of her all the time, what had happened to her, and open the last drawer in his desk at home, where, beneath folders of nothing and old letters he didn't want Marina to see, he kept her bag and her clothes and things in it, which she had left behind. She had vanished and he could not find her. (The answer was, Alma Levine would join up almost immediately with a man she met on the road and take his name and for a few years find joy and purpose in continuing to appall her parents by unsuitably marrying and quickly birthing two fat sons who looked all, not just half, Haitian.)

But now he looked at these things for only a second, and then at his phone. The storm stayed furious. The traffic wanted to kill him. *I wish everything was over,* he thought, and pressed the button.

"Yes?"

Hic-hic-hic.

His father must have known about Gwen. That was why he'd been calling all morning. "Dad?"

Hic-hic-hic, "David?"

The connection was bad. "Not David," Phil Needle said. "This is your *other* son, Dad. I'll call you later. Gwen's going to be fine. I'm getting in the car right now, I can't talk."

Hic-hic-hic, "Gwen?"

So it wasn't that. "You know I can't take it when you're like this, Dad."

Hic-hic-hic. Phil Needle hung up. His father, he remembered, was a racist. And David, his brother, was dead. For years it was a problem he had, wondering where it was his brother was, what space there was for him in the world. And then he had it, sad but certain: he was dead. He could not come to the phone. Phil Needle kept scanning the road. A blur went by in the window, bright like a tropical bird. There was a space for everything, is what the story was, alive or dead, cotton gin or bumper sticker, wherever she was. Wasn't that true? Surely nothing was gone forever. Surely everything—and at this moment, in this version, he *was* crying—could eventually be found.

CHAPTER *11*

Every wall in the police station had posters taped everywhere on it, and in the center was a guy at a desk behind thick, smudgy glass and crisscrossings of metal, with small holes poked into it like an old telephone receiver. It looked like buying tickets to a dangerous movie. The man in front of Phil Needle was giving a long, vague description of a pickpocket while holding his wide-eyed baby away from him, as if he were about to drop it into a vat. The baby kicked and lost a sock. Marina picked it up and starting crying again. Her grip tightened on Phil Needle. He gave the sock to the father. The baby, swear to God, rolled his eyes.

"Can someone help us?" Phil Needle asked. The pickpocket victim headed for the door.

"Yes," the guy said, and nothing else.

"My daughter's name is Gwen Needle," Phil Needle said.

"Oh, yes. You've heard nothing?"

"They told us to come here," Marina said, on tiptoe to talk through the holes.

"That's not necessary," the guy said. He was in his mid-fifties and his eyes couldn't help slipping to a bag of leftover Mongolian beef that his buddy had brought him. The smell was cheery and spicy, and he gestured for Marina to stand down. "I mean, you've heard nothing from your daughter."

"Yes, no, we haven't."

"Okay, the investigating officers are here. Please have a seat just for a minute."

There was a crash, a loud crash, off to the left someplace. People look around when something falls, even when it's nothing they should worry about. "Sorry about this," the desk guy said. Desk *sergeant*, Phil Needle remembered, the sergeant in charge of the desk. "We're a bit off protocol tonight. The media is pouncing on us with a story about this showboat that somebody stole, and three missing children. I'm very sorry. It'll just be a minute."

"Okay," Phil Needle said.

"I have kids myself," the guy said, and looked someplace—at a bag, Phil Needle saw.

"Okay," Phil Needle said again. He had a bag himself, in his hands, a bag from the drugstore that he'd gotten from a bag of bags under the kitchen sink. He could feel the corners of the framed photograph of Gwen he'd grabbed on their frantic way out of the condo. The guy walked out of view. Phil Needle and Marina were now in a room alone, sitting down. Two cops walked in and past Phil Needle to buzz themselves through a door. He glared straight ahead at a poster on the wall, one he had seen thousands of times. It had been taped up back at the radio station in New York, and in offices all over. You could see this everywhere, and Gwen was knocking around unmoored, running loose and unfound. It was worse than the bumper sticker. A row of four identically drawn men were in different poses of hysterical laughter. One of them was laughing so hard he was on the ground.

Marina leaned her head on him and sniffled. It was common in this day and age, when waiting someplace, to look around at your involuntary companions and imagine that you were trapped with them someplace more dire: a hostage situation or a building on fire, something requiring teamwork and survival. Could you build the camaraderie promised in movies about such times, or would you fall apart? Phil Needle looked around and realized, quietly but sharply, that he and his wife would not survive this. Gwen's disappearance would slaughter them.

YOU WANT IT WHEN? was the caption on the poster. It was talking about office work, and the sad fact, true at the time, that people want things right away and that other people don't care about that. The poster reminded people that it didn't matter what you wanted. Where was she? Where did somebody put her? Where were those ragged thumbs of hers, and her odd, tiny earlobes? Was he about to be one of those guys, clutching a photograph of Gwen, on the news every year in support of an extreme new crime law? Were they becoming one of those families used as a murmured example of the wickedness of the world, as a worst-case scenario to comfort those whose daughter was merely pregnant or paralyzed? Would there be a funeral, everyone sweating in black clothes in the summer and squinting in sunglasses? Oh God, would there be a hasty peer-group shrine, wherever she was found, with cheap flowers and crappy poetry melting in the rain? Would her college fund sit forgotten for a while in the bank, like a tumor thought benign, and then be emptied impulsively on some toy to cheer himself up? He had seen in a magazine a handsome automobile some months ago, shiny as clean water. Somebody opened the doors. A man came in a black suit missing a tie, his beard stopping just where the shirt opened to show Phil Needle a gold chain.

"You're the man who lost his son," the man said, very, very kindly.

Phil Needle stood up. "Daughter."

The man frowned. "I heard son."

"Rabbi," said someone new. It was the desk sergeant, now in the room and scratching his head and looking at Phil Needle apologetically. "Not him, Rabbi," he said. "Through here, down the hall."

"I heard right inside," said the rabbi, but he was buzzed in and disappeared through the open door.

"I'm dying," Marina said quietly. "Are you dying, Phil?"

"There's a room for you folks too," the guy said as two new policemen came out to look at them. "Sorry for the wait, but this stolen-boat thing is turning into a circus."

"And three children," Phil Needle said, "you said, missing?"

The two men both shook their heads at the desk sergeant. "I'm not sure," he said, and then coughed a little. "This is investigating officers Jarris and Snelgrave, the primaries on your case."

"Yes," Marina said like a ghost. She had been staring at them. "We've met."

"You know them?"

"Yes, Phil. They're the ones who came to the house."

But they're black! he did not say. He merely stood up and nodded at them and shook their hands and followed them through the door and down a hallway made too narrow by old beige filing cabinets. He felt happier they were black, really. They would work hard and ruthlessly, twice as hard, due to injustice, to find poor Gwen. Wouldn't they?

"We're going to put you in this room for a minute," said Jarris. "We'll be right back with the file."

The room was mostly a table, wooden and pocked, with metal chairs arranged inscrutably as if for a play. Marina sat in one. Phil Needle stood near the mirror, which of course was one-sided, as all mirrors were in police stations, at least on television, at this time in American history. On the other side were stern cops regarding him, surely. Surely Phil Needle was a goldfish in a bag.

"Are you dying?" Marina said again.

"She's fine, Marina," Phil Needle pitched. "She's been rebelling lately, we know that. She quit swimming."

"Stop saying she's fine. It's been more than twenty-four hours."

Twenty-four hours sounded so much longer than a day. Gwen's

photograph sat in its crinkly bag. "Remember that show I did about the Amish?"

"It wasn't your show."

"Well, the episode I produced."

"You didn't produce it. They just had you mix some of the sound last-minute."

"Well, I got a producing credit."

"Because you read the credits yourself."

"Marina—"

"You *did*, into the microphone."

"Marina—"

"How could you even think of such a thing right now?"

The officers came into the room. Phil Needle had not gotten to say what he wanted, but he wasn't going to talk about the Amish in front of black people. "Hello," he said, "investigating officers Jarris and Wellgrin."

"Snelgrave," said one of them.

"Snelgrave."

"*I'm* Snelgrave," said the other one. "We're very sorry for your distress, and we're also very sorry there's been some confusion tonight. Somebody stole one of those boats by the pier, do you know what I mean?"

"What?"

"They use it for a show. *Pirates!*"

The officers sat down. Jarris was folding a folder, and Snelgrave had a lidded cardboard box, as if he had just been told to clear out his desk. Phil Needle was the only one standing. "Pirates?" he asked.

"Please, sit down, Mr. Needle."

Phil Needle sat down but kept thinking about it. He couldn't help it. Just the word was jolty.

"We're just telling you about the boat because the media will make it sound like that's all the police are working on. But that's not true."

"There are," Marina said, "three children missing, you said?"

"Let's concentrate on your child right now," Jarris said, and opened the folder, which had maybe two pieces of paper in it. It was slender, as slender as Gwen. Perhaps they kept it slender to remind them.

"First, I need to confirm her Social."

Marina sighed and then numbly spat out nine numbers, a marking system devised by the government at the time, each digit increasingly wavery.

"And she's how old?"

"Fourteen, we told you." Marina reached across the table and grabbed Phil Needle's arm just above the elbow.

"And you're not sure what she was wearing when you saw her last?"

"No, I don't know," Marina said. "She just ran out to pay the taxi. It was so quick. It was the morning."

"We think we found the driver. If it's him and if it's your daughter, he took your daughter to Octavia Street, but she jumped out and ran into an alley."

The word *Octavia* made Phil Needle think of a pretty girl, but he could not think of where he had met such a person. Marina was frowning.

"That doesn't make sense."

Jarris looked at his paper. "What part of it doesn't make sense?"

"Any of it."

"She paid the driver, he says."

"The driver must be lying," Marina said.

"He kept the money."

"I don't mean about that."

"He identified her from the photo, although you said it wasn't a good photo."

"She's hated to be photographed lately."

"I have a daughter, Mrs. Needle. I know how it is."

"I brought the best one we have," Phil Needle said, and put the bag down on the table.

"Thank you for that," said Snelgrave, and slid it closer to him. "We're just asking about what she was wearing because we want to know if it could have included gray sweatpants."

"Gray sweatpants," Marina repeated.

Investigating officer Snelgrave blinked and frowned, and Jarris made a note. "Yes," he said. "Is it possible she was wearing gray sweatpants?"

Phil Needle moved paper dolls in his mind. It was possible for anybody to be wearing gray sweatpants.

"From where?" Marina said.

"What do you mean?"

"What brand?"

"Well, let's look." Snelgrave tossed off the cover of the cardboard box and overturned it dramatically. Some clothes piled out. A red top. Gray sweatpants. A kind of brown shoe and then another one. Last of all was a pair of panties, small, with strawberries. It was filthy just to look at them, shameful and wrong. The two officers were watching his face.

"Are these hers?"

"You found them?" Marina asked. "How did you find them?"

"Do they belong to Gwen?"

Marina blinked and reached out for them. She picked up the red top and then, with a quick inhale of breath, held it to her mouth before putting it down. "No," she said. "And these shoes—Tox. I refused to buy her Tox."

"Why?" Phil Needle asked, but Marina did not answer. She was crying too hard. Her shoulders were shaking like stormy weather, and her *hic-hic-hic* had turned to something wider, from deeper in her chest. To Phil Needle it felt like not enough to pat his wife from his end of the table and so stood up to stand behind her and put his hands on her shoulders, like he was massaging a prizefighter.

"It'll be okay," he said.

"Where do you think we found these?" Officer Jarris said.

"Those *aren't her clothes*," Marina wailed.

"Where did you find them?" asked Phil Needle.

"Tox are *expensive*," Marina said. "And they're bad for your feet. *Brutal* on them. I saw an article."

"These articles were found neatly folded behind a garbage can on the Embarcadero," Snelgrave said. "Two blocks from your house."

"And right by the water," Officer Jarris said.

"But what does it have to do with anything?"

"Exactly," Jarris said. "Thank you. Exactly my question."

Snelgrave ran a hand through his hair, but it was so curly and cut so short that it was more like he was patting himself on the head. "As far as I can tell, there are only two reasons a teenage girl takes her clothes off. One of them is to go swimming."

Marina touched the top. "What?"

"She *is* a strong swimmer," Phil Needle said.

"We talked to the coach of the team," Officer Jarris said.

"They're not hers," Marina said, pointing at the strawberries.

"Why did they make you cry?"

"Because Gwen is missing," Phil Needle said. He had to let go of his wife's shoulders because his hands wanted to strangle someone.

Snelgrave started to put the clothes back into the box. "There's not much more we can do." He held up one of the brutal shoes. "Finding a missing teenager can be like finding a needle on a sheet."

The image of this, a needle on a sheet, was something Phil Needle thought about for just a second. The sheet was undraped, and the naked figure of Alma Levine stretched toward him.

"And it's especially hard if people aren't cooperating."

Marina rubbed her eyes violently. "Who isn't?"

"Everyone we talk to?" Jarris said. "They say she had a new friend."

New friend? "We weren't sure about that," Phil Needle said, because he had to say something.

"Her friend Naomi Wise said it was a boy. You told us she didn't have a boyfriend."

"She *doesn't*."

"Would you know if she did?"

Marina looked up at him. Phil Needle could see right into his wife's nose. "I don't know," he said, to the little wet hairs, and then looked at the detectives. "She's fourteen."

Snelgrave kept staring at him and put the lid on the box. Phil Needle thought of those clothes, folded on the street, and wondered where she had gone, whoever was wearing them. Had she walked naked through the farmers' market to the touristy piers? Or the other way, it could have been, past his neighborhood, to the confusing and iffy intersections stretching toward the train station. "Did you check the train station?" he asked.

"Do you think she's there? Is that where you think?"

"I don't know."

"And you don't know what she was wearing."

"And," Jarris said, "you don't know who her friends are."

They stared at him, very hard, and Phil Needle blinked back, whereupon the detectives dragged him into another room in Phil Needle's mind and beat him until he was willing to do anything to escape further punishment. In this room they just finally sighed.

"Is her best friend Cody Glasserman?"

"No," Marina said. "*Phil's* the one who likes him."

"Stop saying that," Phil Needle said.

"Is he her lover?"

"Cody Glasserman? Have you seen him?"

"That's what we want to talk to you about," Officer Jarris said, and leaned from his seat to open the door. It creaked, and a bunch of Jews walked into the room. One was a tall, graying man who looked not unlike Phil Needle, and then a muscular, long-haired boy with a large nose and curious eyes, and then a weeping woman with a mass of necklaces around her.

"Phil," the graying man said, and held out his hand. "It's Steve Glasserman. We met at the Swinner."

It took Phil Needle the entire handshake to remember that a Swinner was what All-City called their annual swim dinner at a garish Italian restaurant full of ricotta cheese, out by the water. "Steve Glasserman," he repeated.

"Cody Glasserman has been missing for twenty-four hours," Officer Jarris said. "It was the swim coach who made the connection."

Marina stood up and hugged the woman. They cried together in the crowded room. "This is my wife, Deedee," Steve Glasserman said, "and Cody's brother, Nathan."

"Nathan says his brother got a note," Snelgrave said.

"I'm not sure," said the boy who must have been Nathan, fiddling with his hair. "He said he didn't."

"It must be a swim meet," Phil Needle said.

"What?"

"I mean, is the whole team gone? I don't know what I'm saying."

He sat back down. Everyone was looking. He was a one-cent stamp, struggling and struggling to be of use, and then another man came in who Phil Needle also knew would be useless, even though he was certain he had never seen him before.

"Dr. Donner," Marina said, and Phil Needle watched her gasp.

"Who?"

"Gwen's dentist. If you ever took her, if you showed an interest—"

"Took her?" Jarris asked.

"To the dentist," Marina said.

"What is happening?"

"Dr. Donner's daughter is also missing," Snelgrave said. "About the same time as Gwen, but they didn't call it in until now."

"My wife has been having problems with her. I thought she'd just stormed off. I was on a plane. It's stupid now, I know."

"Oh, Dr. Donner," Marina said.

"David."

"David."

"The Donners live," Jarris said, "on Octavia Street."

"Oh my God!" Marina wailed.

Now Phil Needle remembered that *Octavia* was the girl the man had said, on Memorial Day, when Gwen was stealing and Phil Needle had gotten the call. Octavia, she had called herself. He snapped his fingers.

"The drugstore," he said to his wife.

"What?" Marina said. "What are you talking about, the drugstore?"

"Dr. Donner here doesn't think your daughter was friends with Amber," Jarris said, "but we wanted to check with you. Three teens missing."

"Wait," Nathan said woozily. Everyone waited while he wiped his forehead with his hand. "Amber Donner? With the hair like, sort of, I don't know? She goes to Hill Academy? Yeah, they're friends."

"You're sure?"

"Yeah, I see them all the time. Hanging at that bakery, and all the time in my neighborhood for something."

"My daughter?" Marina said.

"And mine?" asked Donner.

Nathan nodded and grinned as if to agree: *Who would think I'd be useful?* Phil Needle nodded, too, to do something.

"We can move on this," Snelgrave said. "Come with us, everybody."

Phil Needle started to walk. His wife was patting Deedee's face, although he was pretty sure they didn't know each other. The appearance of the Glassermans, he realized tardily, was something of a triumph: Cody Glasserman *was* involved somehow. Also, this meant Gwen was probably okay. She was somewhere with Cody Glasserman, who looked harmless as hell. She had taken her clothes off—no, they weren't her clothes—and was in his skimpy arms, rolling around in a dental chair.

The hallway appeared to have changed while they were in the room, or maybe they were going a different way, because it opened up into a wide area with very low ceilings. Phil Needle ducked instinctively. People were talking on telephones, and a television was propped up in a corner with the sound loud but muffled. A reporter was talking into a microphone, and then the picture cut to an old woodcut image of a pirate ship. It was hard not to watch any television that was turned on, as it always was during this era.

"Are they going to talk about Gwen on the news?" Marina asked.

"When it comes on, yes," Officer Jarris said. "This is just a special bulletin they're doing about the boat. Everyone's into the boat."

"The news will do a report about your children," Snelgrave said, his nod swiveling to encompass them all. "It'll be the top story. We finally got them to knock down the boat. It will include their pictures and a number to call. We'll be charting any sightings on this map."

"Let's take a look at the map," Jarvis said, co-hosting. There was, as promised, a map, the whole of San Francisco plain on paper on the wall. He stepped closer and saw that the city was spotted with tiny holes, as if a hive of bees had long ago stung every block. A lone, long pin, its tip red like a bead of blood, leaned somewhere near the Bay Bridge.

"Every time we get a tip, we put a pin in this map. If you're really sure those were not Gwen's clothes, we'll take that pin out."

(The clothes found at the Embarcadero belonged to a girl of fifteen, whose parents had a strict dress code. Shivering behind the garbage can with her best friend keeping giggly watch, she had put on a short, sheer dress and some glittering sandals, removing her underwear so it would leave no wake on the dress when the boys looked at it. She ditched her old clothes, and they ran off unsupervised into Saturday night to hit a club called Dark Skyes, and it is like this everywhere in the world. For years she would think, shivery and curious, about who in the world could have stolen her stash, and how much trouble it put her in when the night was over.)

"They're not her clothes."

The officer removed the pin. Phil Needle swept the map with his eyes, from his condo down Market Street, sidetracked to the park, out, out, out to the Sunset and his old home. That place had been affordable. He had afforded it. Where could she be, how many places could there be, in this city so expensive, to hide a person? San Francisco had gentrified its empty warehouses and abandoned shacks, all the child-killer haunts with their shadows and meat hooks. There is no escape in San Francisco. Everyone is everywhere. And *Cody Glasserman*, of all people? "What if she's not on the map?"

"Then we get a bigger map, Mr. Needle. And a bigger one, and a bigger one. There's always the globe, if it comes to that. She's still on earth, after all."

"It's a global world," Jarris said thoughtfully.

"And her body?" Phil Needle asked.

"What?"

"If she's not okay—"

"I'm sure she is. We have reason to think they are together. Everyone's phones are off, which would indicate cahoots."

"Cahoots?"

"Runaways are different from abductions, Mr. Needle. They end better."

"*Usually*," said Steve Glasserman.

"Usually, yes."

"But if she's not," Phil Needle said, "how do you find her body?"

"Don't think like that."

"But how?"

Snelgrave sighed. "Her body would also be on a map."

"But the map is all?" Phil Needle said. "It's the whole thing? That's the scheme? Surely you have special satellites you could use to look?"

The Glassermans looked hopefully at him. They hadn't thought of satellites.

"I'm not sure I follow, Mr. Needle."

Phil Needle tried to picture the satellites, although he did not know a thing about them, not really. They brought him phone calls and television and roamed around in circles, out of view even in the night sky. Now Marina touched his shoulder.

"What if you run out of pins?" he said helplessly. "Where is she?"

"Please, Mr. Needle. Can I get you some coffee?"

"*Where is she?*"

"Mr. Needle, I need you to calm down."

"There's only one thing that'll calm me down."

"Help yourself."

"No, it's not coffee," Phil Needle said. "It's my daughter, my daughter on the map."

"Mr. Needle," Snelgrave said, very, very sternly. "I believe your daughter is on this map. Your son, too, Mr. Glasserman, and, Dr. Donner, Amber. Mrs. Glasserman. Mrs. Needle. Nathan." He would not stop saying names.

"Then put a pin in it," Phil Needle said. Everyone in the room was suddenly taller than he was, although he found the courage to admit that this might be so because he was, now, on his knees.

It was Jarvis who helped him up. "You've done all you can here. I'm going to give you my cell number so you can always find me. They're going to air the report and we're going to get calls, and the next few hours will bring us better news."

"The photograph," Marina remembered.

"We'll send it to the network."

"But I left it in the room," said very sad Phil Needle.

"No, Mr. Needle," the black man said. "I have it." He held up the bag and drew out the square frame, and then everyone frowned. It was in a way understandable, although perhaps only if you had visited the condo, as it was the first thing you'd notice, the largest face on top of the piano. It was not a photograph of Phil Needle's daughter. It was a photograph of Phil Needle. The photograph of Gwen, right next to it at home, had not been grabbed in his haste. His own face stared at him instead, smiling confidently, and behind him, outside the frame, a bunch of Glassermans, their similar features almost like the same face—thick nose, curly hair, tired and cautious eyes—pasted in different poses near the map. *You want it when?* Phil Needle wanted all this not to be happening.

×

Where else can an innocent voyage lead? To an uncharted isle and back again. Treasure Island wasn't unknown, but it was often ignored, and late that bad afternoon the pirates, soaked and filthy, were taking turns dozing and spacing out in a grim, flat lot. The storm would soon wreck other people elsewhere, but here the rain was still sheeting straight down, bothering them as if on purpose. They were sheltering in the curve of some muddy greenery, big, flat leaves exhausted from their lives. They weren't keeping dry, and they were too wet to care.

"Are you awake?" Amber said to Gwen.

"Are *we*?" Gwen said. "My head's still all buzzy."

"Like dreaming," Amber agreed. There was a quick snore from Cody. Gwen had never had a dream like this. She could not say where they were, really. It was a bad place. It turned out Treasure Island was really two lands, one high above them, lush and shaded with secrets, and then this place where they'd landed, which either wasn't something yet or had stopped being whatever it was some time ago. Here was flat, very flat, with a chain-link fence all bent out of shape about something. There were several signs posted, but their panels were worn away and missing, and in the middle of the place was a flagpole flying nothing, the wind slapping the ropes and pulleys around in skeleton dance steps. Over the rain was the sound of the sea, or more likely cars going by on the bridge, away and above in a wide stripe cutting across the sky. Yes, Gwen thought, it sounded like bad automobiles going slow. Some huge building loomed closed and rummy, with UNITED STATES NAVY faded on a few walls. And yet, just a short hike away, straight up through underbrush and a steep, spiraling road, was the Treasure Island they had dreamed of, a mass of greenery where anything might be happening. This was what Gwen wanted to look at. She could even see a place where they might keep watch, a bump on the hill shaped like something staring at her. It wasn't a crow's nest, exactly, although crows might live there. It was a spot where they could see where to go.

Their boat wasn't going anywhere, though. The *Corsair* was too run aground to go to sea again, just another piece of nothing amidst all the junk on shore. Its front was a smashed, broken nose. The parrot had fled the coop, the broken cage ribs in the water. They had managed to rescue most of the treasure, sheltered under the overturned rescue boat. It would be a while before it would become necessary, as it had in *The Darkest Wind*, to boil their clothing, so that any spilt edibles could be coaxed into a thin broth, but at this point in history, to think they would be cooking steaks seemed a faraway dream. The sea had stolen all it wanted and left behind whatever was shabby and useless, like props from a canceled show.

"We must go on," Gwen said out loud. "We have to ride it out."

"Verily?"

"Totally verily." It was true. This happened in every pirate history—*any old port in a storm, Cap'n*—but Gwen had not thought it would happen so quickly. These were different times. "When the sun goes down, half of us will scout up there and see where we might hole up. This flat part, whatever it is—"

"Not for us."

"Verily again. But I bet there's a place up there, the hotel or something. Somewhere dry and away. Safe."

"You think? We can still do it? Repair the boat?"

"No, I think steal another one."

"From—?"

"Somebody must come here. We'll hide out in the trees for a couple days, maybe, and then pounce."

Amber looked out at the rainy water. "Sick."

"Yeah."

"Hammocks, maybe."

"We could make those," Gwen said.

"Verily."

"And training exercises," Gwen said, "to keep sharp."

Amber bit her lip. "Gwen, Errol?"

"I know." Gwen looked over at him. His hat was over his face.

"Is there, was there something he took at the place? Like a medicine? You know, that he's not taking now?"

Gwen had not thought of this. Surely there was nothing useful at the Jean Bonnet Living Center. Surely this was a better place.

"I'm just asking because—"

"I know, Amber."

"He's not doing well."

Talk of mutiny, this was also inevitable in such a narrative. Omitted in this narration are Errol's many failings once the *Corsair* was run aground. His walk had become particularly shuffly, and whilst crazy-talking he had dropped two boxes into the water. Gone.

"We'll see," Gwen said. "Now he's sleeping."

"We hope."

"Yes."

"You know I love him too."

"Yes," Gwen said again, and wriggled even closer to Amber.

"And you, wench."

"Me too."

"I don't miss my parents *at all*."

Gwen smiled. "No."

"Tortuga, though."

Gwen reached under her shirt and drew out the *Corsair*'s radio. "Maybe we can find him."

"Yeah, cool, turn it on."

Even out here they could find his signal. They bobbed their heads and listened to him, and the mutterings of lost souls in the microphone booths, until the weather broke and the moon was a skull in the sky. With the radio off, there were noises around, noises of nature but not, to Gwen, sounding natural. Better to look at the lights of the bridge, the flashes of cars braking and moving, dots and dashes of a message trying for home.

"I'm a stranger here," Errol said in the darkness. "Where am I?"

"Treasure Island, Captain," Gwen said. She could scarcely see him, just a standing shadow taking off its hat, next to the silent bulk of Manny.

"Did you come here maybe in the Navy?" Amber asked.

"I don't know," Errol said. "I have a problem with it."

Manny handed Gwen something plastic, light and smooth in her palm like a cheap utensil. It was a flashlight, she could feel, and when she moved the switch, it glared Cody out of his sleep.

"What?" Cody stood and shook his skinny legs. "Oh, yeah," he said in recognition.

"Treasure Island," Errol repeated. "Only in America."

"Only Americans think it's only in America," Manny replied, his bulk huge in the blackness. "Places like this are everywhere."

"What about me?" Errol said. "Where am I?"

"We ran aground," Amber said. "The storm gave us problems."

"I have a problem with my memory," Errol said.

"Gwen's got a plan for what's next," Amber said.

Errol's shadow put its hat back on. "Who?"

"If it's acceptable to you, Captain," Gwen said, "I thought we should send a team to scout ahead in the hopes of finding a part of the world where we might settle ourselves."

"Any old port in a storm," Errol recited.

"Where?" Cody asked.

"Up there." Gwen pointed with the flashlight.

"It's too dark," Cody said.

"Maybe, the hotel on the map," Amber said, "or at least somewhere warm and dry."

"That would be nice," Cody said.

"*Can't hoit*," Errol murmured.

Manny sighed, his silhouetted shoulders a great wave. "I'm out of here."

Gwen's light rose up the bulk of the figure until it hit Manny's squinting eyes. "What?" she said.

"I guess I'm not cut out for this occupation of piracy," he said, his voice lilting in the dark. "I've been thinking about it this whole time."

"But you're *from Tortuga*," Gwen said, and the light shook in his face.

"Put that down," he said, and Gwen lowered it. The first thing in the beam was Gwen's knife, still at her side.

"But you left home," Amber said. "You're like us, you left."

"I had no choice," Manny said. "I was to end up a disappeared man. There was no life for me there, do you understand?"

"*Yes*," Gwen said.

"*No.* I lived under a dictator."

"Same thing," Gwen said, her mother glaring at her in the dark.

"*No*," Manny said again. "I had so many lives before I cleaned up for Peggy. Many things. In Florida I sold eggs, just as I sold eggs to get there. Hid in a rented truck driving north in record heat to become an apple picker. Did windshields and detailing all day. People hire us because we're cheap and that's all. Money under the table, and never what was promised."

"What does this have to do with—"

"Exactly! Thank you! What *does* my story have to do with it? It's not a place for me here. I might now find one."

"*Manny*," Gwen said. She was surprised to find her hand ready with the knife.

"My real name is Myoparo," he said. "Nobody tries to pronounce it in the States."

"I won't let you."

"What will you do?" Manny laughed a little. "Maroon me?"

"I *will* maroon you," Gwen said.

"Gwen—" Cody said.

"Maroon you on a sandspit. You take one more step away and I'll split your gullet."

"Little girl—"

"*No!*" Gwen cried. "I won't have it! You cannot leave! We need you with us!"

"God be with you," Manny replied and rustled away into the bushes.

Gwen felt her anger, clenched and fierce and not enough. "You won't get a stone's throw from here!" she cried, and reached down to find a stone to make her point. But it took a while to find a stone in the dark, and then when she threw it, it just disappeared. He was out of this history, although not out of history at large, as no one is. There was a place for him on the American island. He would meet a girl in an hour, huddled up against a sign. NO TRESPASSING, it said, BY ORDER OF THE UNITED STATES NAVY, but the sign was on the ground, leaned up against a garbage can half-full of water, where some months ago men had thrown away beer cans and forgotten about them. Who watches over places like this? Nobody. Invisible, they broke the law, trespassed back to the bridge together, and in six months Myoparo Bernardin would be made a citizen of the United States. It is quite a story he tells, and most of it is true. Were it cleaned up and broadcast, for a show on American something, it would be an episode to remember. But instead Manny would vanish into the melting pot of what was still called, at this point in history, the American dream: a wife and a child and a legitimate business. And money, of course. He had the twenty-five thousand dollars in his pocket with the catmint tea. Manny was no fool. Even with the radio off, Gwen could not hear him make his way, but she knew how it went. It was the way it always went, in the world and now out of it. Something was stolen from her. Her fingers closed on the knife handle. She would get it back in her clutches.

CHAPTER *12*

The big story on the night in question was the theft of a boat, scarcely seaworthy and not yet discovered in pieces on Treasure Island, but Phil Needle let himself into his condo largely ignorant of the big story. His wife too. He wouldn't have cared if he knew. The condo was dead. It was no longer a home. He put the photograph of himself down on the kitchen counter and watched Marina clack over to the fridge.

"Do you want to eat something?"

A gun, Phil Needle thought, but it wasn't true. He caught a glimpse, out the show-offy window in the living room, at the bridge that had trapped him, glittering into the dark mass of Treasure Island. Man-made. Maybe the map was true.

"*Phil?*"

Phil Needle came back. "What?"

"*Eat something.* Do you want to."

"I'm not—I guess I should," he said to her. "Long day. Just chips at the gas station, was lunch. I woke up this morning in Los Angeles." *Naked*, he remembered.

"And you didn't *fly*," Marina spat, and slammed down yogurt with a happy cow on the label. A steak would taste good. But Marina was done cooking, just moving her hand on the counter like it was pretending to be a spider.

"This is where I last saw her," she said quietly. Toby II emerged from someplace and whined at the glass. Phil slid the door, and he went out to shit. It felt more dramatic than it was: *where I last saw her*. It was a kitchen. "What do you think happened?"

"Nothing," she said, and shook her head. "When I picture it I picture nothing."

Nothing. He stood for a second and pictured it too, and then drifted out of the kitchen and up the stairs to the bedroom, bonking his suitcase behind him. He wanted to shower, but then when he was undressed he kept going and changed into one of many T-shirts he had promoting things. They were mailed to his office all the time, in the hope—apparently prescient—that he would wear them. His favorite sweatshirt, the most comfortable one, was missing from his closet. Could *one thing* be just where he wanted it? He washed his face and felt Gwen's absence in the bathroom opposite his, on the other side of the mirror.

He shouldn't have gone into her room, but he did.

The bed was unmade, with the sheets toppled down one side and a few decorative pillows leaned carelessly against one wall. MY PRINCESS SLEEPS HERE, said one, a long-ago gift, as if Gwen were a princess who belonged to a pillow. Her closet was open—Marina had checked for what she might have been wearing—and her desk was ransacked so thoroughly that it looked for a minute like it was upside down. Two drawers had been pulled from their slots and lay overturned in an X on the frayed blotter. A pile of strange books, both startling and familiar, were scattered on the floor, their covers full of ships and swords. Phil Needle saw a small, folded triangle of paper on the floor, almost hidden behind one of the desk's over-splindly legs.

PERSONAL it said on one side of the triangle.

Dear Nathan,

I can't stop thinking about you all the time and the
way you stole my heart. Your arms, your face, your
eyes, your expression you must have when you play
the bass so good. I know that you're with Naomi so
I probably don't have a chance. But I want to talk to
you alone. I want to make you see that I love you
more and better and everything. I want to kiss you
and other things too. I am a mistake, verily (only
you and me and my parents know this),

and here Phil Needle sat on the bed

and when I think that you won't love me I wish I'd
never been born.

Gwen Needle almost hadn't been born. She was the result of
tsunamis of fertility treatments, years of special diets and false posi-
tives, Marina's feet in stirrups and Phil Needle masturbating into
plastic cups, always with the prim offer, from the brittle nurse, of
"visual aids," which was a stack of pornography kept behind the
gleaming white doors of a cupboard in a room shuddering with the
ghosts of other fruitless fathers with their pants off. The problem
was not his fault, not his fault, not his fault, but Phil Needle had
endured the unspoken question throughout all the consultations:
What is wrong with your fucking? He had almost convinced himself
that children were gratuitous, and that they could sell the house in
the Sunset, its second bedroom gaping empty, and live somewhere
new and shiny and close to the water, the end of the family line,
when finally, in the words of the smirky third doctor they had tried,
it took. The whole time—it must have been nine months,

right?—neither of them drank, Marina so that Gwen would not perish in the reluctant womb, and Phil Needle in sympathetic support, except for the drinks he had by himself while his plump, round wife slept down the hall. In January, the month of Christmas trees in garbage trucks, he could feel movement below his wife's skin. It was the first thing Gwen did: kick, her limbs soon stretching out from Marina's belly like a periscope. Little Baby Submarine, they called it. *Her.* On the drive home from the hospital, with Marina in back and Gwen sound asleep, already pouting, it looked like, in the car seat, Phil Needle thought, *Why use the seat belt? Why strap myself in? If there is an accident the baby will die, and if the baby dies I am finished.*

Three nights later he planted a tree.

She didn't die, though. When she was two, she found Marina's birth control pills and ate nine of them before they found her. They'd induced vomiting by giving her, on someone's advice, a raw shrimp, but she didn't die. She was slow to walk—"Walk to me!" Phil Needle must have said to her a thousand times. She begged to fly kites on windless days. For three days when she was eleven she was a strict vegetarian. She loved to throw bread into the pond in the park, not the part of the pond where everybody threw bread, but where the old men sat frowning at their motorized miniature boats, the bread attracting ducks and gulls, who would splatter around the armadas and spoil the scale of the thing. "Walk to me!" he would say. But she kept moving past him. Phil Needle was so hurt—he knew it was silly—that it was a few seconds before he reacted to the fact that she'd fallen down the stairs. Only two stitches, with a kind of thread that disappeared by itself, although he swore her unmarked face was never the same. It was Marina's idea, it *was*, not to tell Gwen how troublesome it had been to cook her up. She'd take it hard, Marina had said. She'd get delicate. Nathan, Phil Needle remembered, was that insolent older brother, his surfer hair and big nose that would look so terrible on a grandchild. Look where they go, these submarines. They are safe nowhere. No one can save them. Look what happens! Look what happens! Nobody, nobody, nobody should have children.

"Phil!"

"Yes," he said, but quietly. One of the books had a sock on it, Gwen's small sad sock, and Phil Needle thought of Levine's articles, her bag in his suitcase. Underwear, et cetera. It was better to hide them now, those zipped-up secrets, before Marina unpacked and found them. "*Yes!*"

"Where are you?"

He doubled back to his room to grab the crumpled bag, and then back down the stairs. His photograph was back on the piano, smiling and unrebuked. All of them were grinning in front of various backgrounds. What did it mean? One day they were happy, many days, even. Marina had opened the yogurt but then given up again.

"Where were you? Where did you go?"

"I think she's with those other two," he said, holding the note up like a white flag. "We didn't know they were friends, but they are. She knows both brothers. Look."

He almost handed her Alma Levine's bag. She watched him fumble and then took the note and stared at it.

"This isn't—who is this?"

"Gwen wrote it."

"Then why is it here? This is a lie."

"What?"

"It's a lie. She didn't send it."

"My daughter," Phil Needle said, "is not a liar."

Marina widened her eyes.

"I mean, of course she is. But look at it. It's something."

"What is something?"

"Nathan is the brother, I'm saying. She wanted to meet him. She's with her new friends, off drinking together or who knows what. Early rebellion."

"And where were you?"

"Marina, we've gone through this. I drove home because the airports—"

"No, I mean right now, where were you?"

"Upstairs. I was just—in her room. It's where I found this."

She looked up, finally. "Don't give me that. You changed your shirt."

"And then—"

"And *then*," Marina said, "*and then, and then, and then?*"

Phil Needle said nothing. Sometimes they'd take Gwen out to dinner and she'd be the bored silent one at the table while Phil Needle and Marina talked and had drinks. Or Marina would be the silent one while he chattered with his daughter. Or they'd all take a turn being the silent one, all together.

"*Answer me.*"

The only answer Phil Needle could think of was that his wife was an idiot, at least sometimes. She had turned the wrong knob on the oven once—that oven, right there—and cooked the Thanksgiving turkey on the self-cleaning setting. She had once purchased a new bra and then, he saw it on her dresser, filled out a promotional postcard that was tucked inside: *Reason for Purchase, circle one: Gift. Impulse. Salesperson recommendation. Saw it advertised. Wanted to treat myself. Needed new bras.* He was sorry he hadn't flown, and he was sorry about the wrong photograph, and he had said so and still they had to fight. It was like falling off a ladder, twice: you didn't mean to do it even once, but that did nothing to keep you from doing it again.

Marina walked past him into the living room. "If they don't find her I'm jumping through the window."

The window was still speckled with raindrops. Marina was turned away from him, although he could see the ghost of her face in the glass.

"It's safety glass," he said finally, and outside the dog snorted.

"And the veranda is one floor down. You'd land in the garden with a few cuts."

"I'm out of here when this is over," she said. "I'm leaving you. I want a divorce."

"Really?" Phil Needle couldn't help saying it. *When this is over?* It was not even clear to him what *this* might be. Surely if they found her alive and well, it would be a flood of forgiveness and tears, and if not, then it would never be over. How could it be that now, with his daughter out of reach and his assistant's belongings crumpled in his hand, they had reached the timberline of their affection? Marina was already crying, again and relentlessly. Of how little comfort Phil Needle was, even when he walked to her, without hurry but swiftly, and put his hands on her shoulders, to be shrugged violently away. There was nothing to it. It was easy for him, Phil Needle, to shatter his wife.

"I won't come back to you," she said, in sobbing rage.

"I know who," Phil Needle said, surprising himself. "Rafael Bligh!"

"What?"

"You keep in touch with him! I know you do."

"*Rafael Bligh?*" It was perhaps the first time she'd smiled since he got home, even though she stopped it right away. "No, Phil. It's not Rafael Bligh."

"Who is it then?"

"It's no one," she said. "There isn't anyone. It's for *me*." She was pointing to herself like it wouldn't have been clear otherwise. "I know you think one kind note erases everything, but it doesn't."

"I don't. What note?"

"*What note?* I can't lead you through everything, Phil."

"I have no idea what you're talking about."

"Then what good are you?"

Phil Needle didn't answer. He walked away from his wife without a word. He would answer her later, he decided, in the hallway. He opened the door of the office and saw the fake tree, rattling against the fake window. Marina never turned it off. He sat in the chair and reached to turn on the desk lamp, but it clicked to nothing. There is never a good time for a lightbulb to go out. Half-blind, he reached down to open the bottom drawer, deep and cold from being near the outside wall. He moved everything aside to hide Levine's things when an envelope, forgotten and sealed in a reclosable plastic bag, fell out of a folder and onto his shoe. Inside, with a box of matches and some small papers, was about an ounce and a half of marijuana.

He heard Marina stomp up the stairs and did not hesitate. In fifteen minutes the effects of the drug were well under way, and Phil Needle stood up shakily to go outside. He hadn't been stoned in at least a year, since he'd bought the marijuana on impulse, when offered it on the Embarcadero. He had been afraid to tell Marina about it, as it meant that it could also be offered to Gwen when she roamed the neighborhood. He had thought then, *Someday I will smoke this, and sit in my courtyard with my mind hazy and silly, as I did when I was a young man.* And then forgotten about it. No time like the present.

(But before he slipped out the sliding door, Phil Needle, as quietly as possible, opened the door to the other room in the hall and looked at Marina Needle's paintings. Ordinary landscape, ordinary landscape, all ordinary landscapes, either the same paintings he had seen when he'd last peeked, or very similar. Trees and water, hills and sky, sky and trees and water on a hill. She wasn't getting better, though neither was she bad. The paintings told him nothing, he thought in the courtyard, no more than the stars and the clouds. There was nothing as far as the eye could see.)

Outside, the air felt elderly, reluctant to move and cranky at him. He hadn't called his father back. Sorry, everybody. Phil Needle sat on a bench and "(Water on a) Drowning Man" flowed into his head, the tinny, ringing guitar and the full-throated croak of an American legend. It was why he had enshrined it as his ringtone, so everyone reaching him was heralded first by this outlaw. It was his favorite Belly Jefferson song, and he had always wished, whenever he heard it, that he had bigger troubles, real blues troubles, so that it could not be said he was listening to Belly Jefferson undeservedly. But in truth his troubles had always been enough. He hadn't wanted any more, not ever. He wanted out. To vanish like a thief in the night, like it says in the second verse, no, it was the actual song. Phil Needle looked down at his phone. It was real. His own name blinked back at him, as it did whenever they called him from work. Phil Needle Prod, it showed, because there wasn't enough space.

"Hello."

"Phil, it's all of us," came Allan's voice, in the cheap echo that happened when you put someone, in this era, on speakerphone. Past the glass, the kitchen was lit and still like a boring museum. "Barry, EZ, Dr. Croc, and this is Allan."

"I can't," Phil Needle said, "hear about anything about work right now."

"No, no," Barry said, over the chatter of everyone saying "no, no." "Everything's fine. In fact, Incredible Cleaners sent a case of Scotch, the ad's gone so well. But we heard about Wren." Somebody muttered something. "*Gwen.* Sorry. And we're so sorry, Phil. You're in our thoughts."

They were in Studio B, probably, and Phil Needle could not help but think of Allan masturbating. *I want to kiss you and other things too.* He did not want to be in anyone's thoughts. Toby II sniffed near him like a snooty waiter.

"But also we had an idea," said probably EZ.

"It's a good one," Dr. Croc said. "Today's consumers like it."

"We were thinking you should go on the radio and make an appeal," Allan said. "I could get you on KUSA tomorrow."

"Those guys are amateurs," Dr. Croc muttered.

"Highest-rated morning show. They'd have you on, Phil, if you wanna do that. They owe me a favor."

"A favor?" Phil Needle asked. "How do they even know you?"

"I have a show," Allan said, "once a week."

"Three A.M.," Barry said.

Gwen's note was on the counter, next to the yogurt. Phil Needle tried to work it out. "You work at KUSA?"

"We all do," Barry said.

"All of you?"

"Yeah," Dr. Croc said, even him.

"You don't pay us enough," Allan said quietly. "Sorry."

Dear Renée, is that what it was? Money? Aren't you ashamed of yourself? "It's okay," Phil Needle said. "I guess it's true, I should pay you more probably."

"That'd be great."

"I'll make a note about it, clear it with Leonard Steed."

"Sure. Do you want to come to the station tomorrow?"

"When?"

"Eight? Eight in the morning? Seven thirty."

Phil Needle looked at the happy cow. He was free at eight, of course he was. "Okay," he said, and then, so quick it was almost instinct, "Thank you."

"Of course, Phil. What good are we, right? If we can't get our radio boss on the radio."

"What good," Phil Needle said, and hung up. Levine's things moved in his hands, and he left the courtyard in a steadfast blur. In moments they were in the drawer, underneath even the drugs. (He tried, he tried, not to think about the day his father found the cocaine.) Toby II ran around in the kitchen, half-enthusiastically, at all this hubbub. Would they fight over the dog if there was no child? Would he really be divorced, would more young women's toiletries rattle into his life? Or would Marina just be standing next to him on Independence Day, as if nothing had really happened? It was what he could imagine, but so what, what good was that, his wandering mind, the grand late-night schemes of his crew, his straying body in a faraway suite? "No good," he said, answering his wife's question at last, but nobody knew he had even said a word.

×

Dawn came with a helicopter, chipping through the sky around the bridge. Gwen and Amber woke right quick, staring at each other wrapped in sweatshirts. Treasure Island, Gwen saw, sitting up, was where they were. Cody was curled against a shrub with his arms around his knees, like an urchin in a folktale. Errol was off a ways, standing quietly over a puddle. The noise kept up, chopping around the rising sun.

"What is that?"

"Duck," Amber said. "We'd better duck down here." She had already crouched off the concrete into some bristly shrubbery. Gwen could see a small twig scraping at the space between the end of Amber's pant leg and her muddy sock, a patch of skin already prickled and red as a rose garden. They had all suffered.

"I don't think they're looking for us."

"Of course they are, wench."

"They're angled toward the bridge. Traffic, I think it is."

"Like for a radio report? It's Sunday, I think."

Gwen looked up, squinting and wondering where those sunglasses had gone, and then put her hood up and curved it down. "Church traffic," she tried, with a wavery smile.

"We should warn the others."

Others, she said, like there was a teeming band. Manny's departure had made the group into a small batch of parts. Even the rescue boat, still covering their meager supplies, looked smaller now. "Cody," she said, and he rocked back and forth a little. "Captain."

"Aye?" Errol called over, and Gwen pointed to the sky. Errol glared up. "Wings," he said, walking closer.

"We'd best take shelter."

"I'm not afraid of birdlife, grommet. We had a parrot in our crew, did we not?"

Gwen took his sleeve. It was a bad sleeve, wet and torn, but it served the purpose of tugging him into the brush. Cody stood shakily and tried to crawl in after them, his arms and legs every which way. Gwen could not help thinking that Nathan would have done it better. Errol growled a little and knelt down, a puddle rippling around his knee. This looked like nothing, where they were hiding. Tall plants, reeds or just ruined leaves, crossed high in front of them, with shrubs circling their wagons against the wind and grime. The air scutted noise above them. No one would look for them here, Gwen thought, because nobody would look for anything here. Cody sat down next to her. His teeth were dirty and chattering. "Can I talk to you?" he whispered.

"You don't have to whisper it," Gwen said. "They can't hear from up there."

"I woke up with a sore throat."

Amber was fiddling with something in her hands. "Well," Gwen said, "these are dark days."

"Yes," Cody said, and the helicopter took a loud lap while he said something else. Gwen looked at him.

"You can't," she said, and Amber frowned at both of them. "There isn't one."

"I'm sorry," Cody said. "I didn't know it would be—"

"Be what?"

"I didn't know we'd kill people."

"There's not a pirate account that omits bloodshed. None I've seen."

"Yeah, you told me, but Gwen, I didn't read those books."

"You were *invited* to join us," Amber said, finally getting the gist. Errol grunted and bent to examine a thick log with greens sprawled around it like dead string.

"You invited my brother," Cody reminded her, and Amber went back to her fumbling. It was the radio. Gwen put her hand on it.

"No," she said gently.

"Too far above us to hear," Amber said, cocking her head up to the helicopter. "Tortuga would be cheering company."

"We should save the batteries," Gwen said. "They might be failing." *Also*, she thought.

"Worry about your deserter," Amber said.

"I'm not *deserting*," Cody said, and put his hands over his eyes.

"They won't take you," Gwen said, and saw Errol startle back at something. "You've left all bounds, Cody. When they find the wreckage, your family will never utter your name again."

Cody was shaking his head roughly. His eyes threw out another line of tears. "I know I came with you," he said, "and I know I wanted to attack the boat. I know that man was bad. I know we had knives."

"And then?" Gwen asked. "And *then*? *And then*?"

Cody looked desperately at her. "I just want to go home," he said again, and the helicopter roared over them again. It was there for the big story. It was not interested in teenagers hiding in the bushes, probably ducking out of church, or an old man lifting up a log in one shaky hand, scowling, to lurch further into the wild. The aerial shot of the mast of the *Corsair*, leaning out of the grimy water with a few soaked planks for company, would be a successful part of the evening broadcast. But Gwen didn't think of the boat. It was gone. She thought of herself and her charges, beyond the law and looking to stay that way, and waited through the last lap until the sky was empty and the coast was clear, before walking out of the sticks and scratches, onto the flat gray landscape and the fading noise.

"It is an *insult*!" The captain's cry could finally be heard. "It is *all* an *insult*!"

The log thunked to the concrete, splatting mud on Gwen's muddy boots, and Errol followed, crashing through the brush into the morning sun. He looked terrible. It looked, in his snarling mouth, like one of his own teeth had been knocked loose, and his hair was wild with twigs and brambles crowning it, and there were specks of blood freckled down his arms and all over his clothing. Just one sleeve was rolled up, with Errol's thick-banded watch shining like a signal, and the other hand was filthy—the one holding the rusty saw. His eyes were everywhere, darting angrily and accusingly from the trauma of whatever unrecorded battle he had fought in the night. "Scallywag!" he shouted hoarsely. "Rogue! Scum! Culprit! Asshole!"

He had already pushed Cody to the ground. Cody scrambled to stand but once standing he did not run, his expression fearful but stubborn too. He was never one to run away from a bully. He stayed there and got the crap beaten out of him.

"Errol," Gwen said quietly.

"Out of this!" he cried. "I have right of reprisal!"

Cody looked at her. He didn't know what that meant, either.

"Errol," she said, "it's Gwen."

"I know," Errol said darkly. "I've been looking all over."

"We're on Treasure Island," she said. "Remember?"

"I have no home, not anymore. It is all an insult!"

He was pointing at the log, the green stretching out of the sodden wood to offer weird flowers, like ancient skulls.

"Orchids," Amber said. Some stealthy grower, or perhaps some miraculous accident, on a log in a nothing place.

"He took what's mine," Errol spat, "and left me these!"

Gwen looked at the flowers, delicate and hideous, like the whole scheme. "Errol."

"Sold it from under me," Errol said, "and cast me into the diaspora."

"*Captain.*"

Errol looked at her for the first time. "Hello," he said blankly.

"It's Gwen."

"He took what's mine," he muttered. "Sold my house to buy his own and left me stranded with insults of flowers."

"These were just here," Amber tried. "This is not what we're after."

Errol pointed the saw at Cody. "My fucking son," he said.

"I'm not your son," Cody said.

"We agreed until such time that the treasure could be divided. He took spoils. And *now* he talks of desertion, sends a priceful gift as distraction? You will feel the sting of this lash, by Neptune I swear it."

Most of this Gwen recognized from *Treasure Seekers*, but Cody hadn't read anything. "What?" he said. "What did I take?"

"*Everything.*"

Cody found the lever to be fierce, an angry look at the old man, as such generations have given each other since the sea was wet. "Name," he said. "One. Thing."

"I am having trouble with my memory," Errol answered, and then swiveled, violently, to stare at Gwen.

"Please," Gwen said. "Wait. Tarry."

"I will fight any man, with any weapon."

"It won't help to hurt him," she said.

"*Can't hoit,*" Errol said, with a wild cackle. Blood came from his mouth, the hole from the tooth maybe, or some other wound she could not see.

"Captain," she said. "Sailors are a particularly volatile element."

"Agreed. I want him punished for his crimes."

"I think his crimes," Gwen said carefully, "are different from the ones you are thinking of."

"You could say that of any man."

"Yes, but—"

"And no man will believe the whipping my son will receive."

"Okay, but let's try and be reasonable for a second."

Errol let out a ghastly cry, his hands spread wide at the heavens. It was long, loud, lost, frantic, and ended suddenly, as if he had remembered something at that very moment. "*D'ye hear?*" he asked Gwen, although she was the one who had said it. "*D'ye hear? Reasonable!*"

"Just for a second," Gwen said desperately.

He screamed again, and Gwen had to move her hands up to cover her ears. No man should scream like that. It was an untamed noise, separate from whatever containment civilization required. She had felt that scream so many times but never found the voice to let it out. Now she knew why. Because people hated it was why. It drove them mad and angry. "*Reasonable!*" he said, when it was over. "I'll have you know, grommet, we don't sit here to hear reason. We go according to—" and another scream again, short this time, and Errol looked down.

Cody's cleaver was stuck in his leg.

"*Bastard!*" Errol screamed. Cody was panting. Another amateur move, Gwen thought, a rash act from a crewman unready for the voyage. He had come at Errol from the side, the blade now stuck in right below the knee, the handle quaking where the boy had let go. It was a strange, strange place for a wound. It was impossible, even when Gwen could see it plain as day. There was a sharp, bad gasp from Errol's throat, and then for a second it was so quiet Gwen could hear a few birds, and the traffic overhead from the bridge. Cody leaned down and wiggled the cleaver out of Errol's leg. The blood bled. Errol looked at it and then looked at Cody and the swordfight properly began.

In countless histories, the clashing of swords is a battle of wits, barbs tossed down from swinging chandeliers, brash laughter as the heavy curtains are cut to ribbons. They didn't know, Gwen thought. They couldn't have seen one. Errol and Cody set upon each other bestially, the cleaver and saw jerking and arcing not like rapiers or cutlasses but like antlers and claws and teeth. Birds circled and fled as they made their way down the last of the path to the lot. Even the underbrush seemed to shrink from their flailing arms, as if they were unpopular kids moving through a party. They did not have the breath for insults—there was not a shout of "Take back all slander!" from Cody, or "Give back what you stole, knave!" from

Errol—though as Gwen tailed them, she could hear their grunts and squeaks. They were dodgy all the way, neither pirate beaten, ducking away from each mad blow as they circled the provisions still sheltered by the overturned boat. Cody was a scrambler, his feet loosening rocks and garbage, even toppling two cardboard boxes stacked up in the corner of the lot, empty and soaked and never having held anything. Errol was surer but slower, having lost all hesitation about the world, his steps uneven from the first blow. The flat of the saw slapped Cody's face. Errol kicked at the cleaver as it tried another wound, spilling blood from the first one onto the wet ground. Errol found an overturned chair in a mess of grass—as if someone, years ago, had stormed away from the dinner table— and brandished it with his other hand like a lion tamer, its ruined seat cushion flopping to the ground. Gwen tailed them warily. Errol had rumpled Cody's hair on the deck of the *Corsair* at least once. Now they were enemies, unreasonable barbarians. When the chair hit Cody's shoulder, she must have gasped.

Cody turned to glance at her, set his mouth in a tense grin, and then darted from Errol's saw with more grace than was necessary, showing off for his ladylove, ducking under the chair and kicking Errol in the back of the knees. Errol screamed, high and wild like a panicked woman, and moved his saw jaggedly forward—Cody had to pull back his belly to avoid it—before snarling something. It sounded like "Six years." Cody, with a flourish, backed away six or eight steps and quickly tore off the topcoat worn by Captain Scrod, first one sleeve and then the other, then twirled it around the hand that wasn't holding the cleaver, around and around like spaghetti on a fork. Gwen had seen this in movies, a fighter spinning a heavy, mummified hand of cloth, for a shield, she was pretty sure. Cody didn't need to do it. Cody wasn't doing it right. He looked at his hand to see. Errol stepped forward calmly and dragged the saw across Cody's bare arm. You could hear the flesh tear over the traffic, and Cody's scream and the clatter of the cleaver on the ground as the wound widened, his skin opening like an umbrella. Cody went down and Errol stood over him, his bad foot on Cody's chest pinning him down and bleeding away, with his saw up in the air in both hands, angled straight down like an arrow. *You are here.*

"Dead to me!" Errol cried, "and *dead!*"

"*Stop!*" Amber screamed. Gwen couldn't believe it, but Errol did. He stopped and looked over, mid-plunge, at Gwen's best friend. She was crying, Gwen saw, tears long and slow down her face.

And she was holding the gun.

"*I'll shoot both of you.*" Amber stepped closer. Gwen remembered the thing that clicked on the gun when Roger had it. Had it clicked now? What was going to happen? "*Both of you, either of you, I don't care.*"

"Who are you?" Errol said hoarsely. Cody looked grateful and embarrassed both. "Who are you, interfering?"

"One of your crew," Amber said. "We must stick together or die. We run the gauntlet of the whole world, not at each other."

Amber hadn't said it right—a good forger but not a good reader, they would say about her in times to come—but Errol nodded like it meant something. To him it likely did. He put the saw down and kicked Cody's bleeding arm with his other foot, then stepped off him.

"Begone," he said wearily. "You and all who support you. It's mutiny."

"Errol," Gwen said.

"Sell my house and kill my woman. Send your filthy flowers to wash your hands."

"I don't even know," Cody said, breathing hard, "what you're talking about." He tried to stand up but had to slide, bleeding, across the ground to Gwen. Amber followed him with the gun but gave up. Cody put his hand on Gwen's leg and then blinked up at her.

"You, too, Vera?" Errol asked.

"*Gwen,*" Gwen said. "No." But she reached down, and couldn't help it, lifted him up. Blood slid onto her pants, sticky and staining, and in that second she realized she'd die in them, these pants she'd chosen because they were the toughest. Errol tossed the saw to the ground and limped to the water, where the mast of the *Corsair* still stood ready, even as the boat had fallen apart. He pointed at the mast and then said something to himself, his shoulders raising and lowering in argument as he paced on the bank. It was terrible, where they were. Gwen had expected things to go wrong—they went wrong in all of Errol's books—but not this way. She had wanted them to go wrong better.

"He cut my arm," Cody wheezed.

"To be fair," she said, "you did it first."

"I was Singapored."

"*Shanghaied.*"

"I knew it was a city," Cody said, and stood on his own, although he shivered a little, shifting his weight from one little leg to the other. Gwen remembered what he'd told them: that he'd had to wear tights for a school play. A sad performance it must have been. She looked at the blood on her pants and thought, for the first in a long time, of the burn on her leg, while Cody fished into his pockets and pulled out a small square that he smoothed in his hands.

"This is so good of you," he said quietly, and held it up for her to see. Gwen Needle grinned back, in a photograph. She was at her dad's office, where he had been trying a new camera. Allan had made her laugh about something, she remembered. It was thousands of years ago.

"Where did you find this?"

"I stole it," Cody said, promptly and proudly. "From your dad's wallet in the locker room. While he was showering."

Cody naked, amongst other naked men. Gwen could not help scanning them in her head, looking for Nathan.

"I always keep it with me."

"What are you saying?"

"I'm saying—I'm giving it back," Cody said, and tucked it into her hand.

"You're giving me a picture of me?"

"It's like a badge, right? When a policeman quits?"

"Pirates don't wear *badges*," Amber said.

"That's what I'm saying," Cody said. His hands gestured to the bridge, the rescue boat, the distant, muttering captain. "I thought we could get away from stuff."

"We were supposed to get away from *everything*," Gwen said. "This is the same as everything. It's like school is what it is, you giving me back my picture."

"I'm sorry."

"You're sorry? What pittance is that?"

"You know I don't get it when you talk to me like that."

"Leave, then," she said to the boy. "Go home, if that's what you fought for."

He looked wildly around. "I—I don't—"

"Leave or I will drive you from this place."

"There's no car."

"It means *force*," she said, and gave him a shove on his shoulder, just one. He stepped back, amazed, and then looked up at the bridge, back to the buildings, out to sea. His arm dribbled down blood.

"We should have gone to Tortuga," he said weakly.

"You don't know anything," Amber said. "That's too far."

"The show, I mean. At the Fillmore."

"I didn't want a *date*," Gwen said. No one would understand this. It is the presumed mission of all women, a quest for a man, and no amount of bloodshed can dissuade the myth. *For a boy*, people would say to her soon, in disbelief or even in admiration, and they would all be wrong. She had written notes to Nathan, yes, but she had not been so dim and reckless as to send them. They were safe and sheltered in a drawer. Gwen dropped her hands. She had been,

she was stunned to notice, tearing out her hair, and now her hands
hung down at her sides, the knife on one side and nothing on the
other. "What good are you," she said, "offering these nonsenses in a
time of genuine strife?"

Cody didn't say anything to her, not ever again.

"*What good are you?*"

Cody headed for the big buildings. Gwen and Amber watched
him go. It was difficult to tell who was marooning whom. In a few
months it would be as if she had simply shared an elevator with this
story. Amber she would remember, and their mad captain still
muttering by the shore, but Cody would fade away and then everything would fade away and Gwen would remember mostly her own
disappointment, and the silent, pleading faces of the dead. God,
God, she was tired.

"I hope he comes back," Amber said.

"Really?"

"With breakfast," Amber said, with a small grin. "Even the
pirates on that lonesome raft, at the end of that thing, had grog,
remember?"

Grog sounded good. She was thirsty and wanted to feel the
blur, the rush, that drunkenness promised. She should have saved
some bottles, when they were attacking *The Wild Lady*. She should
not have let all that go up, she thought, as Cody slipped around a
building and out of sight, in smoke.

"I think there's orange juice," Gwen said, and they trooped
over to the overturned rescue boat. They flipped it over and looked
at what they had.

"Soda, I thought maybe," Amber said. "The juice is gone. It
was in a carton. There's tonic."

"Ginger ale."

"Oh, I want that."

They shared a bottle. It fizzed at them snobbily, as if to say,
We're doing fine, all we bubbles.

"We weren't supposed to use anything," Amber said, with a guilty glance at Errol, down by the water.

"Yeah," Gwen said. "Until such time that the treasure can be divided."

"We're divided enough," Amber said. "Half our crew is exiled away."

"Quiet, wench."

"You're the wench," Amber said, and then, after a minute, "I wonder what happened to them."

"Them?" Gwen looked back at where Cody had disappeared.

"The ones on the boat," Amber said quietly.

Gwen did not want to think about them. The way the man had looked at Amber. The screaming girl they could have silenced, maybe, instead of torn apart.

"It's okay. I don't want to talk about it either."

"Then why did you—"

"I don't know, okay? I had to say something."

Gwen finished the bottle and threw it to crash on the ground as she put her arm around Amber. "Thank you for what you did, with the gun."

"I wasn't thinking."

"It worked."

"I'm not even sure it would have gone off."

"It's okay."

"You think? Maybe I should have let one of them kill the other one."

"No."

"It would have fixed things between us, maybe."

"What?"

"Not *us*. *All* of us. Because it's splitting. Dispersing, like you read to me. I mean, these are the only people I love in the whole—" She flailed uselessly at the water.

"I know. Me too."

"I was miserable before I met you," she said. "I know I pretended like I had something, but that day at the dentist I would have gone home and, I don't know how, got dead."

Gwen looked at the little scars on Amber's ankle.

"I mean, even my ex, when he was my *boyfriend*. Even he called me Monkeyface."

"What?"

"Don't say you don't notice."

"Amber, you don't look like a monkey."

"The Stepmonster said"—Amber was crying again—"she'd never seen anyone uglier."

"She's a—" Gwen said, "bitch and liar."

"I have nothing if we go home."

"We're not going home."

"I mean it."

"So do I."

"We can't steal a boat. That idea's over. There's no hotel and no treasure."

"We have a boat," Gwen said, and pointed to the boat.

"That?"

"That."

"In the sea."

"Yes, straight out, through the Golden Gate."

"We wouldn't last. Not long."

"I didn't say *long*. I said *out*."

"West."

"Yes. Wait. Yes, west."

"Straight off into the sunset."

Gwen thought of the Sunset, her old neighborhood. A better place, a better life. She nodded fiercely. She did not know what would happen, but she knew how it would go.

"Okay," Amber said slowly. "*And*, we're taking the captain, right?"

"Of course. What did you think?"

"I don't know. He's getting up there."

"I know."

"If *we* won't last long."

"Yeah. But we're not marooning him."

"No, no, I know. I just wanted you—"

"To be ready."

"To be *sure.*"

"Yes."

"Okay," Amber said. "You tell him."

"We should do something about his leg."

"Bandages? There's a clean T-shirt, at least. I'll load up a few things."

"Yes."

"Okay."

They did not move.

"Okay," Amber said again. "*Now.*"

Gwen moved, with one glance at Cody. He was long gone. (By the time the remains of the rescue boat washed ashore, Cody was watching his parents' arrival, via four-wheel drive, at this desolate place. A dog walker, with a cell phone and the milk of human kindness in his veins, was about to see his stumbling figure now.) She tramped through a puddle of worry and made herself think of her old house again in the Sunset, an incongruous but convincing fantasy of where this last stage of the trip would take them. Things added up in her mind, but nowhere else. She had a clean T-shirt in her hand, and that was all. She wished she could just take a wand and make everything good like that, because otherwise it was the same question she'd asked Cody.

What good was she?

Errol was standing silently next to two heavy planks, bright and new as if from a lumberyard, but quite wet. He was decompensating, is what it was called at this point in history. His leg was bleeding. His face was flushed. He was hotheaded, hot-everythinged.

Gwen knelt next to him and looked at his bleeding knee. The wound scowled back. Gwen wiped at it with one end of the T-shirt, and Errol groaned and looked down.

"What's that?" he said.

"Hold still," she said. "I need to bandage you up." She cupped one hand into a puddle, but the water looked dirtier than the knee. She tied the shirt around his leg anyway, as tightly as she could, which was not very tightly, and the blood moved through it almost right away. *Waterlogged,* she thought, and then looked down at the planks. Would waterlogged matter if they're going to be oars?

"It hurts," he said.

"Yes," she said, and lifted one plank. It was wet, but not weak.

"Somebody did this to me."

"Yes," she said again. "We have to get out of here, Captain." Gwen listened, not for the first time, for sirens heading down the road from the bridge. Nothing, though.

"I know you."

"Yes," Gwen said very sadly. "Gwen."

"My dearest."

So she wouldn't cry, she heaved one of the planks onto her shoulder to carry it, and Errol looked at her approvingly. "Tell me something," he said. "How did we meet?"

"Right now we need to leave," Gwen said.

"No."

"Come with me."

"Tell me how we met."

"You're my *captain*," Gwen said fervently, "and Captain, it's time to go."

Errol just shook his head. "It's two thirty is what it is," he said, looking at his watch. Gwen knew it was morning and not two thirty. The watch had stopped, at another time.

"Please come with me," Gwen said, but she could not carry both planks and tug on his sleeve, too.

He shook his head and shook his head and shook his head, faster and faster and faster, and then stopped and peered at her. "Where?" he said finally, as if through fog. At last it was something someone else might say in conversation.

"The sunset," she said. "On the thing we took. The rescue boat."

"That's not right," he said.

"It's the only place to go," Gwen said. "They'll find us soon otherwise."

"Triemiola?" he said.

That was a warship, often used to combat piracy. Gwen nodded quickly.

"All right," he said.

She walked behind him with the planks, herding him toward the boat. *Rescue* boat wasn't right, she realized. It was *life*.

Amber smiled at them when they arrived. They dragged the boat down some rocks to another part of the shore, so they wouldn't get caught up with the *Corsair* and its detritus. The lifeboat, their livelihood, was carrying just one box of some food and one bottle of water and the two makeshift oars Gwen had found. And Gwen had her knife. And Amber had the gun. And the radio. The lifeboat squealed over a rock and then they helped Errol inside. He looked so done and lonely, sitting in an open boat on a sea that had no friendly shore. But then they joined him, crowding into the boat and using the planks to push themselves off Treasure Island and points west, as best they could. The three last pirates cast off and stayed with their history and their final odyssey. It was why they had come, Gwen thought, so they could leave again, this time farther out and farther away into the enormous part of the water, wide and empty like a painting of a landscape. The big picture, Gwen thought, the big story of our lives. It was, finally, the answer: what good we are.

CHAPTER *13*

T his history is not a tragedy, despite its gore and its finale, and neither is it a comedy, although there is something funny, Gwen knew, about a lifeboat drifting in a bay, the prevailing current immune to whatever thrashings they gave it with their planks. At the time the story takes place, it likely would have been classified as a human interest story, on the grounds that humans would be interested in it. Phil Needle imagined pitching his morning, the story of what he decided to wear when he rose, foggy and thirsty, to plead for his daughter's return on the radio. He wavered between shaving and not shaving, torn between looking presentable and authentically panicked, and in the time he spent wavering at the mirror he lost the time to shave. He let himself out and took to the streets in his rented car. (His real vehicle was still in short-term parking and would soon be chained to a yellow truck and dragged through the streets to the city's municipal vaults, joining his wife's towed car, for ransom.)

KUSA was in a transitory part of town, where Marina met Old Mason, on the edges of a vast park that once had been a military base and was, at the time this story takes place, something else. Highway 101 veered nearby, and to the north was the beach where people took their dogs, and a harbor where small yachts, including at one time (though never again) *Outside the Box*, awaited their well-fed owners. The offices were located in a small complex of shady buildings with a cart outside selling strong coffee. Phil Needle had never been to KUSA and had plotted his route out on his device. It got him there a little early, but he did not get himself a coffee. It would look unseemly to arrive, a stricken father, with a paper cup, steaming and foamy on the top. He bystanded for a minute or two, watching nothing in the fog, and then just went inside, up two flights of stairs to a glass door with the call letters, KUSA, stenciled on them, a kind of door Phil Needle longed to have for Phil Needle Productions. He had missed the elevator, or there wasn't one. He tried the door and then made a face to the girl at the desk and the door buzzed and he tried it again and walked in.

"I'm—"

"Yes, Phil Needle, we've been expecting you."

"I know it's not eight yet."

"Yes, well, we were expecting you at seven thirty."

"What?"

"We were expecting—"

"Allan told me eight."

"Well, it doesn't matter. You're here."

"But I could have been here—"

"Yes, well, let me get our producer. We've moved from morning news to the zoo hour, so it's a little—it doesn't matter. We're happy to help, of course. We were, I was so sorry to hear, I should have said first thing."

"Thank you."

"Is there anything—do you want coffee?"

"No, actually yes, thank you."

She left. Her name was Ellen, said the thing on the desk, but then came a woman Phil Needle did not want to see.

"Phil."

"Um, wow."

"*Wow* what?"

"I didn't know you worked here."

"The guys didn't tell you?" she said. "Dr. Croc got me this job."

"Really?"

"He's been kind of a mentor to me," she said. "A resource. Phil, I'm so sorry to hear about your daughter."

Dear Renée, I have nothing to say to you at this time.

"We have a slot for you to talk live, Phil, and we'll record it and replay your message on the hour. We'll give our toll-free number at the end and relay any messages to you, of course, and to the police. Are you interested in a reward?"

"What? Gwen."

"*Offering* a reward, I mean," Renée said, and clicked her pen— *off on off on off on*—in a way Phil Needle had forgotten about and was annoyed by again. "The police always say it isn't worth it for the crazies it attracts, but I don't know if you know that we found Casey Rittola last year."

"Who? Yes. No."

"The reward helped. So maybe you want to."

"Twenty-five thousand dollars," Phil Needle said from nowhere, and took a cup of coffee from the other girl. It would surely be possible to get such a sum.

(Alma Levine was standing in her apartment, staring at that exact sum laid out on the bed while a man made tea in her kitchen.)

"Good, and there's just one more thing. A song?"

"What?"

"If Gwen had a favorite song, something we could tie it to. I mean, if she doesn't or you don't know, okay, but if it were something, I know it sounds awful, that KUSA might play. We can cross-pollinate this way."

"You're a good producer," Phil Needle said, as slowly as he realized it. "That's—that's a smart idea."

"I've had good teachers."

Off on off on off on off on. She hadn't meant *him*, of course.

"I am sorry I fired you, Renée."

"I *quit*," Renée reminded him gently, "a long time ago. Do you have a—"

"The Tortuga song, she loves that." He remembered suddenly, slowly, the tickets to the show. Of *course* that was where she went. Call the police. After his broadcast. He would write this down so he wouldn't forget, on his hand, except his hand was holding a cup of coffee.

"Which one?"

"The one she likes, I don't know. Thump thump thump."

"I think I know what you mean," she said. She leaned forward at an odd angle, like she was about to sip from Phil Needle's cup. "We're going to find her."

"Okay," he said. The radio started playing a commercial for back-to-school supplies.

"I hear you were at RADIO when you found out."

"Yes."

"How was it this year?"

"Failure," Phil Needle said, because why not say such a thing?

"I don't believe that," she said. "You're a good producer, too."

Phil Needle didn't believe that either. "I should have been home with her," he said.

"Nonsense," she said. "I have three myself. They always say that rabbits are the most powerful influence on children's lives, but once they hit teenager it's their friends."

Parents, was what she said. "Okay," he said.

"I'm going to put you in the booth," she said. "You'll have a few minutes to collect yourself. There's paper there if you haven't written it down."

"What?"

Renée put her hand on his hand on the coffee. "What you're going to say," she said. "Have some more coffee, Phil."

Phil Needle sipped gratefully as he was led. Coffee and *food*, was really what he wanted. If she were gone forever, he would never be able to put honey on toast again without thinking of her stomping down the stairs—he would have to sell the condo—to grab it every morning. It was always the same, Gwen thought. He always put on too much butter, and too much honey. She was hungry, but not hungry enough to be homesick.

"What do we have to eat?"

"Not yet," Amber said. "It's only been, like, an hour."

"The wench is right," Errol said. "Let's not eat our seed corn."

Gwen did not know what seed corn was. She splashed another oar. It did not seem that anything they did had any bearing on where they were going, but through the fog she felt the fuzzy warmth and glare of the sun, almost right behind them. They were going west, at least. All progress was incremental. It seemed to Gwen, from the occasional noise to her left—portside—that they might be too close to shore, but it was too foggy to tell. Off the starboard side, there was a shadow that might have been Alcatraz, trailing them like a detective, and here and there the bottom of the Golden Gate Bridge would peek out from the shifting walls of fog, as if it were on a flickering screen. Gwen thought of the cameras in the drugstore and felt caught again. Was it really possible they could make it to the bridge? And then, and then?

"It's open," Errol said. He scratched again at the dirty bandage Gwen had fashioned. They would raid another yacht, Gwen thought, maybe two miles from the harbor, and conscript a doctor into service. He would have supplies with him, and would be handsome and ruthless. "I'm too warm, help me get this off me."

"What's open?" she asked him instead.

"That," he said, pointing just off the bow.

"The sea?"

"Sure, the open sea." He coughed once but did not take his eyes off the surface. The oars rippled the water. "I know you," he said.

"Yes."

"You're my—my—my—"

"Yes."

"You're my grommet."

"And you're my captain," Gwen said soothingly. "My old sea dog."

Errol smiled, with a sad shrug. Gwen watched him look at his watch. It was still, to him, probably two thirty, to everyone else maybe eight A.M. The bridge rippled closer, and Gwen wondered if there were people up there, if anyone would be looking down at them as they headed out for their exodus. "This is our last chance to send a message home," she said.

"Message in a bottle," Amber said, "if we have another ginger ale quick. I could forge it. It could be from anybody."

"I'd want to write it myself," Gwen said.

"You're thinking about Nathan Glasserman."

"Am not."

"*Verily.*"

"Verily *not*. Well, not *just*."

"Your parents."

"They used to take walks across the bridge sometimes. We all did. So I was just thinking."

"What would you write them?"

"They're worried, I guess."

Amber smiled. "*And?*"

"*And*," Gwen said, "I'm never going to see them again," although this didn't feel true. Somehow, no matter what happened at sea, surely she would live to scowl at her parents once more.

"So what would you say?" Amber asked.

Gwen tried to think.

"*I* would say, 'Fuck you for not making me learn how to swim,'" Amber said.

"You can't swim?"

"I told you."

"I don't think so." Gwen could not picture not swimming. What could that look like, just falling in the water, straight down?

"Yes," Amber said. "Maybe you didn't hear."

"Like when I said about Nathan," Gwen said, "instead of his brother." They smiled unhappily at each other, and then Gwen leaned over and kissed Amber on the mouth, something she'd wanted to do. It was romantic, but it didn't last forever. "So if you fall," she said at last, pretending it was a normal world, "overboard, I mean—"

"Throw me a rope," Amber said quickly. "We still have rope, I think."

"I can't swim either," Errol said. "Never learned."

"In the *Navy*?"

"Two tugs on the rope means pull me in," Errol said. Gwen moved the rope out of his reach.

"How about, no matter how many times I pull on the rope, pull me in?" Amber said.

"Definitely," Gwen said.

"When that time comes," Amber said. "Swimming won't help, right?"

"I don't know," Gwen said. She didn't want to talk about it, *that time*. She rested her plank for a minute and turned on the radio. A beat emerged, familiar and angry.

"Cool," Amber said, leaning into the speaker. There was a foam cover over the microphone, yellowish and dusty like a dead parrot, and the glass walls of the KUSA booth hadn't been cleaned. Why had it come to this? There was a way it had gone, and now the way, Phil Needle saw, was this bad booth, wrong. How was he to know, when he should show up, how he could do better? It wasn't as if he had heard a voice, telling him the right thing to do, that he had ignored. He put on his headphones.

"Phil, will you say something into the mic? We need to check levels."

"Check levels," he said.

"Keep talking," Renée said. "You know the drill. You're a radio person."

"I'm a radio person," he said dumbly.

"Are you okay, Phil? I mean, considering?"

"Yes," Phil Needle said, and then he considered. "Yes."

"Do you need more time?"

"Yes. No. No."

"Okay, stand by."

"Standing by," Phil Needle said.

"The commercial's winding up. I'll tell you when to start talking."

Phil Needle tried to think.

The commercial wound up. They were already at it with back-to-school, when it was July—no, June still. *Leave us alone*, Gwen thought, *why don't you all leave us alone?* Her angry fingers moved the dial and then she fell back in surprise, dropping her plank into the water. It did not float but drifted straight down, a ghostly rectangle fading quickly to the water's gray. It was the voice on the radio that had startled her. It was the voice of her father.

"Hi, I'm Phil Needle, award-winning radio producer and head and founder of a company moving towards excellence, and I have something to say."

Errol spat into the water, his chin quivering. "I had suspicion of spying," he said, "indeed to goodness I did."

"When Incredible Cleaners asked me to produce a commercial for them, I could have offered them all the bells and whistles that you hear in local business ads a million times a day."

The air filled with bells and whistles, and Errol stood up in the small boat. "I knew it," he said, and pointed at Gwen with a grim finger, bloodied from picking at his wound or perhaps some new injury she had missed. "I knew I should beware the impatience and injustice of youth!"

"But I'm here to tell you that Incredible Cleaners doesn't need any bells and whistles, no catchy jingles, no clever slogans and no statements of purpose from the Incredible owner. So the only sound I'm putting on this ad is my own testimonial. I'm putting myself, Phil Needle of Phil Needle Productions, on the line for this one. Because I'm not just a radio producer for Incredible Cleaners. I'm a customer. And why am I a customer? Because Incredible Cleaners is absolutely incredible. Thank you very much."

Errol was trying to pace up and down the boat, but the boat wasn't big enough for pacing. It rolled dangerously with each stride. Gwen hardly noticed. She was still staring at the radio and listening to her father's cross-pollinating ad. Nobody had ever reminded her of the very simple fact of recording and duplication, and so she saw her father in a booth, not worried sick at all, just reciting lines into a microphone and thinking about his stupid job, his glamorous radio world in New York, regretting his mistake—

"*Gwen.*"

—and glad to be rid of her.

"*Gwen.*"

"What?"

"Do something," Amber said quietly. For Errol had stopped mid-stride and had slid his saw out of his coat. Gwen could have sworn it had been left with all the trash on the island, but there it was, still bloodied from the swordfight and swinging in Errol's hands like a pendulum.

"Errol," she said.

The radio identified itself as KXKX, cool jazz for the cool city. Errol sneered and flicked the radio overboard with his blade. As it hit the water, Gwen had the fleeting and wrong suspicion that the entire ocean, all its fish and rare treasures, would be electrocuted. But instead all was silence.

"*Captain,*" she tried.

"*No!*" Errol screamed. "There will be *no talk* until I get my satisfaction! This is betrayal! Infidelity! What is the word!" He slashed in the air again, and Gwen felt her cheeks burn. They must have been red. Errol took another step. "My resolution is immovable," he said immovably. "Stealing is wrong. If caught, you should be punished. He stole from me, that man's voice. He stole my house after they killed my Vera, those murderers. They slaughtered her and I vowed revenge on all his kind. And you, you Jewish cunts, in cahoots you are! *Errol*, eh? *Captain*, eh? I am deaf to your pleas and blind to your suffering!"

"*Grandpa!*" Gwen cried, and felt tears on her face.

It was true. Errol Needle's first symptoms had been racist remarks, broadcast under his breath at family lunches and then plainly out loud at larger gatherings, until Phil Needle, his surviving son, told him he was no longer welcome at cocktail parties or barbecues, and hired a lawyer recommended by Leonard Steed to gain control over his father's finances. It would not be accurate to call this theft, and neither would it be false. It is the course of the world. Before long the son had the father moved to the Jean Bonnet Living Center and sold his house out from under him and used the money to buy a home he could not afford. By then Errol's symptoms were worsening. He was enraged by his son, and his son's wife, the staff at his new home, his clothes, anyone on the phone, the color orange, television, certain music, his doctors, dogs, fancy food, Judaism, pants, hairdos, spit, children, long sleeves, and everything else except a handful of old sea stories on his bookshelf. His fantasy that he had once been in the Navy, instilled by endless rereadings of *Captain Blood* and the others, was so fervent and unclouded that Phil Needle believed he was learning something about his reticent father. He had fallen, and after the Fall everything had been taken away. Errol railed against this injustice, against all injustices, but only Gwen, forced to serve as her grandfather's companion as punishment, listened to his increasingly far-flung claims. Phil Needle just sent orchids, phoned occasionally and impulsively, and waited to be phoned himself someday, knowing, as Gwen knew now, that dead men tell no tales. Errol growled at her again and swung the saw. Amber dropped the other plank onto the floor of the rocking boat, and Gwen saw something equally fierce in her friend's eyes.

"Errol, stop it."

"Take me prisoner, eh?" he said. "My person. The only thing left to steal. Trick me aboard and bury me at sea in an unmarked grave."

It was true, Gwen thought, keeping her eyes on the blade. He would not survive this. We don't survive anything. It all, looking at the calm and endless water, just keeps going. He raised his hand to her again and something clicked this time.

"*Stop!*"

It was the gun. Amber was holding it on Errol with two shaky hands, and her eyes were shaky too, moving from Errol to the saw to the water to Gwen, her friend, with a very small smile.

"Amber."

"No," she said. "He cut you. Look at yourself."

The water was too cloudy to see her reflection, so Gwen put a hand to her stinging cheek. It was not tears on her face. He had raised his hand to her and carved a small wound.

"I'll trim you both of your lives," Errol growled. "My resolution is immovable. You stole from me. I'll trim you both."

"Gwen, think what he did. To Cody, I mean. We can't do that here. The boat's too little and we're all in it."

"You stole from me."

"Errol, put the saw down or I'll fire this weapon."

"My resolution is immovable."

"I will shatter your heart, I will *do it!*"

"I have a problem with my memory," Errol said.

Gwen took a gentle step toward him and he slashed at her again. He missed, but she found herself fallen in the boat anyway, her eyes blinking at the plank, which Amber was kicking with her foot. It lurched halfway past the rim like a seesaw, a makeshift runway for any plane set to depart.

"Off the boat," Amber said.

"I know you," Errol said. Gwen sat up and saw he was looking at her.

"Walk off the boat, Errol," Amber said.

"I know you. Tell this wench to drop her threat. I know you."

"Yes," Gwen said, "Gwen."

But that was all she said.

"*Off the boat!*"

"*I,*" Errol said, just as fiercely, "*have a problem with my memory!*"

"*Walk the plank!*"

"It *bothers* me," Errol cried. It *was* tears on his face. He swung the blade. Amber pointed the gun straight up and pulled the trigger. There was nothing. She opened her eyes and moved the gun back down to look at it. Errol saw this opportunity, maybe. It may have been that he started to pounce when the gun fired straight down into the lifeboat. It split, so fast, and vanished as the recoil from the gun blew Amber into the air, surprisingly high, surprisingly far, and then down into the water, off somewhere. They were all in the water. The instant wreckage of the lifeboat closed around Gwen and Errol like a flower, rubber and plastic everywhere her limbs struggled. It was so cold. There is no one who has not been to sea who can imagine the sheer freeze of the unexpected water, and Gwen lived shivering in it for a minute, like a girl in a coffin, before she came alive and found the sputtering surface. She breathed and reached out both hands and found Errol's shoulder.

"I'm cold," he panted. "I'm cold!"

"Hang on to me," she said, but in her hands he was so heavy. A burden. Errol shook his head.

"I don't want to be," he said, "out of the water. I don't want to be on the boat anymore. I want to get off for a while."

"Grandpa—" Gwen said, and took another cold breath.

"Let them steal it," he croaked, and let go and disappeared down. Gwen's hands closed around nothing and then just the bandage, soaked and trailing upward, like a tattered white flag.

They were very, very close to shore, close enough that they would have been tracked had it not been for the fog. The bulk of the lifeboat washed up some hours later, right where Marina met Old Mason, but Gwen was a little further down the beach when she was spotted, standing up and heaving with breath on the sand. There were many men on the shore who saw her emerge, like an apparition on the half shell, walking their dogs mostly, with coffee in hand from a nearby cart. She was recognized almost instantly from the television, a powerful medium at the time. They did not need to see the picture in Gwen's pocket. It was so good of her, now soaked and sorry-looking. Gwen was sorry about it. She was sorry for everything. Sorry teachers and coaches. Sorry friends and enemies. Sorry for those who died and for those who mourned them, sorry for anyone who lost their home or their wife or their husband or their children. Sorry for anyone upset or inconvenienced, sorry for any victim of theft or murder or jealousy. For unrequited lovers she was sorry. For anybody who ever got a cut on the arm, sorry you got a cut on the arm. For the wealthy on boats, for the schmucks stuck in traffic, for the famous and the infamous, sorry you treacherous, wounded bastards, I am so sorry.

"We've got 'em," somebody said. They took her down. Amber's limp form was lifted away from her, and there were so many hands on her arms and she was helped forward and reattached to the land of the free. More men came. It was a commotion, down by the water, that might attract anyone who had stepped outside. It was a human interest story. She collapsed for a moment, and her head almost hit the sand. A few grains whirled up and stuck to her heaving face. All the despair in the world, cold and final, was thrust upon her. Later it was reported that she was kissing the ground. In *gratitude*. The things they got wrong, she thought, sitting in bed in the middle of the day. The rain had stopped like they'd made it up, and the sun glared in each square of the window like a finished round of tic-tac-toe, a game, played at this time in history, in which opponents filled in squares one by one, everything marked with an X or a zero. Most times nobody won. Gwen was not an outlaw. She lived with her parents in this condominium, and no part of it was Gwen's. She was up in her room for the entire barbecue, even when the sun set and all the people strolled inside. When I saw Phil Needle last, he was standing at the sliding door with everyone who wanted to be where the action was. The moon was large and far over the busy bridge, and then the fireworks, with all the bells and whistles, sprouted in the sky like sudden dandelions of light, challenges to the darkness that wilted away in seconds, all traces disappearing and leaving all the stars in their place.

Phil Needle had a call from Leonard Steed that afternoon.

"Who am I talking to?"

"Phil Needle."

"Good, good, good. Listen, Needle, how is your emergency?"

"Good."

"What?"

"Over," Phil Needle said, and covered his eyes. The fake tree fluttered.

"Good. Listen, I've managed to hold off the buccaneers."

"What?"

"That's what I like about me. I'm fast on my feet."

"What?"

"Of course, it's if and only if you have a pitch."

"What?"

"The perfect pitch, Needle, an American outlaw story."

"What?"

"Stop saying *what*. Be fast on your feet too. Do you have that, Phil Needle? Do you have that for me? A human interest story? The big story that people might actually tune in to?"

And it is evidence, reads the last page of a book discarded from Errol's shelves, *that notwithstanding these follies wasted the population of the world, squandered its treasures and infected us with new vices and diseases, they tamed the ferocity of man's spirit and established a base for permanent prosperity.*

"Needle?"

Phil Needle thought of his daughter.

It was strange how ungrounded things could become and not overturn. Dead men tell no tales, so Errol Needle was scapegoated for everything. Phil Needle finally learned of his father's disappearance from Peggy, who dithered for nearly a day, terrified of lawsuits, and then phoned Phil Needle crying, mistakenly calling him by the name of his deceased brother, David. Finally the story was put straight. Obviously it had all been Errol's idea, though it was also obvious it was beyond his reach. He had kidnapped his granddaughter and some of her friends when they had sneaked off, the three of them with two free tickets, to see hip-hop at the Fillmore, and he had murdered two people while holding these youngsters prisoner. The *San Francisco Chronicle* never put two and two together about the fierce letters they'd been getting for the past month, and Errol's death was labeled, ambiguously or maybe tactfully, the result of natural causes. Rain vanished the fingerprints. Phil Needle was recognized several times in the weeks to come, not as an award-winning radio producer, although Incredible Cleaners ran the ad through September, but as the father. A new Haitian tea place opened on Octavia. The parrot died in a tree and the contact lens was vacuumed up from the carpet, and the rest is history. Nobody wanted to know more. Except me. As independence boomed across the sky, I went upstairs uninvited. No, this was their room. No, this was a bathroom. And then I knocked.

"It's open."

Gwen was on her bed, unmade, with the pillows scattered angrily, MY PRINCESS SLEEPS HERE. She was painting her toes, her legs bent oddly beneath her. She was wearing a T-shirt from a radio station, and as shorts a pair of men's boxers, probably her father's. She appeared to have a burn on her leg. A dog, also banished, watched me from its place on the floor. *Thank goodness*, I confess I thought, *she's home safe*. Her room had been righted somewhat, the drawers back in their slots and the clothes hung up, but the waste-basket was far too full, wrappers and love notes overflowing onto the floor. Gwen didn't care. It had taken a long time, days, for her love to die, but it had. She didn't think about Nathan Glasserman, and the Glassermans were so eager to bury the story that Nathan never thought of her either.

She didn't acknowledge me, except to hide one hand under her legs so I couldn't read whatever was written there. The window to her room was open, and through some trick of acoustics you could hear every word of the party below. She must have heard it, I thought, when it was said. *We are pirates.* But Gwen just kept flipping through her new television, a gift of gratitude maybe, or apology, or just because Phil Needle had come into more money.

At first it was some sporting event, with a bunch of guys running around, never never never even one girl except for the ones with boobs and skirts on the sidelines, but then she changed the channel. Women were in prison, and the moon was full. Veronica, who had been framed by her boyfriend after the opening credits, cowered in her bunk as the strange noises slithered closer. In seconds she would awaken to the shriek of the warden's whistle, and no one would believe her. Of course it was a dream. She could not have seen vampires in a women's prison. During the day, where could they go? But Veronica's eyes shimmered with fright and glit-ter. "Help me," she moaned, badly dubbed in a voice Gwen could not place. Vampires, then, I thought, if pirates have been taken away from her. Some wild story, some chance for escape. "Help me! Help me! *Help me!*"

It was what Gwen always remembered. She did not always

remember the boom of the gun, or the freeze that was everywhere on her skin. She did not remember giving up completely and deciding to sink, as it was useless to do anything else and there was nowhere else to go. Errol was gone and the boat was gone and the cold water rushed around her and she did not draw away from its grasp until she heard Amber's faint and frantic cry, and then followed the course she had taken, required even of synchronized swimmers. The course was on water safety, and had reminded everyone that if you're lost underwater, look what direction the bubbles are going. They will always be rising. Look for your breath to save your life, or the lives of those you love.

"Help me!" Amber was screaming when Gwen reached the surface. Her grandfather was below her somewhere. It was like the problems they gave everyone at school, as if school didn't give you problems enough. *You can swim and your grandfather can't and your best friend can't, but you don't have time to save them both.* "Help me! Help me! *Help me!*"

Gwen reacted, just as the Stepmonster would overreact and, to have morality and sense replace rebellion and ingratitude, enroll Amber in Immaculate Conception Academy, as if such a thing could be taught. Gwen and Amber would be seen as victims, but not quite blameless ones, bystanders who should have been more innocent, and so denied phones and watched like hawks until Gwen started college, a year late, shortly before her parents' twenty-fifth anniversary. It is useless, at the time this story takes place, to say they never saw each other again. They were on the grid, photographed and tagged, and whenever curiosity bit at them, alone at a screen, they could look at updates, postings. Everybody could do this with anybody. They did not lose each other, although they never again spoke, because they could not get lost. Phil Needle stood in the parking lot, suddenly grasping that this was so, that nothing is lost in a world utterly mapped, that nothing is rogue with everything cross-pollinated, as the shouts on the beach lured him across the street to the sand. He still had coffee in his hand. An accident, he thought, mistakenly. A fresh disaster. Something new and unconnected to himself. But then he saw his sweatshirt, his favorite sweatshirt, on a figure on the beach. It was like seeing a cotton gin in the lobby of a building, something snatched up from its rightful owner and moved to a new place. He blinked in disbelief and then Phil Needle connected, dropped the coffee cup to be swept later to sea, and ran down the sand to his daughter. There she is! There she is! There she is! This was his day, his chosen time. He was sick with luck, surprised and grateful that the world was his oyster after all. There she is! Thank you God and the men standing around wondering what to do! Thank you to the map in the police station and all its pins, thank you to the ambulance, to the open sea with its wide arms tossing everything back to land! To my crew at Phil Needle Productions, thank you! To the microphone in the booth and the waves in the air, and thank you to the radio audience, anyone out there listening! He kept broadcasting it in his head, all down the beach, until he had her in his arms. "We've got 'em." All the happiness in the world, all that was denied him, had come into his possession at last, pouring onto him like water on a drowning man. It was what he always remembered, returning to the moment like a treasure in his chest, his destiny, the pure and purloined joy in his heart as Gwen collapsed onto the sand. We steal the happiness of others in order to be happy ourselves, and when it is stolen from us we voyage desperately to steal it back. We are pirates. It is the course of the world, and we may think that we can travel out of the world's reach, but anyone who thinks that, Gwen always remembered, is a mistake. You can swim as long and as hard as you like, but you will be giving up one life in order to save another. She found Amber in the water and grabbed her as Errol settled to the bottom. She pushed her to the surface, and Amber stole a first breath from the air as the water stole Errol's last. She brought her to shore and gave her up. She stood alone, Gwen Needle, and thought for a moment she could go somewhere else, but then she was in her father's arms and it was over. The world was her home, she could not leave it. She was found, she was lost. She was safe, she was doomed. She was history.

AUTHOR'S NOTE

This book contains bits lifted from the vast treasure troves of pirate history, lore, literature and film. Acknowledging the sources of such material would be contrary to the spirit of the pirate and literary traditions both, but the author would be remiss if he failed to salute Rafael Sabatini and Richard Hughes for *Captain Blood* and *A High Wind in Jamaica* (or, *The Innocent Voyage*), respectively.